This was the woman Dottie had given his house to.

Serena had ruined his homecoming—and his Christmas. Jonas couldn't forget that. But he didn't like the tired lines under her eyes. He disliked even more that he cared about her exhaustion at all.

Best stick to the basics. "ID?"

She handed over her military ID card and her son's.

Jonas's fingers flew over the keyboard as he automatically typed in the last name, the active-duty sponsor's social security number—

His hands stilled.

Delgado, Philip. Gunnery Sergeant, U.S. Marine Corps. Deceased.

He knew Serena was a war widow. That she had a son. But to read it, in black and white, made him wish he could have been there and been the one to save her husband. Anything to take the sorrow from her eyes.

He glanced over at her. Her gaze was intent on her son, and Jonas waited for her to look back at him. When she did, he saw the cold edge of distrust on her face.

His mind kept going over his last conversation with Dottie.

"You'll love Serena. It's as though she's always been here."

Dear Reader,

I was delighted when Harlequin Superromance asked me to include another World War II subplot for Navy Christmas, much as I did with my very first book, A Rendezvous to Remember. In Navy Christmas, we meet Dottie Forsyth's parents and find out how her family settled on Whidbey Island over a century ago. Dottie isn't even in the contemporary story—she's already passed on. But as the story between her stepson, Jonas, and niece, Serena, progresses, it becomes certain that Dottie had a hunch they'd make a good pair. Because of reservations on both their parts, it takes them a while to acknowledge their romantic feelings for each other. Serena is a war widow and not looking for a new father for her six-year-old son. Jonas is fresh back from deployment and still smarting over Dottie's amendment to her will—leaving Serena the family house instead of Jonas, as she'd once promised.

Serena discovers, along with the reader, the history of Dottie's parents, which includes her father's service as a Flying Tiger in World War II.

When the opportunity arose to donate to a fundraiser for the National League of POW/MIA Families (www.pow-miafamilies.org), my editor suggested I donate a character's name for Navy Christmas. The successful event found Dawn Dempsey as the winner. Dawn graciously gave the name of her grandfather, Charles G. Dempsey, for a World War II sailor. Charles served in the navy during WWII and in the Pacific theater. You can find out more about him on my website (and on the following pages!). While my characterization of Charles is fictional, I used details of his life that Dawn provided to make the character authentic. I hope I did his memory, and Dawn's family, proud.

If you like reading about Whidbey Island during Christmas, don't miss Navy Joy, a novella in the anthology Coming Home for Christmas, which also has stories by sister veterans Lindsay McKenna and Delores Fossen. It's out this month, too.

I love hearing from you—please reach me via my website, www.gerikrotow.com, Facebook, Twitter or Pinterest. Don't forget to sign up for my newsletter and be automatically entered into the Geri Krotow Loyal Reader program, where you have a chance at winning a signed book each month.

I wish you and yours a very Merry Christmas, and may the peace of the season find you wherever you are, whatever your walk.

Peace,
Geri Krotow

GERI KROTOW

—

Navy Christmas

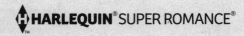
HARLEQUIN® SUPER ROMANCE®

Recycling programs
for this product may
not exist in your area.

ISBN-13: 978-0-373-60883-6

Navy Christmas

Copyright © 2014 by Geri Krotow

Printed in U.S.A.

ABOUT THE AUTHOR

Former naval intelligence officer and U.S. Naval Academy graduate Geri Krotow draws inspiration from the global situations she's experienced. Geri loves to hear from her readers. You can email her via her website and blog, www.gerikrotow.com.

Books by Geri Krotow

HARLEQUIN SUPERROMANCE

HARLEQUIN ANTHOLOGY

HARLEQUIN EVERLASTING LOVE

*Whidbey Island books

Other titles by this author available in ebook format.

Don't miss any of our special offers. Write to us at the following address for information on our newest releases.

Harlequin Reader Service
U.S.: 3010 Walden Ave., P.O. Box 1325, Buffalo, NY 14269
Canadian: P.O. Box 609, Fort Erie, Ont. L2A 5X3

To My Loving Family Steve, Alex and Ellen.
You've given me the best Christmases of my life.
I love you with all my heart.

CHAPTER ONE

Whidbey Island
One week before Thanksgiving

"MOM, MY EAR IS *FINE*. How much longer do we have to wait?"

Serena Delgado looked up from the pair of socks she was knitting. Her six-year-old son Pepé's brown eyes and earnest expression looked so much like his father's it made her smile.

A smile was a big improvement over the heart-crushing pain the thought of Philip used to bring.

"Pepé, we have to be patient. I brought my new knitting project to keep me busy. Look, they're the Army-green socks you asked for."

"Mom."

Pepé wasn't impressed by her intricate stitches, or the fact that she was knitting both socks at once on her circular needles.

"Are you that bored with your video game already?"

"This waiting is taking a long time, Mom. I'd rather be playing soccer."

Serena checked her watch. She'd never attempted

two-at-a-time socks before, and her absorption in the task must have been deeper than she'd realized.

They'd been sitting in the pediatric waiting area of Naval Hospital Oak Harbor for forty-five minutes. Located on Naval Air Station or NAS Whidbey, it was the only military medical facility on the island.

"Maybe you're right, *mi hijo*. Let's go see if we can find someone to help us. They may have lost our paperwork in the shuffle."

She stuffed the needle and yarn into her tote and grabbed each of their jackets. They walked past the empty reception area and Serena's hunch that they'd been overlooked grew stronger. She knew patients weren't supposed to enter the hallway where the examination rooms were located without a nurse or corpsman to escort them, but since it was a Friday afternoon, she'd take her chances. She was as eager as Pepé to start the weekend.

The first few exam rooms were empty, lights out.

"No one's here, Mom," Pepé whispered, as if they were going on a spy mission.

"We'll find somebody."

Light spilled from the room in front of them and Serena paused, her hand on Pepé's shoulder. She didn't want to barge in on someone else's exam.

Pepé stilled next to her and a conversation became clear.

"This is crap, Doc, and you know it." A deep voice filled with frustration rumbled from the room.

"You're back home, Jonas. In case you haven't noticed, there's no battlefront here at NAS Whidbey."

Jonas.

Serena's spine stiffened. The one "Jonas" she knew of fit this scenario too well....

"I'm putting you where the Navy needs you, and right now I need you in the regular pediatrics clinic for the next few weeks. You'll treat the routine cases. When Petty Officer Reilly isn't available, you'll have to check in the patients, too. If you have any problems getting used to the system we've upgraded to, ask HM1 Reilly. I don't think you will—it's all pretty straightforward."

"I'm trained for so much more, Doc. At least put me in the E.R."

If this was the Jonas she had heard about— Jonas Scott—he had an awfully sexy voice. Nothing like his brother Paul's, whom she'd met in person.

"Mom, that's Doc Franklin!" Pepé whispered his recognition of the second voice, but his excitement threatened to break his self-control. Besides being his beloved pediatrician, Doc Franklin shared the name of one of Pepé's favorite heroes in American history. Pepé loved Dr. Benjamin Franklin, from the moment the Navy had assigned him to the family. Serena liked him, too, mostly for his easygoing manner with Pepé. She'd never heard this side of him, however. Military medical officers were more than doctors; they had to lead, too. And Jonas didn't sound like he wanted direction from anyone.

"Shh, we shouldn't interrupt them." Her lawyerly instincts seemed to vibrate as she did her best to ignore the twinge of guilt at admonishing Pepé. She was eavesdropping, pure and simple.

But if Dr. Franklin was indeed speaking to Jonas Scott, the one man on Whidbey Island who could change Serena's life, it behooved her to listen.

Just a bit longer.

"You can rotate through the E.R. as needed, but not until after the holidays. Peds isn't always boring, Jonas. Right now, take advantage of being back from deployment. You weren't even due to report to work until next week, after the Thanksgiving holiday."

"Sitting around my house isn't a whole lot of fun."

Regret pierced through Serena's stoic attorney mode. It had to be Jonas Scott. It had been as much of a surprise to her as it had been to Jonas that his stepmother and her biological aunt, Dottie Forsyth, had willed her family farmhouse to Serena. The tragic circumstances of Dottie's unexpected death hadn't helped. Dottie was supposed to grow old in the farmhouse, not be murdered by a crazy woman the previous summer.

"I'm sorry, Jonas. It's a crappy time of year to be single and alone."

"It's not about that, Doc. I'm over it."

"I know you're over your ex, Jonas. What you're not over is deployment and the constant insane pace. You're done deploying, trust me. With the drawdown in Afghanistan and your rank, you could finish out the rest of your time on shore duty. And what about your stepmother's death? You've got a lot to process."

It *was* Jonas Scott, Dottie's stepson.

He had an ex?

"I'll deal." His voice was little more than a growl.

"I have no doubt that you will. But it won't hurt you to scale it back a bit and enjoy the lighter schedule. Give yourself time to grieve, Jonas."

"There has to be something I can do besides weigh in snotty-nosed kids whose mothers are overreacting to the common cold."

Serena's face heated as she fought her maternal anger.

"Save the tough-guy routine for someone who doesn't know you as well, Jonas. You're great with kids or I wouldn't have assigned you to my unit." Dr. Franklin's tone reflected compassion. As if he knew Jonas better than most.

"Give me a break, Doc. These folks wouldn't

know a medical emergency if it bit them in the ass. Did you see that last family? They had all three of their kids still on bottles, and the youngest was two. I don't have time to treat overpampered, over-fed, sugared-up kids whose parents need a lesson in nutrition and physical fitness. For heaven's sake, Doc, I was stopping Marines from bleeding out less than two weeks ago, and the kids I treated had real, often life-threatening, needs. Now you want me to hand out cartoon-hero stickers?"

Serena grasped Pepé's hand. Enough was enough. Pepé didn't need to hear any of this.

That's what she got for snooping like the law-yer she was—she'd exposed her son to a post-deployment tirade he'd had no part of. She bent to his ear.

"Come on, *mi hijo*. Let's find out what happened to our appointment."

Doc HAD GONE quiet and Jonas wondered if he'd pushed his boss too far. Doc Franklin was an easy-going guy, and Jonas had enjoyed working with him overseas, in a combat zone. In war, they were teammates fighting to save every life, every person who came into their unit. And even back home where Doc was a pediatrician, he was still a naval medical officer. He thought he had the most im-portant job in the world.

"Well?" Jonas prompted.

Doc's stare should have tipped him off. Too late,

the hairs on the back of Jonas's neck rose and he knew someone was standing behind him.

He mentally groaned and turned around, expecting HM1 Reilly, or worse, the naval hospital's Commanding Officer.

Instead, he found himself looking into the deepest, darkest mocha-brown eyes he'd ever seen. They sparked with anger and a knowing he couldn't quite identify... He shook his head to clear it.

The stunning woman in front of him had night-black hair that fell in a straight sheet past her shoulders, skimming around her generous breasts. Breasts that were covered snugly by her purple turtleneck. She didn't cover up her sensuous figure with the added layer of a sweater or pullover like a lot of women, either. He gave her points for that. Her bottom was just as sexy and he couldn't miss how her jeans emphasized every curve.

This was a woman who knew her power over men.

He knew it wasn't some sort of vision brought on by deployment fatigue. But even in his dreams he'd never conjured up an image quite this...distracting.

"Hey, Dr. Franklin!" A black-haired boy stood next to the woman, his enthusiasm for Doc making him bounce up and down while his mother held his hand.

"Pepé, Ms. Delgado, how is my favorite Marine

Corps family?" Doc walked next to Jonas and kneeled down to the boy's level.

Delgado.

Son of a bitch.

Not only had he shown his worst side to Doc Franklin, he'd made a mess of things with the one woman he needed to treat right, the one woman who had what he wanted so badly, what he'd waited to have for so long. He knew more about her than she knew, and they hadn't met in person yet. Until now.

How much had they heard?

Serena Delgado. And her son, Pepé. The family living in the farmhouse that Dottie had promised him.

Pepé yanked his hand out of Serena's and ran over to Doc.

"We're great, Doc! We're going to Friday Island for Thanksgiving. I might get to swim in the heated pool."

"It's San Juan Island, Pepé. Friday Harbor is the town." Her voice matched her looks—deep and harmonious with a side of sexy.

Serena Delgado kept staring at Jonas as she gently corrected her son. The daggers of light in her eyes were anything but gentle. If he were to guess, she was sorely pissed off.

At him.

And she had every right to be.

"You're Serena."

He'd planned to introduce himself in person to her later. After he'd been back long enough to get over his jet lag.

More like get over your wounded ego.

"Yes."

Her eyes reminded him of an iced coffee. Dark and rich, with a bite.

Jonas held out his hand. "I'm Jonas Scott."

"I know who you are." She flicked her gaze at his hand long enough to make her point. She wasn't going to shake his hand or make this any easier for him. Why should she?

"I'm not sure how much you heard of what I said—I'm sorry and please understand that I was just being a pain in the, um, you know."

"It's clear you don't usually work in pediatrics." Her tone remained grave but he caught the slight tic at the corner of her mouth. "I hope I'll be able to control myself. Being a mom and all, I never know when I'm going to get all hysterical and go crazy on you."

He wasn't sure if her attractiveness or the fact that she was enjoying his discomfort rattled him more.

"Touché." They continued to stare at each other.

He'd be turned on by any attractive woman after being downrange so long. It was just his luck that it happened to be the woman who'd upended his whole life.

Unexpected disappointment punched him in the gut.

Even if their shared connection hadn't been so ugly, so life-changing, he wouldn't stand a chance with her. Not after she'd overheard his harsh words.

And the boy—Pepé. Jonas didn't like the twinge of envy he'd felt when Pepé smiled and ran to Doc Franklin. He used to be the practitioner kids loved, the one who loved taking care of kids, but after the past several months of deployment, he couldn't look at a child and not feel the immediate wash of sorrow that'd become too familiar to him.

"Please call me Jonas. I'm sorry I haven't contacted you yet. I've been home a short time, and I didn't want to stop by the house without calling first."

Had she heard him stumble over the word *house?* Or was it just his imagination that referring to the farmhouse as anything but his or his family's caused him pause?

She held her hand up to stop his meager attempt at an apology.

"I think we've said all we needed to in our emails, don't you?"

"No, not at all. Six months ago we were both in shock, and an email is never the same as meeting in person."

He looked over to where Doc was goofing around with Pepé.

"I don't want to have this conversation now, Serena—can I call you that? Not with Pepé here."

"I imagine it would be difficult for you to ask me to give up our home while Pepé's within earshot."

Frustration made his vision blur as the goddess turned into a witch. An immediate ache in his chest opened up, spewing the ugly visions of children he hadn't been able to save. Damn his post-deployment emotions. His ability to compartmentalize, the usual method of coping with unwanted emotions and allowing a warrior to focus on a mission, seemed to have evaporated the minute he landed back on Whidbey last week.

"I may deserve that, *ma'am,* but trust me, I'm not the bogeyman. I understand that you and Pepé have been through a lot. More than your share."

Those brown eyes remained steady on him. Measuring him, assessing his integrity. He'd had stares from top admirals that weren't as unnerving.

"As have you. And yes, you can call me Serena."

Her tone held no recrimination, no pity. Dottie's claim that Serena was "a gal with real class" rang through his mind. Thinking of Dottie, of her death, made him want to put his fist through the clinic wall.

"Dottie loved you so much. She never stopped talking about you." As if she'd read his mind. As if she knew he needed that reminder of Dottie's love for him.

"Funny, because she was the same way about you—she went on and on in her emails and our few phone conversations about how thrilled she was to finally have met you, to have closed the family circle by meeting her long-lost niece."

Her eyes narrowed and she took a step back. "You're right, Jonas. We need to have this conversation elsewhere."

Her anger had melted into another emotion he didn't want to consider. Sadness?

"Mom, Doc Franklin says I can go back to soccer next spring!"

"That's nice, Pepé." Her shoulders sagged and Jonas made a conscious effort not to offer her an arm, a shoulder of his own.

"What's going on with Pepé?" If he was going to check her son in and probably see more of him in the clinic, he'd better do his best to be professional.

"He's had a rash of ear infections. The last one took him out of the second half of soccer season. He loves soccer, as he'll be sure to let you know any minute now."

Her exasperated expression reflected her obvious love for Pepé.

"I understand. I get antsy when I can't get to the gym. You two must have a special bond."

A small line appeared between her brows and

Jonas swore he tasted the bottom of his uniform boots. How many times could he say the wrong words in one afternoon?

"I'm sorry, Serena. Obviously small talk isn't my forte any more than pediatrics is."

She opened her mouth to speak but Doc interrupted them.

"Commander Scott, this is Pepé, my main man. I've known this kid since he moved on island last spring. He's a champ. Pepé, this is Commander Scott, and he's going to take care of you." Doc raised his hand for Pepé's high-five slap.

"Yes, sir."

Jonas gritted his teeth for the fifteenth time in as many minutes. This wasn't going to be easy. If Doc Franklin had made the connection between Serena and Jonas, he wasn't talking. And Jonas wasn't about to mention it now, not after already shoving his foot down his throat twice.

Jonas walked Pepé and Serena back to the check-in station. He gestured for her to take the seat next to the computer desk as he smiled at Pepé.

"Go ahead and scoot up on the table for me, buddy."

"Am I going to get a sticker?"

"After I check your ears, sure."

"You sounded angry about the stickers, Mr. Scott."

"It's Commander Scott, Pepé."

Serena's smooth correction made Jonas smile. He had to hand it to her—she was raising the boy to show respect and courtesy.

"If it's okay with your mom, you can call me Jonas, Pepé. I'm not a doctor like Doc Franklin. I'm a nurse practitioner and I can take care of you, too."

"Mom, is it okay?"

"Sure, *mi hijo.*"

Jonas didn't like the tired lines under her eyes. He disliked more that he cared about her parental exhaustion.

This was the woman who Dottie had given his house to.

Best to stick to the basics.

"ID?"

She handed over her and Pepé's military ID cards.

Jonas's fingers flew over the keyboard as he automatically typed in Pepé's last name, the active-duty sponsor's social security number—

His hands stilled.

Delgado, Philip. Gunnery Sergeant, U.S. Marine Corps. Deceased.

He knew Serena was a war widow. That she had a son. But to read it, in black and white, made him wish he could have been there, could have saved her husband. Anything to take the sorrow from her eyes.

He looked back at her. Her gaze was intent on

her son and Jonas waited for her to look back up at him. When she did he saw the cold edge of distrust in her eyes.

She'd never believe his thoughts—she'd assume he wished her husband had lived so that Dottie wouldn't have left the house to her. As he typed in the pertinent information about Pepé, his mind kept going over his last conversation with Dottie.

"You'll love Serena. It's as though she's always been here. And her son, Pepé, is a doll."

"Mom, I don't understand why you never met her before now."

Dottie had been his stepmother but he'd always called her "Mom."

"Your uncle was a troubled man ever since he was a teenager. My father sent him to his family in Texas to get his life together after his Navy time was up. Instead of working on the ranch, making a living, he got a girl pregnant—Serena's mother—who never wanted anything more to do with him. Her family supported her and her new baby. Serena didn't know she had a biological family on her father's side until your uncle died."

Dottie's heart had been so big. She'd been a successful Realtor—a single, never-married woman, liberated for her generation. Until Jonas's widowed father, more than a decade her junior, showed up with four little boys. After that, she'd become a devoted wife and mother without missing a beat.

It had always been understood that Jonas would

get the farmhouse. Dottie had repeatedly promised it to him. She'd planned to move into a more senior-friendly condo in downtown Oak Harbor once he returned from his seven-month deployment.

Instead, she'd died at the hands of a murderer soon after changing her will to leave Serena and Pepé the house.

Would Dottie have done that if Serena had a husband and home to go back to in Texas?

They'd never know.

SERENA WATCHED JONAS'S face closely. Only a quick intake of breath, a scant second's pause, as he read over her military dependent ID card. She forced her shoulders to relax—he knew about her and Pepé; there was nothing to hide. His emails inquiring as to whether she'd be willing to sell the house to him hadn't surprised her, but the strength of her reaction had.

She'd made it clear that it was her house now, and it wasn't for sale. It was going to stay in the Forsyth family as Dottie had wished.

He'd never replied in full to her last refusal of his offer, sending her a one-liner stating that he'd come to meet with her once he returned from downrange.

When he looked back up at her now, she tried to glance past him at the computer screen, anywhere but at the eyes as blue as Texas bluebonnets, blazing with an intensity that made her blood feel like lava in her veins. This heat didn't come from the anger she'd experienced moments before. It was the kind of heat that two people share when they're attracted to each other.

Her hormones had been relatively dormant since Phil's death. Why did they have to start humming now? With the man who wanted to take Dottie's house from her?

Not for the first time since Dottie's will was read, Serena wondered what Dottie had been thinking. She must have expected her change of plans to upset Jonas, her stepson. She'd betrayed the man to whom she'd originally promised the house.

Jonas handed her ID back to her and she reflexively reached for it. But he held on to it for a moment, and she forced herself to look at him again.

"Again, Serena, I'm sorry. I'm afraid you've caught me at my most butt-faced moment."

"Hey, you're not supposed to stay that word!" Pepé said in his high-pitched voice.

"You're right, Pepé. I'm not using my best manners today."

"You need a time out." Pepé spoke matter-of-factly and Serena winced at how closely his tone mimicked hers. Did she sound that stern with him when he acted out?

"I need more than that, my man." Jonas swiveled his stool in front of Pepé, who sat on the small, kid-size examination table.

"You're not a doctor, right?"

"No, like I said, I'm a nurse practitioner, and I'll be looking after you."

"Okay." Pepé's ever-practical acceptance never ceased to awe Serena. Acceptance saved one from a lot of grief and sorrow.... "Pepé, what have we discussed about correcting adults?"

"You have to listen to your mother, buddy, but you're a good man to call me on my bad language." Jonas smiled at Pepé and Serena curled her toes.

Jonas Scott wasn't so easy to write off as a man who'd get over the loss of the house once he adjusted to her and Pepé living there. He was fully alive, fully present. And she found him as handsome in person as the photos of him in Dottie's house had hinted.

She gave Jonas credit; he didn't cover it up when he made a mess of things. She'd keep her observation to herself, though. She didn't know him well enough yet. He hadn't been able to make it home in time for Dottie's funeral; he'd been too far downrange, too deep in country. He'd told his brothers to go ahead with it and not to wait for him. The oldest brother, Paul, was an attorney and kept her informed all along of the process of Dottie's murder investigation, Serena's initial status as a possible suspect and then the reading of the will.

Paul had supported her because, by blood, Dottie was her aunt. Dottie had loved her and Pepé as if they'd been a part of one another's lives forever and not the short six months they'd shared before Dottie died. Because Dottie had vouched for Serena and introduced her to the other Scott brothers and their families, Paul believed in her innocence. Serena had been quickly removed from the suspect list by the island sheriff, so she hadn't needed Paul's legal support, after all. But it had been nice to know someone had her back.

Paul had warned her that Jonas was a little more than surprised that the house wasn't his. They were all shocked by it, in fact. Dottie had promised it to Jonas when he was a teenager, after his father died and left Dottie a widow.

"I was going to call you, Serena. I've only been back a little more than a week." Jonas's deep voice stopped the flood of memories.

Before she could reply, he turned his attention back to Pepé.

"Ready for the machine?" Jonas grinned at Pepé, who smiled.

Serena knew she should be grateful that at least Pepé was still around military men. As if it would somehow help keep his few memories of his father alive. Sadness welled and she cursed the ache in her heart for what might have been.

What *should* have been.

"Sure, Jonas!"

Jonas placed the small cuff on Pepé's upper arm and pressed the button to start the blood pressure reading.

"Open up."

Pepé opened his mouth, all the while staring at Jonas. Pain mingled with the regret she'd feel the rest of her life for what Pepé was missing by not having his own father around. The only emotional balm in all of it was that Phil had died when Pepé was barely four, so he didn't remember a whole lot about his dad—and the memories of grief would fade. They'd already faded for him.

Unlike her.

"So what are you here for, buddy?" Jonas had pulled the thermometer out of Pepé's mouth and entered the results into the computer.

"I had an ear 'fection but it's better now. No more yucky medicine!"

"Okay, well, let's see what your ears look like. He get a lot of these?" Blue eyes. Unblinking. Professional. No further discussion of the house they both wanted. That she owned. Not here.

She wanted to grab him and make those eyes glaze over with lust for her.

Maybe it was time to start dating again. Not Jonas, of course. Another man, who wasn't off-limits to her.

"Ear infections? Not until we moved here over a year ago. This is his third one since then."

"What convinced you to stay on Whidbey? It couldn't have been just the house."

She heard the veiled cleverness behind his casual conversation. As if he didn't know.

"Life. Getting the house from Dottie was a dream come true." That was plain mean. She opened her mouth to apologize, to appease her twinge of guilt.

"Well." His eyes stayed cool and made it clear that, like her, he wasn't going to share anything more personal. His focus was on Pepé.

Serena knew a moment of unabashed shame. She should give him a break. The poor guy had just come back from war, for heaven's sake. His stepmother had died while he was gone, and he hadn't been able to say a proper goodbye to the woman who'd raised him. Serena remembered seeing him in photos Dottie had scattered all around the house. In one photo, he'd been tall and well built in his Navy dress uniform, at his brother's wedding.

All the photos were gone—the brothers had come and collected Dottie's most personal belongings before Serena had a chance to take possession of the house. They'd left behind Dottie's collection of knickknacks and a house that was falling apart at the seams, if she were brutally honest. It wasn't anything she blamed Jonas's family for, though. Dottie was too busy making the most of every single day to concern herself with the daily maintenance of an old farmhouse.

Dottie's will and the fact that she'd given the house to Serena had become public knowledge only after Dottie's funeral.

He'd been at war. He deserved to know why she was the one who'd gotten the house. Problem was, she didn't know why Dottie had left it to her and Pepé, either. A legacy gift, yes, but at the risk of so much dissension in his family. Especially with Jonas Scott.

A quick knock sounded and a hospital corpsman popped her head around the door.

"Your next patient is ready in exam room three, Commander Scott."

"Thanks, I'll be there soon." Jonas proceeded to examine Pepé's ears, ignoring her presence.

Serena's chance to smooth the way with Jonas evaporated.

CHAPTER TWO

Whidbey Island
January 1941

SARAH FORSYTH HAD seen a lot in her twenty-one years, more than most girls from Whidbey Island, Washington. She'd also found the love of her life in her husband, Henry, and enjoyed a life with him and her daughter that she had no desire to see upset with one of Henry's crazy ideas.

"I'm a pilot and I'm the best man for the job, Sarah. My two years of college are all I need. I'm going to be an officer."

Sarah tried to assimilate Henry's words while keeping an eye on their daughter, Dottie, who was occupied with her rag doll near the woodstove. Their dinner plates were still on the table where they'd left them after Henry spoke the words that shattered their domestic tranquility.

"We agreed that you'd keep flying whenever you had a chance to make extra money, as long as it didn't keep you gone for more than a week at a time. Now you're talking about, what, going all over the world to save people? You have a family *here,* Henry. Your daughter needs you. She's not even five yet!"

"Our *country* needs me, Sarah. If we don't all pitch in, the Japanese are going to take over. If not them, the Germans. Do you want Sarah learning anything but English when she starts at the schoolhouse next fall?"

"I want Sarah to have her father!"

Rage welled in her, worse than when she'd fought him about moving back to his hometown in Texas instead of Whidbey Island. When he'd agreed to move to her family's farmhouse in Washington State, she'd thought the flying bug was out of his system.

"Honey, I knew Texas was too far from your family, and I knew you wanted to move back to the farm. I'm happy here, and we'll all be happy here again, when I get back. When this damn war is over and we can live in freedom again." His eyes blazed with a conviction that made her shudder. This wasn't another of Henry's whims.

"But we're not even in the war yet!" Why did Henry have to jump the gun on everything? "How much freedom is it for me to have to raise Dottie all by myself, Henry?"

"You have your family here with you, Sarah. You're not alone. The farm's pulling in good money with the milk and eggs. Your job at the library is going to work out for you, too."

"But Dottie…"

"Has a good mother who will take the best care of her."

"Momma, can I go play with my doll in my room?" Dottie never liked being around her parents when they argued, no matter how innocuous. She enjoyed the make-believe world she lived in with her Raggedy Ann.

"Sure, honey. Be a good girl and put your nightie on, too." It was best that Dottie didn't hear all of this.

Sarah looked at the man she'd fallen in love with when he was still so young. That was more than five years ago, when she'd been sixteen and he was eighteen. Henry Forsyth had grown into a solid specimen of manhood. *Her* specimen. She didn't want him to die.

"You don't even know if they'll take you."

Henry was much older than the local boys she'd heard had gone to Seattle to enlist.

"The Army recruiter said I'm a shoe-in with my flying experience. I have to sign the papers by tonight."

Those commitment papers required him to complete Army Air Corps pilot training, or, if he flunked out, agree to serve as an enlisted soldier for a term of three years.

Three years wasn't forever; she knew that. But it was more than half of little Dottie's life at this point. What about a sibling for her? When would that happen?

Sarah knew that if the Americans joined the war Henry's three-year commitment could turn into forever.

In the worst way.

"You're lying. You already signed those papers while you were down in San Diego!"

He looked guilty, which gave her hope for his soul but didn't make her any happier about what he'd signed up for.

"I should've insisted that you help Papa on the farm full-time when he asked."

"You know that would never have worked for me, Sarah. I have to be in the air. Plus the extra money I've pulled in hasn't hurt, has it? I'll be making more money in the Army Air Corps."

She knew it was true. He'd learned to work as a crop-duster in his early teens beside his daddy and older brother back in Texas. During the dust bowl years, Henry had gone west and found work flying crop dusters up and down the coast, from California to Washington. She'd met him by chance on the dance floor at the Washington State Fair in Puyallup. Lucky for her he'd been on a break from flying and in search of some fun.

He'd been so handsome, his face all lit up by the lights from the amusement games of chance. Each booth had bright white bulbs that glowed yellow at night. The night felt soft—the sun took longer to set in midsummer, and it had been so warm on the mainland, far away from Whidbey.

Papa had taken their entire family off the island for the whole day. He'd used all the money they'd made from selling milk and told Mama "more money will come in. The kids need to see there's more to the world than Whidbey Island."

They hadn't counted on their youngest daughter, only fifteen, falling in love with a complete stranger. A stranger who showed up on Whidbey Island six months later to woo her. He caught flights up and down the west coast, arriving on Whidbey every few months.

Sarah had been a senior in school the last year they'd dated and hoped to go to college some day. History had always fascinated her. She planned to work a few years after high school and save enough money for classes. But love won out— she and Henry had made a baby one night under the apple tree in Papa's orchard. On the quilt her grandmother had hand-stitched for her hope chest. She'd snuck it out of the cedar box Papa had built, knowing the night was going to be cold. Knowing she wanted Henry to kiss her again and again.

"You're a good husband, Henry. And a good father. That's why I don't want you to go." She wasn't manipulating him; she meant it. He'd made enough money for them to live very comfortably on the land her father had given them, including the small cottage they lived in. He promised her the farmhouse once her siblings were married off, when he and Mama were ready to switch and take the cottage. Papa believed the farmhouse should always be for a growing family, and he wanted to keep it in Forsyth hands.

Henry made sure she got her dream. Well, as much as she could, being a new mother and all. He helped her take correspondence courses so she could work at the town library as a clerk. He went to night school, hoping to one day have a four-year degree. They'd done well so far.

Sarah loved books, stories, facts, history. And if the accounts of World War I that she'd recently read were any indication, she might never see Henry again.

"Henry, remember hearing about how hard the Great War was on our families?"

His expression softened, and for the first time since he told her he was going to fly for the Army Air Corps he looked doubtful.

"Yes." His grandfather had died in the trenches at Ypres, and her father's older brother had come back shell-shocked and never quite recovered his original wits.

"I don't want anything bad to happen to you, honey." She walked up to him and threw her arms around him. He held back for just a split second and she knew.

He'd already started to make the mental preparations to go. He had to. He was a man who loved his country and wasn't going to let some crazy dictators around the world ruin it.

Sarah laid her head on his chest and listened for his heartbeat. It was the one thing that could soothe her. When she'd started her labor with Dottie all she'd wanted was to rest on her side, her ear to Henry's chest, the steady *thump-thump* taking her thoughts away from the excruciating pain.

"Sarah. I love you so much, darling." He raised his hand to her hair and stroked it away from her face.

"I know you do, Henry." She raised her lips to his and they shared the kiss that a couple does before a long separation. Deep, loving and warm. Never enough.

"I'll help you pack later, after I get Dottie to bed."

"I don't need to take much. They're giving me a whole new wardrobe!"

He tried to amuse her, to crack lighthearted lines here and there while they gathered his few personal items and stacked them neatly in the small duffel the Army recruiter had given him.

"How long before you ship out?"

"I'll probably get through the flight training pretty fast, and then be out there before the end of the year."

"Where's 'there'?"

"Somewhere in the Pacific."

His expression was as neutral as stone and she knew it pained him to leave her, to leave Dottie. She also saw the pilot's anticipation simmering in his eyes. Henry was gearing up for a fight, for the war they likely faced. Her heart squeezed with longing as she acknowledged, at least to herself, that it could indeed be the fight of his life.

HENRY HADN'T TOLD Sarah everything. He couldn't worry her. Besides, he would come back—he was the best pilot he knew, and nowhere did he feel more at ease than in a cockpit.

The recruiter had been slicker than any of the politicians he'd had occasion to ferry from town to town when his crop-dusting jobs had petered out midwinter. But Henry saw past the Army haircut and the quick talk. He saw a chance to really make a difference, to maybe even have a career that he could bring Sarah and Dottie along on.

Sarah never wanted to leave Whidbey; he knew that. Yet with a little time and some persuasion from him, he thought she'd be willing to move. The recruiter had said he could get stationed in Hawaii! Why wouldn't Sarah want to join him there, to have Dottie run on hot sand instead of freezing wet grass most of the summer? "I'll send you my paychecks as soon as I get them. My pilot training is going to be at Moffett Field, in California. I'll be an aviation cadet, enlisted, because of my high school diploma. But I'll become an officer if I can, Sarah." He watched her long fingers hover over his freshly pressed undershirts, her lips wobbly as she tried not to cry.

Dear, sweet Sarah. She was tough as nails one minute, a complete cream puff the next. It was part of what he loved about her.

"That's not necessary."

"Sure it is. You can save it all, or use it to buy yourself a pretty dress."

She threw down his one pair of pajamas and propped her hands on her hips as she faced him.

"I don't need a pretty dress, Henry. And I can make enough off the farm and my library position to support Dottie and me just fine. But I don't give a darn about any of it. I want you to come back safe, do you hear me?"

He stared into her green eyes and knew he'd come back. He didn't have a choice; they were meant to be together.

She'd said "come back." So she'd accepted that he needed to do this; he needed to go.

Unlike the reaction he'd expected, her capitulation didn't make him feel jubilant. The reality of the months, possibly years, apart made his chest feel as it there was a huge weight on it.

"I'll come back better than ever, Sarah Jean. You just watch me."

He smiled at her, the way he did after he brought her to climax, the private smile that always made her blush. When her cheeks turned rosy he grabbed her hand.

"Is Dottie asleep by now, do you think?"

"She closed her eyes as soon as I turned out her light."

"Come to bed with me, Sarah. Love me."

"Oh, Henry."

She trembled with her need and he knew he'd remember this night through all his days away. He unbuttoned the six tiny red buttons that ran in between her breasts and slid his hand over her breast, encased in a simple white cotton bra. He teased her nipple through the material and she bit his earlobe.

"Don't torture me, Henry." Her breath was sweet and her skin hot as she unbuckled his belt and unzipped his pants.

"There's nothing here but pleasure, darling." He hiked up her dress and pulled it over her arms, which she'd lifted to help him. Her dress and his pants hit the pine floor of the farmhouse at the same time, followed quickly by their underwear.

Sarah turned to clear the bed of his luggage.

"Wait."

She turned back to him. "What?"

"Let me do this for you, before we go to the bed."

He knelt down in front of her and she sighed, her hands massaging, then gripping, his shoulders. Henry had to have all of her tonight. As he breathed in her essence and used his mouth to make her cry out, he prayed it wouldn't be the last time.

CHAPTER THREE

Whidbey Island
Two days before Thanksgiving

SERENA LUGGED THE last of the attic boxes into the spanking new climate-controlled storage room she'd had built as an extension off the garage. Both were connected to the farmhouse by a small mud-room. It was the only structural change she'd made since she'd inherited Dottie's house.

"It's *your* house now," she muttered under her breath. It took time to adjust to the fact that she was a homeowner, and not only that, the home was where the woman who'd given her and Pepé comfort and unconditional love had lived her entire life.

It was already more than six months since Dottie's death and the house still felt lonely without her. As if somehow the house itself wasn't finished mourning the woman who'd filled it with so much love for so many years.

Nevertheless, Serena and Pepé had made it their home and the rhythm of their life had settled into a comfortable, manageable zone.

Until Pepé's doctor's appointment last week.

Running into Jonas Scott at the clinic had been her roughest time on Whidbey so far. Not counting the day, of course, that Dottie had been murdered at the hands of a psycho.

It stung that she was attracted to Jonas—attracted with a capital *A. Of course* the first man to get her blood going since Phil's death had to be the one person she had nothing in common with. Except for Dottie….

Besides, no matter who Jonas was to her, it was too soon to think about a new relationship. Her body was only starting to wake up after her grief.

Her back ached painfully, the muscles tight and weary after moving what felt like a ton of knick-knacks. Aunt Dottie, and probably her mother before her, had had a penchant for collecting curios. Unable to fathom sorting the monstrous collection so soon after Dottie's death this past summer, Serena thought her idea of placing the decades-old boxes in stackable plastic bins a stroke of genius. Until she realized each bin weighed a minimum of twenty-five pounds. And she'd had to purchase dozens of them.

"I am crazy." The boxes were stacked neatly against the far wall of the storage room, but it was only a prelude to the inevitable chore.

Sorting.

"Mom! *Mommmm!*" Pepé's cries grew louder as he zeroed in on her location. Like a bat, Pepé had his own kind of echolocation when it came to Serena.

Especially since Phil had died.

"Here, *hijo*." She wiped her forehead and placed her hands on her hips. She'd gotten to know Dottie only in the last months of her life, and Serena's appearance obviously came from her Hispanic mother. Dottie had been tiny and petite whereas Serena's curves resembled her mother's.

Mama. Juanita Rodriguez was her rock, to this day. Serena had been all but abandoned by her biological father but Juanita had made up for it, as had her *abuela* and her *tias*. She missed her mother and made a mental note to call her later. It was time to start building the bridge between them that the pursuit of her biological father's family had severely tested.

"Mom, look!" Pepé ran into the room with an action-hero figure, his focus entirely on the red plastic toy clutched in his small fingers. "I can fly!"

"Wonderful, Pepé, just watch out for the— *No!*" She lunged forward to catch him as Pepé's arms flew out, his toy launching through the air as he landed on the box she had yet to stack.

The plastic bin toppled over and its cover popped off, spilling piles of crushed newsprint onto the tile floor.

"Pepé, are you okay?"

"I'm fine, Mom. Where's my hero?" Pepé scrambled to his feet as quickly as he'd fallen, his gaze intent on the stacked boxes.

"Oh, no, you don't, Joseph Peter Delgado. I'll find it, but for now, help me put this box back together. Carefully."

Pepé frowned as he bent down to help Serena. He knew she only invoked his full name when he'd pushed it. He was a sweet little boy, *all* boy. The dull ache of loss pounded in her rib cage, though it had faded from the life-changing pain that had engulfed her when the uniformed U.S. Marine Corps team had knocked on their door in Texas two years ago.

"Slowly, Pepé." She showed him how to pick up each wad of paper and check to see if anything delicate was wrapped inside. Most of the paper was yellowed newsprint that had protected Dottie's precious memories.

Under one larger bunch of paper she saw a red knitted sock peeking out. Serena carefully pulled the paper away to discover a good-size Christmas stocking. It seemed to be hand-knitted, with the name "Henry" embroidered across the top in white and navy blue stars embellishing the foot. The yarn was scratchy and rustic. Serena wondered at the hands that had knit with such rough fiber. She enjoyed knitting but preferred the newer fiber blends like alpaca that felt like silk against her fingers. This stocking was a labor of love.

"Do you think there's anything in it, Mom?"

"Maybe." Probably spiders and other creepy-crawlies. She bit her lip as she reached into the Christmas stocking and felt a slight bulge in the toe.

"Let me see, Pepé." She opened the top and saw a piece of paper that, once she pulled it out of the stocking, revealed itself to be a black-and-white photograph. It was reminiscent of a tintype in the way the sepia colors highlighted the image of a Navy sailor.

Serena flipped over the photo, looking for identification. All that was written on the back was "Charles—the man I wrote you about." She placed the photo on a box and pulled out another. This one was of a small, happy family, the man in an Army uniform, a beautiful woman and little girl next to him, with "Graduation from Aviation Cadet Flight Training, August 1941" written on the backside.

"Can I look inside the stocking, Mom?"

"Sure, honey. But be careful—if anything bites your fingers, pull your hand out!"

Pepé giggled as only a boy can at the thought of a bug.

He thrust his hand into the stocking and it swallowed up his arm, almost to the elbow. His few remaining baby teeth shone as he smiled in triumph, pulling out his treasure.

"Mom, look!"

Pepé held up what looked like a toy airplane. "Can I have it, Mom?"

"Let me take a look at it first." She rocked backward from her heels and sat on the floor. The ceramic tiles were hard and cold, but she remained focused on the tiny plane.

"It has some writing on it, and look who's flying it, honey." She angled the tiny toy so that Pepé could see Santa Claus waving from the cockpit.

"There's a wreath on the tail, Mom."

"And a name." She couldn't clearly make out the scrolled name on the side of the aircraft but it looked like "Dottie." The ornament was light but solid, as if carved from a single piece of wood.

"What kind of plane is it, Mom?"

"I don't know, honey, but we'll find out, okay? As soon as we get the rest of this box put back."

"Let me look to see if anything else is in there, Mom." He made a point of carefully inspecting the box, removing each crumpled paper and smoothing it on the table. Just like she did.

She smiled as Pepé imitated her mannerisms. "Okay, but I think it's empty."

He made a show of reaching back into the stocking. Serena studied the tiny airplane in her hand. Who had carved this for Dottie? When?

"Mom, there's more paper!"

"It's to fill out the toe, honey."

"No, I think…" Pepé pulled out a scrunched-up wad of paper that he unfolded.

Serena grinned. "You were right, Pepé. What is it?"

"It's an angel, Mom."

In his little hands was an angel woven from some kind of straw.

"Look, it's been glued in several places. It's old and fragile. Let's take it in the house with us and put it in a safe place."

"What about the airplane, Mom?"

"We'll take that with us, too." She shivered. "It's getting close to dinnertime. Let's go back into the house."

Serena had to wonder if they were about to find out more of Dottie's history than even Jonas and his family knew.

"SERENA, I'M NOT angry with you, *mi hija*. I understand that you had to make your own way. You know, I envy it. I never had that kind of freedom. You have a degree, a career. You can support Pepé as I never could have supported you." Juanita Rodriguez spoke to her on the phone as Serena prepared dinner.

"I'm glad you're not mad, Mama." Serena didn't believe for one minute that her mother was completely over Serena's taking Pepé thousands of miles from the family, but she did hear Juanita's love in the softly spoken words.

"When is Pepé going to Skype with me again?"

Serena laughed. "Mama, you're going crazy

with your tablet!" Serena had given Juanita a wireless tablet for her birthday this past summer, and Juanita's first request had been to connect regularly with her grandson.

"Did you know you can read on them, too? I read my sexy novels on the apps."

"Don't let Red hear you say that!" Red was Serena's stepfather and she loved him dearly. He'd treated her as his own daughter her entire life.

"I like it when she reads those books!" Red's voice boomed in the background.

Serena groaned. "Mama, I don't need to hear this. I'm happy for you, but let's keep your love life out of it."

"Can I talk to Abuela?" Pepé stood in front of her.

"There's a young man here who'd like to speak with you, Mama."

"Put him on, but first, *mi hija,* know that I send you a thousand *besitos* and I love you, sweetie."

"I love you, too, Mama. And kisses to you, too. Here's Pepé."

Serena handed the phone to Pepé and watched as he animatedly described his school day to Juanita, leaving out no tedious detail. Gratitude filled her heart. Their life wasn't perfect by far, but they had more than most. They had Serena's loving upbringing and the love that Juanita had taught Serena to share.

"MOM, IT'S THIS ONE." Pepé's enthusiasm lightened Serena's mood enough that she was able to ignore the handprint he left on the computer screen over the photo of a World War II aircraft.

"The P-40 Warhawk. Yes, I think you're right, Pepé." She scrolled through photos of the plane that almost perfectly matched the tiny wooden version of it that sat on the desk next to the computer mouse.

"I like its shark's teeth."

"That's how they painted the ones that were in a special squadron called the Flying Tigers. They're tigers' teeth, actually."

She should let Pepé think the plane was a shark and not a machine designed to take out the enemy with its powerful engine and deadly armament, but she owed it to him to be straightforward about historical fact.

You can't protect him from reality.

Unfortunately, the reality of war had taken his father from him, too soon.

"When was world war, Mom? Is it the one Dad died in, with the bomb?"

Why couldn't World War II have been the last war ever?

Sorrow tightened around her throat and she paused to take a deep breath, a practice she'd learned during many similar conversations. Pepé would hardly remember Phil as he grew older, and his grasp of war and how his dad had died was nebulous at best.

"No, honey. Daddy died in a different part of the world, in Afghanistan. It wasn't a bomb that hurt him, but a bullet."

"From a sniper."

"Yes."

Pepé's gaze remained on her but she saw his eyes shift to the airplane ornament. While it saddened her that he'd know his father mostly through the memories she shared with him, she was grateful he hadn't suffered the grief an older child would have.

"What was the world war?"

"There were two world wars." She picked up the wooden model, willing it to tell her its story.

"This plane was flown in World War II, in the Pacific, from what the internet says." She held it in her hands, wondering again why Dottie had kept it. She knew virtually nothing of her biological aunt's younger life.

Had it been from Dottie's father? Her biological grandfather? Or was it another item Jonas Scott would demand she turn over to him and his siblings? Based on how long the ornament had obviously been packed away, she'd be surprised if Jonas or his brothers knew about it.

At the clinic Jonas had caught her off guard. She'd had to remind herself that he was the same man who had become her nemesis from the moment Dottie's will was read six months ago.

Serena had been asked to attend the reading of Dottie's will, much to her dismay. She hadn't expected anything, especially not a house. Jonas wasn't at the reading, of course, since he'd been downrange. In a war zone.

He'd emailed her almost immediately, offering to buy the house.

Unlike his siblings, Jonas hadn't been interested in getting anything from Dottie's estate, which had been considerable. He'd walked away with enough money to build his own home on Whidbey, and a nice one at that, or at least pay off the mortgage on the small town house his brothers told her he had.

She understood how easy it was for him to see her as nothing more than an opportunist who'd bamboozled Dottie. She'd had the opportunity—Dottie had received physical therapy at the clinic where Serena worked temporarily as a receptionist until she was sure she wanted to go back to practicing law full-time. Serena clenched her teeth at the memory of how damned rude he'd been in his last email to her, and the letter he'd sent registered mail, indicating his intention to contest the will if they couldn't reach an agreement. In other words, if she didn't accept his offer for the house.

He hadn't legally, officially, filed an appeal for the will. She was certain it was only a matter of time. He probably thought that once he was back on island he'd be able to convince her to give him the house.

The Jonas she'd met at the base hospital didn't resemble the 100-percent jerk she'd imagined him to be, although his comments about working in pediatrics put him in that category. It was easier to think of him as the man who wanted her house.

The Jonas she'd met appeared genuinely apologetic for his harsh words to Dr. Franklin. She'd glimpsed compassion in his eyes as he'd checked Pepé in for his examination.

He knew she was a lawyer, but hadn't pressed the point. His brother Paul had indicated he'd hire her when she was ready to practice law again. Had he told Jonas?

Serena loved the law and had applied for her Washington State license, which would take another month or so to come through. She still wasn't certain if she'd seek a job with Paul Scott's firm, though.

She'd taken the job at the physical-therapy clinic as a distraction when she and Pepé had first moved to Whidbey. She hadn't been ready to commit to full-time work yet, and she had several months of transitioning her legal license from Texas to Washington, which included exams.

She'd come west to get to know the other half of her biological family, a family she'd never even known about until after Phil's death. She wanted to keep her focus on that, rather than her law career.

Phil's death had hit her mother hard. Serena had been surprised and then shocked when Juanita showed up at her door after Phil's burial, with the announcement that she did indeed know who Serena's biological father was, and that he, too, had died within the past year. It had been a bitter pill at the time, but now that she'd had the chance to know Dottie and find out about her family, her resentment toward her mother had lessened.

Serena couldn't let any other people die before she had a chance to get to know them. What had started as a short trip west to meet Dottie and find out about her biological father had turned into an entrée to a new life.

Dottie had died before they'd had a chance to go through Dottie's entire life history, but she'd recounted a lot about her stepsons, especially Jonas, over dinners and picnics. Even better, the bond Dottie and Pepé shared had been immediate. Dottie said that Pepé looked just like his grandfather, Dottie's brother, Todd.

Serena's biological father.

"Hey, Mom, can we go swimming on Thanksgiving?" Pepé stood next to her at the computer desk, dressed in his *Frozen* pajamas.

"I don't know, honey. It's too cold if you ask me."

"But they heat the pool at Beyond the Stars." His eyes were big as he questioned her logic. She giggled.

"Yes, but it's wintertime, sweetie. It'll probably be too chilly, so don't get your hopes up. Besides, you'll be too busy eating the *gobble-gobble!*" She tickled his tummy and he shrieked with glee, snuggling into her.

At almost seven years old, his snuggle time with her was limited. Yet it was hard to imagine a day when her little boy would reject her hugs.

She gave his head a kiss and patted his back. "Go brush your teeth and I'll be right in to read with you."

"Okay, Mom."

He darted out of the office and she stared at the computer screen.

BTS, or Beyond the Stars, was the special resort for military Gold Star families to find peace and rediscover themselves after the initial shock and grief of losing a loved one to war had passed.

She and Pepé had been to BTS for a week almost two years ago and it had made a world of difference for both of them. She'd only just found Dottie, and Pepé was still struggling with the fact he'd never see his dad again. The staff of counselors and social workers had been so compassionate with Pepé, and Serena had left with her own batteries recharged. It was where she and Pepé had found the courage to live life on life's terms.

They were going back for Thanksgiving at the invitation of the owner and director, Val Di Paola, and her husband, Lucas. Located on San Juan Island in the middle of Puget Sound, the resort was magical in its setting.

What it had done for her and Pepé was nothing short of a miracle. The staff had become good friends, almost like an extended family, to them.

Thanksgiving at BTS was going to be wonderful.

CHAPTER FOUR

Moffett Field, California
August 1941

"HENRY!"

Sarah yelled as loudly as she could, knowing that her voice could never carry over the marching band and cheer of the crowd as the aviation graduates marched in front of them to the center of the field.

"Momma, where's Daddy?" Dottie's face was screwed up in a scowl. It was hard for her to tell one man from another when they all had crew cuts and wore the same uniform.

Sarah took her little white-gloved hand.

"Here, honey, I'll help you point to him. He's in the first row, third over—the tall one."

"I see him, Momma!" Dottie giggled, and Sarah's heart swelled at how cute she looked with her blond curls and the red, white and blue beret she'd knitted for her. Shirley Temple didn't have anything on almost-six-year-old Dottie Forsyth.

"I'm sure you do, sweetie." Sarah didn't think Dottie could actually see her father but she wasn't going to question her now. They hadn't seen him since he'd left in January, and the day was going to be special; Sarah knew it in her gut.

Her mind drifted as the man in charge of the ceremony talked about courage and honor and duty, and handed out diplomas to each aviator. Henry had told her she'd be the one to pin his wings on, and she couldn't wait. She also expected that he was going to announce that she and Dottie could travel with him. Move with him and live on an Army post wherever he got sent. He hadn't said it but she'd read in the paper at the library that a pilot's family could move as far as here in California or even Hawaii.

Sarah smiled. Henry thought she'd never be willing to leave Whidbey Island again, not after his brief time in Texas in the army, and then his flight training here in California. But she'd realized during their separation that being anywhere with Henry, together as a family, was more important than being in the house she'd grown up in. The house would wait for them. They wouldn't be gone forever. Henry had missed flying and surely it couldn't take very long to get it out of his system. Not considering how often the Army had him up in the air.

"Second Lieutenant Henry Forsyth."

"That's your daddy!" she whispered in Dottie's ear while squeezing her hand.

She watched him walk smartly across the small platform and salute the commanding officer before he reached out to receive his diploma. Pride roared in her ears and she couldn't keep the widest grin of all time off her face.

"Just look at your daddy, Dottie girl."

"Go, Daddy!" Dottie whisper-shouted the words, always mindful of her manners. Except when she wasn't, like the day she'd snuck out of the house and played in the puddles left by a storm last week. It'd taken three tubs of water for Sarah to get the dirt out of Dottie's mud-soaked skirts.

Henry turned toward the audience and Sarah waved. It felt as though her heart would pound right out of her ribs, and it wasn't because of her tight dress. As soon as he saw them he waved back, his teeth white in the afternoon sun. The day couldn't be more beautiful.

It passed in a blur: Sarah and Dottie standing next to Henry, Sarah pinning his wings to his uniform, the lovely reception afterward where she met other wives who'd come to see their husbands get their wings, the walk back to the quarters where they had a small room together as a family. Henry didn't have to stay in the barracks any longer—he was under orders to go to his next duty station.

Which was why, after they'd ensured that Dottie was sound asleep and they made tender, hello-again love, Sarah was puzzled to hear Henry announce that he was resigning from the Army.

"I don't understand. How can you? You owe them time."

"I can and I have. The president is making sure the right pilots sign up for this special mission I'll be part of. I'm working for a civilian, a contractor, who has a flying mission overseas that'll pay way more than the Army Air Corps, and I'll get experience I'd never get Stateside. I can always go back to the Army Air Corps after this."

"Can we still move overseas with you? I thought American civilians weren't going to Europe anymore, not with the war and all."

"No, honey, you and Dottie can't come with me. You knew that, Sarah. I'm headed for the Pacific."

She bit her bottom lip and couldn't keep the tears from spilling.

"But you said…you said it would all be okay once we saw each other again, Henry. You said you might be a career man and they'd send us all together to the same places."

He raised her chin and wiped the tears from her cheeks.

"Isn't it good, this time together?" He kissed her.

"How long will you be gone?"

"A year at the most. I ship out to Burma within a week or two, and then I'll get so many flight hours back-to-back I won't have to stay that long."

Doubt weighed down her joy at being with him again.

"You can't possibly know how long it'll be, Henry. These past eight months without you have been awful."

"I know, Sarah, and I can't thank you enough for being such a wonderful wife, waiting for me, and for being such a good mother to Dottie. She's so beautiful, Sarah. I hope we get to have more babies together."

"I do, too."

"We will, honey, as soon as I get back. Listen, I'm going to be making a lot of money. I want you to save it up for us, and when we get back we can build an addition to the farmhouse. It'll be the biggest house on Whidbey! And use it for your parents, too, Sarah. They've worked hard to be able to give us the place. I want to thank them somehow."

"Thank them by coming back as soon as you can and making their daughter happy."

"I will, I promise."

As they made love, Henry's hands caressed her as if she were the most precious woman in the world. As if he couldn't get enough of her. She had no doubt that she was the woman of his dreams. That he loved her beyond measure.

But it wasn't enough to keep him home.

Mingaladon, Burma
January 1942

THE AIR SIREN woke Henry from a dead sleep. He jumped out of his rack and shoved his socks on before jamming his feet into his flight boots.

"Let's go, let's go, let's go!" Cappy Smith sang out with glee. Cappy was his new best friend since they'd gone through Army Air Corps training together and both left the Army to join Chennault's Flying Tigers. They all lived for the missions. Mingaladon, Burma, was hot, muggy and tens of thousands of miles from home. Not what any of them had signed on for. They'd volunteered to fight the enemy.

Since last month their enemy in the Pacific was clear: the Japanese.

It still stung that they'd been hit on U.S. territory, in Pearl Harbor.

"Wake up, Henry!"

"I'm up, I'm up!" He zipped up his flight suit on the run. They all slept in their suits when they were on ready alert, prepared to go in an instant. Gravel and jungle compost crunched under his feet as he pounded toward the runway.

Fifteen pilots crowded into the ready room, a makeshift shack near the end of the runway.

They all stopped in shock as they recognized their briefing officer.

General Claire Lee Chennault. Founder of the

American Volunteer Group—AVG—that made up the entirety of the Flying Tigers. General Chennault was famous for showing up, unannounced, for briefings just like this one.

The mission had to be crucial.

"You're launching in five minutes, gentlemen. The Japanese are on their way to take out Rangoon." Rangoon was a port city crucial to the Allied war effort. Henry and his colleagues were silent. While no mission was ever the same as the last, their past several had been to protect Rangoon. Three of their P-40 Warhawks hadn't come back in the last mission he'd flown, thanks to the murderous pilots who flew highly maneuverable Ki-43s against them. It was overwhelming to think about the sheer numbers of war machines, both on the water and in the air, that the Japanese had. But one good hit could take an aircraft out. That was Henry's job and what he had to stay focused on.

He wanted to get in, take out as many of the enemy as possible and get back to base before they even knew what hit them.

The general finished his briefing and within twenty minutes Henry was clawing for altitude in his P-40 Warhawk on Cappy's wing on the way to Rangoon. It was pitch-dark, but by the time they got there, the morning sun would be their guide to the bombers they'd take down.

Henry didn't like the transit part of any mission.

It allowed too much time to think, even during the short twenty- to thirty-minute run to Rangoon.

He pulled out the photo of Sarah and Dottie that he kept in his front right chest pocket and gave it a quick kiss before turning to the last leg of their ingress.

"Bandits ten o'clock!" Cappy's voice crackled, and Henry watched him break hard to port to go after the Japanese fighter. Another Ki-43 was headed straight for Henry. He aimed, fired, and knew a bittersweet satisfaction when the aircraft took a hit and started to spin out.

"Cripes, they're hard to hit!" he shouted into his mike, warning his squadron mates that the Ki-43 was every bit as maneuverable as the general had warned, and a challenge to the AVG. On previous missions the Japanese Ki-21 "Sally" bombers had been unescorted by the Ki-43 fighters and been easier targets.

Henry took out two more fighters, maneuvering to get the enemy bombers in his sights. One was in his line of fire but he needed to close the gap. After a tense five minutes of outshooting a second Ki-43, Henry fired on his first bomber of the mission. It didn't go down right away, but when his ammo hit its fuel tank, a fiery ball engulfed the aircraft. Henry throttled back and turned to starboard, avoiding the debris of the explosion and coming face-to-face with a second bomber. He had to fly under the belly of the bomber and throttle back before he could line up on the bomber, firing into the cockpit as he raced by the port side of the war bird as it jerked into a nosedive.

"Come on, where are you?" Henry looked for more fighters to take out until the second wave of Japanese bombers showed up.

Thwack.

It was much quieter, stealthier, than Henry would have expected. His bird had been hit, and he watched in horror as smoke from the burning engine began to fill up his cockpit. He'd lost control of his plane, and was headed toward the ocean at deadly speed.

"No!"

He had to get back to Sarah.

The fighter who'd hit him was below him to starboard, obviously not concerned that Henry had a chance at survival. With what little maneuverability he had left in the bird, Henry tilted the wings to give him a chance of hitting the bastard. Henry gritted his teeth and pulled up on his throttle. Nothing.

"Damn it!"

He wasn't in a dive; that was a small consolation. He'd lost too much altitude to bail out, however. He was going down with the aircraft.

The ocean raced past him and he made out several spots of white sand circling lush green growth on the horizon.

"Aim for the islands," General Chennault told

them during training at this last brief: if they had to go down, land on one of the uninhabited islands that surrounded southern Thailand.

Henry aimed for the one with the widest beach and prayed he'd be able to land without the bird flipping over and trapping him in the cockpit during the inevitable crash landing.

He had minutes until his fate was determined. Seconds, perhaps.

Sarah was going to kill him. If the crash didn't.

CHAPTER FIVE

Whidbey Island
Thanksgiving Day

JONAS GROANED AS his oldest brother Paul swiped the basketball from his sweaty palms.

"You're not going to get the house back, bro." Paul dribbled the ball in the corner where his garage met the driveway. Paul's know-it-all-attorney smirk irritated Jonas.

"Watch me." Jonas held up his hands to catch the swift pass Paul attempted to make to Jim, and loped up to the basket to dunk the ball.

"Let it go, man, Paul's right." Jim caught the rebound and winked at his girlfriend, Lucy, before he attempted a long shot. Jonas intercepted the ball as it bounced off the rim.

"Stop showing off for your girl, fire-boy." Jonas loved teasing Jim, the family fireman. Jim had always been fascinated by explosions as a kid—including blowing up their Lego models with firecrackers. The name had stuck when he went to firefighting school.

John, a successful landscaper and closest in

age to Jonas, hovered behind Jonas, not allowing him to attempt a basket. Jonas long-bounced the ball to Paul.

Jonas had been back an entire two weeks from deployment, and they were all gathered at Paul's house for Thanksgiving. He finally felt as though he was shaking off the last of his jet lag. He'd even made it through his first week at work. He laughed at how good it felt to be with his brothers, all four of them in the same place again. Thanksgiving dinner was going to be brutal when they sat down to the turkey Paul's wife, Mary, was preparing with John's wife, Jackie, but Jonas was grateful they were doing it together—all four of them in the same place again.

It was their first holiday season without Dottie.

"Are we sure they got the right person?"

Jonas's question was as effective as a fire hose as his three brothers froze in their places. No one else had mentioned the arrest, the trial or the sentencing of the mentally imbalanced woman charged with Dottie's murder. Apparently they didn't expect him to, either.

"Go help Mary and Jackie in the kitchen, will you, Lucy?" Jim, the second oldest, spoke quietly to his girlfriend.

"Of course."

They waited until the storm door closed and Lucy was safely out of earshot.

"Why the hell are you asking that now, Jonas?" Paul took over his eldest-brother role.

"Yeah, happy effing Thanksgiving. Pass the gravy." Jim dribbled the ball.

"Give him a break, he wasn't here." John was quick as always to stick up for their little brother.

"Why don't you all just kiss my ass? I was gone and I only know what you told me, which wasn't a whole hell of a lot."

"That's because you were at war and didn't need the distractions. The psycho woman who killed her was deemed mentally ill. Jackie has to diagnose these kinds of folks all the time." John owned a thriving landscaping business on Whidbey. Jackie was a psychiatrist.

"Does that mean she's locked up for life?" Jonas hated opening the wound for his brothers, but he had to ask the questions that email, internet searches and long-distance phone calls couldn't answer for him. He needed to be with them, see their expressions. Needed to know that everything that could be done was done.

"She should be. Laws change all the time, and where she'll be incarcerated may change. She's criminally insane. She also got away with proving she never intended to kill Dottie." Paul, ever the lawyer, kept his voice low, his expression neutral as he delivered the bombshell.

"What?" Outrage blasted through Jonas. "How

do you kill someone deliberately by drowning and get the jury to agree that it was a *mistake?*"

Jim put a hand on Jonas's shoulder. "You're not asking anything we haven't all gone over more than once. Dottie could conceivably have had a stroke while she was on that underwater treadmill."

"AquaTracker." Paul spoke up. Paul ran a good-size legal firm on Whidbey and knew the case inside out.

"Yeah, the AquaTracker in the physical therapist's clinic. The murderer set Dottie up to go under the water, supposedly just for a few seconds. But it ended up being minutes, and at her age, Dottie didn't stand a chance."

Jim shook his head. "I was there with our fire engine, Jonas. Dottie was gone before we started CPR."

"I'm so sorry I wasn't here to help you all through the trial." Jonas meant the words more than he was able to express. They sounded inadequate to him, though. They didn't truly describe his visceral reaction to the murder of the woman he'd loved so much. The woman who'd taken him in and given him what he'd lost when their mother died unexpectedly, leaving their dad a widower at forty-four with four boys to raise.

"It's worked out, Jonas. Believe me, it's better that you, of all of us, weren't here. You would've beaten yourself up for not being able to save her yourself." Paul knew what it was like to hear about a death that could have been prevented with the right people there.

"It took me a long time to get over seeing her in that way, man." Jim ran his fingers through his hair.

"You're probably right. But still, I hate that you all had to handle it without my help."

"There wasn't anything to do. By the time we got the call..." Jim spun the basketball on his index finger, his expression blank.

Jonas took it all in—his three brothers, the crisp air, the scent of roasting turkey coming out of the house through the chimneys and back door.

"It's just not right. Dottie should be here."

"We're lucky we had her as long as we did." Ever the optimist, Paul shoved his hands into the pockets of his hoodie and rocked on his sneakers. "As horrible as how she died was, we didn't have to see her suffer for years with an awful disease."

Anger mixed with the frustration that simmered in Jonas. He saved people for a living but he couldn't change what had happened to Dottie. "And now I find out I don't have the house I always thought I would. The house she promised me. What have I missed?"

"You need to get over it, brother. Dottie wasn't crazy and I'm sure she had her reasons." Jim tossed the ball to Jonas, who grasped it to his chest. Just above where the ache was from all the loss. Dottie was gone, his career was in for a serious plateau during the next three years and his dream of refurbishing the family home had disappeared.

"Serena didn't grow up with us, but Dottie had the right to leave the house to whoever she wanted to." Paul's deep voice rumbled with emotion. "I realize that's easy for me to say—Dottie's place wasn't the first home I remember."

"No, it's not." Jonas dribbled the ball three times and then passed it to Paul. "I don't even remember our mom—Dottie's always been my mom."

"Are you still set on trying to buy the house back?" Jim had expressed his opinion that he thought Jonas was causing himself too much grief when Jonas emailed them all and said he'd try this tactic.

"Call me crazy, but yes, it's worth a shot."

"Serena and her son have been living there for over six months. Doubtful that she'll up and sell it to you." Jim stared at Jonas. "And she's got something with Dottie none of us ever had—a blood connection. By rights she's a Forsyth, and Dottie's father always meant for the farm to stay in the family."

"Dottie accepted us as her family the minute she fell in love with Dad." Jonas couldn't shake the image of Dottie's grief when his father had passed away—he'd been her one true love.

"Winter's setting in. When she sees how cold it

gets, and once we get a good rainstorm that gets the roof leaking like it's bound to, she'll be happy to move out. This isn't Texas."

"I represented Serena during the initial investigation until she was cleared of any wrongdoing. Serena's a nice woman, and her kid is sweet. She's a Marine widow. It's what Dottie would have wanted. They deserve a new start, and I'm glad she had time to get to know Dottie even if it was too short."

Leave it to Paul to defend the interloper.

"Shut up, Paul. Obviously you've been listening to Mary. Mary thinks everyone deserves a second chance. If you're so crazy about the lady who stole our house right out from under us, why didn't you invite her to Thanksgiving?"

Jonas's heated comment made the others laugh. Mary was a social worker who'd worked with many of the same clients as the physical therapy clinic had.

"Mary did, in fact. But Serena already had other plans."

"Probably to redo the entire house." Jonas knew it was her house, no matter how much Dottie's not leaving it to him stung. But he couldn't budge from his position, not in front of his brothers.

"Quit it, Jonas." Paul was in full oldest-brother mode. "Serena is a great woman, and it wasn't her fault that Dottie died, nor is it her fault that our uncle was her biological father. Shit happens."

"Do you have the hots for her, man?" John looked so sincere Jonas almost laughed...while he waited for Paul's answer.

"Give me a break, you squirt. You know Mary's the only woman for me. Serena's got a legal résumé any firm would scoop up. I hope it's mine that gets her."

"You want to hire her?" Jim's curiosity was more ambivalent.

"I offered her a position at the firm whenever she's ready to get back to the law. Although with the way some of us are behaving, I'm going to lose her to my rival firm in Langley." He referred to the city on the south side of the island, closer to Seattle, as he shot a mean stare at Jonas.

"Whoa, I didn't mean to rile everyone up. You want to hire her, go ahead. I don't want to get in the middle of her life. I'm still sore about the house. But you're right—she's a nice lady. Her kid's cool, too." He looked at each of them for a moment. They needed his sour attitude like they needed dried-out turkey.

"So you've seen her since you've been back?" Paul missed nothing.

"She and Pepé came by the clinic. I should go visit her at the house and let her get to know me better. Hopefully she'll realize I'm not some ogre intent on stealing her new home."

"Aren't you, Jonas?" Paul's voice reflected Jonas's conscience.

He sighed, spinning the ball on his finger. "I was, I am— If there's any chance she'll give the house up, I don't want to risk it going to some stranger."

"I still think Dottie had some reason for doing this, other than Serena showing up. Dottie could have left Serena the money and you the house. Why didn't she?" Jim cocked a brow at Jonas, his knowing gaze annoying as hell.

"Let's leave the problem-solving to Paul. Dottie wanted the house kept in her family—her biological family." As he said the words Jonas didn't completely believe them. Dottie had always had a motive for her actions. She hadn't become the most successful Realtor on Whidbey Island for nothing.

He looked at his brothers. "It is what it is. Nothing we can do right now. So…let's play ball."

Jonas tried to get his mind off his heartache and his brothers off the topic of the house and back onto basketball. But he made a mental note to ask Mary a few questions about Serena. It never hurt to go into battle with an assortment of ammunition.

CHAPTER SIX

Whidbey Island
Friday after Thanksgiving

SERENA LISTENED AS Pepé sang along to the music from Walt Disney's *Frozen* while she drove them back on island. They'd spent Thanksgiving Day at Beyond the Stars as planned.

Since they'd lost Dottie this past summer, she and Pepé were alone on Thanksgiving. She could have taken them back to Texas, but she wasn't ready to face her extended Mexican-American family at a big holiday. Not yet. She and Pepé needed time to forge their own traditions, their own family way of doing things. She sent up a silent prayer of gratitude that Juanita had been so gracious about her decision to stay on Whidbey through the holidays. Otherwise, it would have been hard to fight her mother's pleas to come home to Texas for Christmas.

Pepé had made many friends in his school on Whidbey and their families had in turn befriended Serena, so she never felt alone.

But when Val Di Paola, the director of BTS, had

sent out the Thanksgiving invitation, Serena had jumped at it. Pepé had been excited to go back to San Juan Island, too, where he'd learned to jump off a diving board into the deep end of a pool.

Serena smiled. She could still hear Pepé's squeal of delight when he found out that Val kept the BTS pool and sauna tub heated and running year-round, at her husband Lucas's insistence. Pepé had frolicked in the water, and made Serena stay in the pool, as well, until they'd resembled the dried cranberries that had been in the turkey stuffing.

The air was crisp and clear and she was glad to be off the ferry after their rough crossing. Ferries were a necessity in Puget Sound, but Serena was a land girl through and through—give her a four-by-four truck any day. She drove the crossover hybrid, a fuel-conserving SUV that she'd traded in her truck for, off the ferry with care. The water was beautiful but bouncing around on it when the gales blew wasn't her idea of fun.

Black Friday—the American shopping holiday. Back home in Texas she'd be standing in long lines as she and her sisters strategized which department stores had the best deals for Christmas gifts. She'd be tired and annoyed that she wasn't back home with Pepé, who'd be curled up with her mother, his beloved *abuela,* while Serena shopped. A prick of guilt made her realize how much Pepé needed his family, all of it. She'd planned to spend this Christmas with Dottie, and her step-cousins.

Paul Scott had been wonderful to her from the minute she'd met him at his law firm. The other brothers hadn't completely warmed up to her but she'd hoped they would, in time, and with their shared memories of Dottie's magic smile.

It hadn't turned out as she'd hoped, but in some ways it was better. She and Pepé were cementing friendships all over the Puget Sound area, and she'd made strides toward mending her relationship with Juanita.

Nevertheless, Serena needed to figure out what to do to make her Christmas with Pepé extra special.

She pulled onto the long drive to the house.

It had been only been six months but she was proud of the progress she'd made on the property. Dottie had been a skillful gardener and landscaper, but her age and busy social life meant the grounds had taken a backseat during the past few years, at least since she'd been widowed. Serena knew that was eighteen years ago. Her stepson and Jonas's older brother, John Scott, was Dottie's personal landscaper but the grounds required more regular care, in Serena's opinion.

The flower beds were covered with mulch and leaves for the winter, but in the spring they'd burst with daffodils and tulips, if squirrels didn't eat the hundreds of bulbs that she and Pepé had planted last month.

The fir trees were naturally Christmassy and

the way they lined the drive was so attractive. She'd found twinkling lights at the dollar store that she planned to wind around the lower trunks of several this weekend.

Doing everything on her own wasn't easy, but she didn't mind it, either. Serena was happy to spend time with herself. Dottie had understood—the first person to "get it" since Phil died.

That was another thing she and Dottie had shared—they'd both been unexpectedly widowed. Dottie's only husband had died of cardiac arrest with no warning. Dottie had never married until she met Louis Scott, a real estate colleague who'd been widowed with four sons to raise. Dottie had kept her name, Serena's biological father's name, Forsyth.

Even so, she'd raised the Scott boys as her own. Jonas must have been particularly close to her as the youngest. Dottie had mentioned Jonas to Serena time after time, saying he and his brothers were the children she'd never had, and how grateful she was to have been able to be a mother to them. She'd told of how Jonas had taken to her and started calling her "Mom." Serena blinked back the tears that the memory of the warm conversation with Dottie evoked.

But it was difficult to imagine Jonas Scott as anything other than the devastatingly, annoyingly handsome man with the surly attitude she'd met last week.

He hadn't had an easy life from the bits she'd pieced together. His biological mother had died when he was two years old, and his father married Dottie within eighteen months of that. Louis, his father, had died when Jonas was still a teen—before he'd left for college. It had obviously been a crushing blow, yet Dottie and the stepsons Serena had met seemed to love one another and be happy in their lives.

Unlike Serena's mother, who'd always been bothered by the fact that she'd gotten pregnant by a stranger in her small Texas town. She'd never forgiven herself, and this had passed the sense of shame down to Serena.

Serena thanked God every day that she'd gotten out of that Podunk town to go to college and then ended up married to a military man whose job took her around the country. She'd hoped to see more of the world, but so far Whidbey Island was as far as she'd come and she was happy enough with that.

Jonas had looked chagrined when he'd realized that she and Pepé had heard his harsh words to Dr. Franklin.

She really should have announced their presence sooner. It wasn't fair of her. He'd just returned from his deployment, and Serena remembered how tired and scatterbrained Phil had been after long months downrange. It always took a few weeks to wake up to the reality of a more civilized lifestyle.

But Jonas had been such a "butt" as he'd said himself. He'd stirred her anger to a froth she hadn't experienced in what felt like forever.

Once he made the connection he'd been much nicer, charming even. Of course he had; he wanted the house and he had to go through her to get it.

A jolt of awareness made her sit up straight. She'd thought of Phil without the usual sense of longing, of sorrow. It was the second time in the past few weeks.

Dottie had told her that one day her deep grief over her husband's death had lifted and she saw life in full color again. She'd said it would happen for Serena, too.

Jonas Scott's male energy certainly hadn't been lost on her.

She looked in the rearview mirror at Pepé's sleeping form in the backseat.

"Wake up, sleepyhead."

Ronald barked at her as if the request was a command for him and not Pepé. The fawn-colored Weimaraner/Labrador-mix puppy they'd rescued last spring was coming into his own as a full member of their family.

Pepé didn't stir as she maneuvered the SUV into the driveway. Even though it was almost noon, the lull of the ferry and motion of the drive always made him sleepy.

"I'm hungry, Mom!"

Serena laughed. "How do you go from sound asleep to full-throttle in less than a heartbeat?" She roughed up his hair with her hand.

"Quit it, Mom." He unsnapped his seat belt and was out of the back car door before she had time to turn around again, Ronald racing ahead of him.

She watched their forms streak across the fog-dampened ground toward the front door.

And the tall man who stood in front of it, his back to her. They weren't used to drop-ins.

She felt a stab of fear and scrambled out of the seat.

The recent headlines across the local paper roared in her memory. The island was having a rash of break-ins, often motivated by an addict's search for prescription narcotics.

She should have had the dead bolt installed as she'd planned.

"Pepé, wait! Ronald!"

But Pepé didn't turn back toward her, didn't acknowledge he'd heard her. Ronald skidded to a halt in front of the man and she heard the dog's strident bark.

Who was the stranger at their door? What if he wanted to hurt Pepé?

"Pepé!" Her voice was sharper, the edge of fear stoking her anger.

"Mom, it's Jonas!"

Breathing hard, she stopped running before she

got too close. Close enough that anyone would see the fear and anger on her face.

"Jonas." She welcomed the relief that it wasn't a complete stranger.

"More like your sort-of cousin, isn't it?" He shot her a lopsided grin and just like that her hormones were off to the races. She really needed to start thinking about dating again. Then she wouldn't have such an overreaction to Jonas, the last man on earth she wanted to be aroused by.

"Sorry—we don't usually get surprise visitors. Ronald's protective of Pepé."

"You mean unannounced visitors. I would have called, but it's against HIPAA for me to look up your number in your records and use it for personal business. You didn't give me your phone number yourself."

"I appreciate your professionalism, uh, Commander Scott—or was it Captain?"

"I'm a Commander." His mouth twitched.

"I didn't want to demote you. I'm not familiar with medical practitioners for the most part, and then when you add the Navy, I get even more confused. We're used to being around Marines. Well, we were."

"Understood."

She took a step closer. "Ronald, it's okay."

Her words were superfluous as Ronald had already deemed Jonas safe with an invisible doggy stamp of approval. He lay at Jonas's feet, his belly exposed for a rub. Jonas obliged and she didn't miss how nice his hands looked against Ronald's silver-brown coat.

Couldn't the dog at least pretend to have more of a vicious edge around strange men? Step-cousins included?

"We're not blood relatives, not cousins, by the way." There. It was out; let him go after her about the house.

"You mean like you, Pepé and Dottie."

He looked up at her as he spoke, continuing to stroke Ronald's underside. When he stood she had to look up. He was at least a foot taller than she was. And his gaze—a girl needed to watch how she interpreted his attention. Why couldn't Jonas look more like a toad?

"I didn't let you off the hook at the clinic. I'm sorry." She owed him that much.

"Don't be. I earned your wrath. And although I don't deserve it, I'd like to start over with you."

Serena smiled.

Jonas responded with a grin and held out his hand. "Jonas Scott, Dottie's youngest stepson. Pleased to meet you."

His hand was warm and strong as it enveloped hers. She liked his firm handshake—certain but not overbearing.

"Serena Delgado. Dottie's biological niece."

She met his gaze at the same moment a spark seemed to travel from where their hands joined up her arm. Judging from the interest in his eyes he'd felt it, too.

This wasn't what she'd bargained for, this instant attraction she was experiencing with Jonas.

"Hey, what about me?" Pepé stuck out his hand in front of Jonas.

"Nice to see you again, buddy." Jonas shook Pepé's hand with the solemnity reserved for equals.

"Mom, can I go inside and play?"

"Sure, but no computer or television. Keep it to your toys or books."

"But it's a holiday vacation, Mom!"

"Take it or leave it, *mi hijo.*"

Pepé ran back inside, Ronald on his heels.

"You're good with him."

"Hmm." Serena shifted on her feet, not sure where to go next. She didn't remember ever feeling so completely exposed with another person.

Jonas was practically a stranger, yet he knew her life. He knew her father had abandoned her before she'd even been born, that she was a widow and single mother. He'd drawn conclusions about how she'd come to have the house. He probably thought she'd finagled it out of Dottie.

Yet she knew so little about him. Except for what Dottie had told her. Dottie had made Jonas out to be perfect.

Serena knew *that* wasn't possible.

At the clinic he had played the straight man, the

professional. He didn't dare comment on her role in his family's business in that setting.

Except for the venting session that she'd overheard, he'd behaved.

"You know who *I* am, Jonas. You know my family situation. You might even think you've figured me out. But I don't know a whole lot about you."

His blink indicated she'd hit her target. She hadn't meant to sound so harsh but it felt good, if just for a moment. Let him judge her; she had as much right to be here as he did.

Didn't she?

They might be unofficial cousins, of a sort, but the attraction between them glittered. Maybe she had too much Christmas on the brain, but she was mesmerized by the vision of a long, gold tinsel garland wrapped around both of them and drawing them closer.... Who needed mistletoe?

"Mom, is Jonas related to Auntie Dottie, too?"

"I thought you were playing inside, Pepé. This is an adult conversation." She studied Pepé, his eyes wide. If he could raise his ears like a dog to listen better, he would. Her little sponge was taking it all in.

Pepé held up an apple and a cheese stick. "Can I have these?"

"Yes. At the table."

"*Auntie* Dottie?" Jonas didn't have to raise his eyebrows; his tone of voice made clear that his judgment of her was as clichéd as the gesture. Let him add the assumption that she'd used Pepé to gain an inside track to Dottie's will and the house.

"We had a chance to get to know Dottie before…before last summer." She stared at him.

"I never heard of you until six months before she died." He shoved his hands in his jeans pockets. His nicely formed, masculine hands.

"No reason for you to." She shrugged. "I didn't want Dottie to bother her family, your family, with what I came out here for—to find out about my biological family. It had nothing to do with you until…until she died."

"And left the house to you."

Anger grew from a curl of tension in her stomach to a python gripping her throat.

"It's really none of your business. Dottie was my aunt and had information about my biological father that I couldn't get from anyone else, as all of their relatives are gone. As I'm sure you know, Dottie was the last one. And, as I'm sure you also know better than I do, genetic medical information is invaluable. I met with Dottie as much for Pepé as myself."

Her throat ached even more and she wanted to punch the side of the house. She would *not* cry in front of this virtual stranger.

Jonas remained quiet, watching her.

"It didn't make sense to draw you and your brothers into my sordid family life."

"Who said anything about 'sordid'?" Jonas

flashed that handsome smile again. Aware that Pepé could be within earshot, absorbing their entire conversation, she kept herself from shoving Jonas and telling him to shut up.

"Not to be rude, but why exactly are you here, Jonas?"

He shrugged. "I came out to introduce myself properly, and to see if there's anything you need for the house."

"Anything I need?"

He had the grace to look away.

"My brothers have, um, indicated that you haven't asked for any help fixing up the place. We know Dottie wasn't able to keep up with it the past several years. And she wouldn't let us help out like we wanted to." He looked up at the house. She followed his gaze and saw the peeling paint, the hole in the eaves where a bird had made a nest last spring.

Discomfort made her wiggle her toes in her faux shearling–lined boots. He wasn't going to get under her skin this way, no matter how hard he tried. She'd fix the house on her own.

"It looks worse than it is. This place is over a hundred years old. It's been through a lot. I've painted the inside and ripped up all the old carpets." She'd found beautiful pine flooring underneath, which she'd refinished in October, thinking her family might come out from Texas for a visit. Of course her mother hadn't been willing to make the trek, not even for Pepé. Not yet. She was still too raw about the fact that Serena had come west to learn about a man who'd never taken the time to know his daughter or provide child support to a teenage mother.

"I'm not criticizing anything you've done or not done to the house. Carpentry, woodworking, cabinetry—they're my hobbies. I know this place as well as Dottie did. It'd be my pleasure to help you get it in tip-top shape."

"Is that a Navy expression?"

He looked at her questioningly. "What—tip-top? Yes, I suppose so. Look, I realize you don't know me, not yet. But I'm the one person who could give you a hand bringing this house back to its full potential."

For the first time since she'd inherited the place, Serena felt a strong surge of possessiveness. This was *her* home. Hers and Pepé's.

"I've gone over it pretty thoroughly the past several months. I've got an extended list of what I'll update and when." She crossed her arms. What was it about this man that brought out her defensiveness?

"No doubt you've made a great start, Serena. But an old place like this has secrets that are hard to find. For example, have you uncovered the buried treasure yet?"

His eyes twinkled. Serena clenched her hands

as she heard Pepé's feet stomp on the floor inside. He appeared at the open front door.

"There's a buried treasure in our house?" Pepé's eyes were wide and Serena wished to heaven and back he didn't have that enthusiastic grin on his face.

Jonas nodded. "When I was a boy I found a special place to hide my treasures from my three brothers. Maybe you've found your own nook for your favorite toys?"

Pepé shook his head. "No, not yet. But I love my room!"

Now Pepé had twinkles in his eyes. Serena wanted to scream but instead pasted on a killer smile for Jonas. He was on *her* turf.

"Mind if I take a look inside?"

"Of course not." She paused. Aside from his brothers and the contractors, Jonas was the first man she'd allowed in their home.

But it wasn't as though he was a man in *that* sense—she wasn't going to start anything with him. He was a sailor from the base and he was practically family. The drug-related burglaries on the island were definitely making her paranoid.

Would her fear of living out on this remote property ever completely vanish?

Jonas had even passed Ronald's appraisal.

It'd be easier if he hadn't. Then she could chalk up her body's response to him as nerves and not the blatant sexual attraction she knew it was.

She saw in his eyes what she'd felt in her heart too many times to count. Self-assurance with a hint of sadness.

Why was she being so tough on him? Jonas was no more responsible for her inheriting the house than she was. They were both surprised by Dottie's decision, and affected by it. One more happily than the other.

"I'm sorry, Jonas. This isn't easy for you, is it? You didn't get a chance to say a proper goodbye to Dottie. It all must seem surreal to you. Do you want to have some time alone in the house?"

"I appreciate it but I don't need to be alone, Serena."

That she understood.

CHAPTER SEVEN

"I DIDN'T SAY anything at the clinic because I didn't think it was appropriate. It's my place of work, and your son was there." Serena sat across from him in the family kitchen, the kitchen in which he'd watched Dottie bake dozens upon dozens of Christmas cookies. He drummed his fingers on the table. "It wasn't the time to bring up Dottie's death, or your involvement in it."

They were alone at the oak table while Pepé played in the next room.

She'd made them coffee and put out pumpkin bread that he hated to admit was as good as anything Dottie had ever baked.

Serena's eyes flashed a warning.

"I had no involvement in Dottie's death. Except that I went to answer the phone for my boss, which left her alone long enough for…for…" She looked down and the waves of regret were practically tangible as the remorse rolled off her.

"I know you didn't have anything to do with it. And I shouldn't have pressed you in front of Pepé. Sorry about that."

"Thank you."

She leveled a steady look at him. Her emotional strength impressed him as much as it made him uneasy, and it seemed to drive his inexplicable urge to make her understand why he was so wary of her.

"Can you blame my family for being suspicious of you? You blew in here from out of nowhere, and within six months Dottie was dead. Murdered. And, oh, yeah, she left you, a stranger, the house that had been in our family for generations."

"She left me the house that had been in *her* family for decades, yes. She was murdered, yes, by a psychopath who used to work at the clinic. I'm not responsible for Dottie's actions any more than I am for those of her murderer."

Her skin developed a dusky rose flush at her cheekbones and her eyes blazed with warning. His awareness of her startled him. When his brothers had said "Dottie's long-lost niece is a Marine widow from Texas," he'd pictured a nondescript middle-aged woman. Not the sexy beauty who sat in front of him.

"We didn't know you *weren't* responsible for her death, not when it first happened."

To keep from staring at her, he glanced around the kitchen. It seemed larger, warmer, than he remembered. The dark cupboards had been painted white and their trimmings were red. The woodworker in him hated any natural wood painted over, but the kitchen looked years newer. Children's artwork, obviously Pepé's, was taped to every cupboard door. The countertops used to be butcher block but now were hard marble or granite—he wasn't a connoisseur of home decorating. They looked updated, clean. He liked it.

"I'm sorry for your loss, Jonas." As much as her pride must have stung at his comment, the gal had class.

"Thank you. It was a huge shock."

"It was for all of us. The clinic staff was like a family, and our clients were part of that family. Not to mention Dottie *was* my family. If I'd stayed in the room instead of answering the phone—"

She shook her head as if to clear out ugly thoughts, memories that burned. Jonas knew the feeling. Multiple wartime deployments didn't allow him to ever pretend bad things didn't happen to good people.

"The physical therapist gave me the job as a favor to Dottie, since she was one of his favorite clients. I didn't need the money, and I'd planned to go back to practicing law at some point. But I needed something to do while Pepé was in school, and this allowed me to meet a lot of the people in our community."

He wondered if she realized she'd referred to the Whidbey Island community as "our." This wasn't a woman who was going to pack up and leave anytime soon.

It didn't mean she had to stay in *this* house, though.

Serena's hands were wrapped around her mug and she stared into her coffee. Her silence reverberated with grief. Jonas had to fight like hell to keep from reaching across the table and grasping her hands.

What was wrong with him?

He wanted to comfort *her?* Serena? The woman who'd been all but responsible for Dottie's being left alone with a murderer. The woman who'd walked away with the prize of his childhood.

While Dottie had left him a more than generous amount of cash, she'd gone back on her promise of leaving him the house. Did Serena know why? He forced himself to look anywhere but on her. He noticed that the kitchen wall was bare where it had once held several shelves.

"Wait, what did you do with all the frogs?"

"Frogs?" Serena frowned and he realized he'd spoken too loudly.

"Sorry, I have a bad habit of doing that. It's from dealing with trauma situations where there's always a lot of noise. I'm used to shouting medical orders over the din." He consciously lowered his voice. "What did you do with Dottie's frogs?"

Serena looked over her shoulder to where his gaze aimed at the bare wall, then turned back to him.

"Most of her figurines and wall hangings were

gone by the time we moved in. Your brothers came and got all the family items that meant anything to them. I stored what they didn't want, until I have time to sort through it all. She had a lot of knick-knacks!" Serena smiled.

Jonas scratched his chin. "She had a collection of frogs. They were her favorite. I loved buying them for her." He fought back his defensiveness. Of course his brothers had cleaned out the house before Serena and Pepé moved in.

He'd have to find out who got the frogs. He'd loved Dottie's frogs as a kid, and had given her many of them for her birthdays and Mother's Day. One of his brothers had probably boxed them up and forgotten it.

"I know. She had us out here a lot. Treated us like family right from the start." *Unlike you and your brothers*. He heard the unspoken accusation that glowed in her eyes. Serena squared her shoulders. "Mary took the frogs, against Paul's wishes. She loves the frogs, too."

Jonas snorted. Leave it to Mary to convince Paul they needed the frogs. She already had a house full of collectibles, on top of the two kids.

"I don't want to be rude here, Jonas, but what do you really want from me?"

Strike. Preemptive at that. Uninvited respect for Serena pushed at his pride.

"What, don't you think that family should get to know one another at holiday time?"

She didn't take his bait.

"I'm sorry, Serena. I always seem to say the wrong thing with you. What I'd really love to know is why Dottie changed her mind about the house. I get that she wanted the farmhouse to stay in her family, but she'd always made clear that my brothers and I meant as much to her as any blood relative. It wasn't like her to go back on a promise, either. She'd been a top Realtor on Whidbey, and the main reason for that was—because her word was golden."

"I've asked myself the same thing. If she hadn't left you the cash settlement, I wouldn't have taken the house, Jonas. I don't expect you to believe that, but it's true. As it is, she took care of you. I have to believe she had valid reasons for her decisions."

Pepé played with Lego in the family room, which was visible from the kitchen now that Serena had torn down a wall. The wall the family photos had been on. Jonas didn't think Pepé could hear their conversation, though. Serena kept her voice low, forcing him to lean in to listen to her.

"I've already been through all of this with your family. I had no idea Dottie was leaving me, us, the house. There was no reason for her to—Pepé and I are financially secure, as I'm sure you're aware."

"No, I didn't know that."

"Oh, really? You don't realize that military survivors get pretty decent life insurance? Or that I'm a successful attorney? I have a hard time believing Paul didn't mention any of this to you." She shook her head. "I only worked at the PT clinic while I was applying for my Washington State law license. It gave us extra time to get to know Dottie, too. Besides, Pepé needed me around more, at first."

"What kind of lawyer are you?"

"Family practice. Not the typical mother who brings her kid into the clinic for a runny nose, am I?"

Ouch.

Another verbal punch to the gut. Serena had overheard more of his conversation with Doc Franklin than he'd realized.

He needed her to understand that he had nothing against her or Pepé.

"I asked for Whidbey as my shore duty station before I left on deployment. Usually I'm at a more demanding duty station at a larger hospital. I'm an emergency-room trauma nurse practitioner." Damn it, why did he feel he had to give her his entire professional résumé? Why did he care what she thought?

"I imagine you've seen a lot." She stood up from the table and took her cup to the sink.

He chalked up the long look he allowed himself at her bottom, displayed to perfection in her jeans, to having just gotten back from deployment.

It'd been a few weeks. What was he going to do when he'd been home for several months, been on dates with different women, and Serena still turned him on?

Because deep in his gut he had a hunch that his attraction to Serena wasn't something that was going to fade easily.

She turned around and he took in her full beauty. Damn it if she didn't look like she belonged in this house, too.

His house.

"Did you want to walk through the rest of the house?"

Her posture was casual as she leaned against the kitchen counter, her blue denim in sharp contrast to the white porcelain sink's apron. He didn't miss how her smoky-gray blouse accentuated her breasts and the curve of her hips.

His body reacted like he was fifteen—immediately and without thought. The man he'd become in the Navy knew he'd just lost the day's battle.

"Sure, that'd be nice."

Did he want to see the house? Of course—and he wanted to be the one to update the rest of it. At the rate they were going she'd never let him back in here. He'd never get her to sell the house to him.

Of course money was a factor and he was willing to offer her a hefty sum for his childhood home. Only a fool would turn him down.

Serena was no fool, but she wasn't like any other adversary in his life to date. Argument was her profession.

He didn't miss the unsaid portion of her query. Did he want to see the rest of the house in order to say goodbye to it?

THEY WALKED UP the narrow staircase in silence. Serena was eye level with Jonas's butt—and a nice butt it was. He dressed simply in jeans and a thermal under a ski jacket. He looked like he skied; his long legs and light step fit his athletic build. She'd noticed his quiet strength at the base hospital, too. But she'd been too upset by his verbal slams against military spouses to pay much attention to his body.

Now she sought anything to keep her attention off her own body's awareness of him. It wasn't a surprise; she'd known that her grief for Phil would eventually lessen and she'd find herself attracted to another man. It was just a shock that *this* was the first guy who'd turned her on. The man who wanted to take back the one thing she had as a permanent reminder of her father's family.

Once they reached the landing Jonas went straight to the room at the end of the hallway, Pepé's room.

"This place seemed so huge to me when we moved in here." Jonas's tone reflected the awe of the little boy he would've been.

"You were what, two or three?"

"Four. I remember it as though it were yesterday. My brother John and I got this room, and my two older brothers were in the bigger room. I didn't complain—their room scared me with all the dormers and eaves. To me it looked like a haunted castle."

Serena laughed. "Pepé said the same thing about that room."

"No, I didn't, Mom. I didn't say it was a castle." He'd come upstairs with them.

Serena smiled at him. "You said it looked like the Haunted Mansion at Disneyland."

"Well, it did."

"Same difference, kiddo." She ruffled his hair and he squirmed away, not wanting to look like a little boy in front of Jonas, or so she surmised.

She turned back to Jonas. "I made the scary room into my office. I haven't had time yet, but I plan to hire a contractor to put in some shelves, to make it into more of a library. I don't want to change the lines of the house at all. Simply add to it for comfort as needed."

"This house could bankrupt a person."

"I think I can handle it."

"It's not just any old house. It goes back—"

"It was built in 1908 by Dottie's grandfather. He and her grandmother, along with their young children, had previously lived in a smaller place on the southern part of the island. He brought his dairy cattle up here. Later, Dottie's father let the dairy business go and made a living as a potato farmer. Your uncle was born here, a surprise midlife baby for Dottie's parents. He was stationed in Texas for a short time when he had a tour in the Army. That's where he met my mother."

She didn't mention that Jonas's uncle, her father, had left Whidbey to go back to Texas after her birth, to see if the woman he'd met during his military time was still there. He'd said that he'd never stopped loving her. Serena felt her mother had still loved him, too, but he'd been too deep into his drinking by then to be the kind of husband Juanita Rodriguez would accept. Juanita had seen their reunion as closure. She'd refused to marry him unless he agreed to stop drinking. Unfortunately, it left her a single mother with Serena.

"My uncle Todd was the nicest man when he was sober."

"I imagine he was. I wouldn't know."

Jonas turned stormy eyes on her. "If he thought for one minute that he was worthy of your mother's love, I know he would've gone back to Texas and claimed you. He wouldn't have given up so easily."

"You can't know that—none of us can."

"He died a horrible death." Jonas said what she already knew from Dottie. Her father had died of cirrhosis of the liver.

"Alcoholism's an ugly disease."

"I take it you're not a medical professional? With that gentle bedside manner?" Jonas kept his tone light but the steel blue of his eyes warned her—*don't judge my uncle.*

He'd been her father.

Serena shook her head. "I prefer to deal in facts. I'm a lawyer."

Jonas's head moved back. Slightly, but she saw it.

"Fair enough." Now he tilted his head to the side. "So tell me, what was a lawyer doing working in a PT clinic as a receptionist? Why didn't you get a job assisting in a law firm until your license came through?"

"I told you, I wanted something to do when we first arrived here. Pepé was in school full-time, and while I didn't want to hang out all day, I wasn't ready to dive into law again. I wasn't sure we'd be staying, either." She didn't rehash the fact that she'd failed as a receptionist—at least as far as Dottie was concerned. Jonas knew that part.

She'd never forget it.

"Did you practice law in Texas?"

"Yes, I'd been working at a family-owned legal office out in town, off base. They provided family law services to many base personnel. Not too different from Paul's practice."

"What kind of family law?"

She looked at him. It was the second time he'd asked. What was his motive for finding out more about her?

"Family court, estate planning, small civil suits. I never wanted to be tied down to a corporate position, not once we had Pepé." As she said "we" she realized it was merely from habit. She wasn't thinking about Phil, and more notably wasn't feeling the pangs of regret she'd experienced throughout her grieving process.

Jonas had her complete attention.

This is a first.

She looked around for Pepé.

"He went back downstairs." Jonas interpreted her body language correctly. She wanted to toss *him* down the stairs.

"Thanks." She looked at Jonas. His eyes were still on her but when she met them he shifted his gaze to something outside the low-slung window in Pepé's room.

"I used to sit on that window seat for hours and imagine what kinds of ships were out there. When it's clear, you can see the gray whales migrating. You need binoculars, of course."

"I'll have to tell Pepé. He'll be thrilled." And he would be. Pepé had taken to their surroundings like a native. He was more fascinated by nature with each hike, each trip. Puget Sound and the ocean yielded breathtaking displays of killer whales, gray whales and other sea creatures. The tidal basins along the coast became teaching laboratories for the elementary school at low tide. Serena had accompanied Pepé on a field trip with his class and had fallen in love with the assortment of starfish, mussels and crabs that lived in a two-foot basin.

She had to remain focused on Pepé and ignore the way Jonas aroused her.

"So you really want to stay here? This far from Texas, from your family?"

"Pepé's my family." She'd parted on bad terms with her mother after finding out she'd lied about her biological father all these years. That was finally mending. But for now, she needed to find out more about who she was. Who Pepé was, too.

"Let me guess—your mother never wanted anything to do with my uncle on account of his drinking?"

"I don't see how that's any of your concern."

"Just as I don't see how you can be comfortable taking a home that's been in a family for over a century when you only knew Dottie for, what, half a year?"

"Need I remind you that, technically, this home and the Forsyth family is more mine that yours? You have zero Forsyth blood pumping through your veins."

"Actually, right now it feels like I've got piss pumping through my heart."

"What?"

Jonas grinned. "It's my deployment mouth, sorry. The expression's an old one, though. You've never heard of 'my heart's pumping piss for you'? Meaning, I have no sympathy for you whatsoever."

"Can't say I've ever had a need to learn Navy slang. And I'm not asking for your sympathy. I'm telling you that Dottie's will was legal and just. I was as surprised as anyone that she'd leave the farmhouse to us, but the longer I'm in it, the more sense it makes. Pepé is the fifth generation Forsyth under this roof."

"Dottie was very generous. Maybe she thought you and Pepé needed a house, a home? Did you lead her to believe you were in financial difficulties?"

"You know that line you shouldn't cross?" At his blank expression Serena jerked her thumb over her shoulder. "It's way back there, buddy. I'm happy to show you the house, and I've given your brothers any of Dottie's possessions they've asked for. You can go through anything that's still here and take what you want, too. But this house is mine now, and someday it'll be Pepé's. Besides, none of your brothers wanted the place— they didn't want the responsibility of dealing with the renovations."

Renovations that were going to end up costing twice the worth of the house if she followed the specifications needed to keep the home on the state and national historic registry. But she wasn't about to discuss that with Jonas Scott.

"Why do you want this house so badly, Jonas?"

"I *wanted* it. And yes, I still want it." With his hands at his sides he looked relaxed. Except for his words, the taut tendons at the base of his neck and his narrowed eyes. "Like I said, I can help you with the repairs, and make sure you don't inadvertently damage anything that will make the house lose its historical status."

What, was Jonas a mind reader, too?

Anger flared, making her stomach hot and her throat dry. She took a step toward him.

"You don't save every patient who comes your way, do you?"

He blinked, then frowned, highlighting his suspicion of her. "No. You don't win every legal case, do you?"

"No. Think of this house as one of your patients that didn't make it—the patient who came in too far gone, where nothing you did could make a difference. It's not your fault. It actually has nothing to do with you. It. Just. Is."

It was hard to tell in the upstairs light, dimmer than downstairs with its big picture windows, how red the skin over Jonas's cheekbones had become.

Their eyes locked and behind his anger Serena thought she recognized the same thing that she hadn't been able to shake the entire time he'd been here.

Awareness.

She should be nicer to him. God only knew what he'd seen downrange, how many warriors he'd treated. Some might not have made it. And he'd offered to help her with the renovations— no matter his reason for wanting to help with the house, he could be exactly the contractor she needed.

"Wait, that sounded a little harsh. It's the lawyer in me."

"Save it." He took one last look around the dormer room before he strode to the door, not sparing her a glance.

"Thanks for the tour. I'll see myself out."

Serena stayed in the room for a long time. Funny thing was, as angry as she'd made him, some crazy part of her thought that for a moment Jonas was going to kiss her.

CHAPTER EIGHT

As HE DROVE HOME, anger tightened across Jonas's chest like an unwanted bear hug from a creepy neighbor. His brothers had told him Serena was nice. They said she'd been apologetic about getting the house. Not enough to refuse it, however.

He turned the bend at the end of the farmhouse's driveway and eased onto the country highway toward town.

"Sure she was sweet and sorry, six months ago." When maybe he would've had a chance to get the place back, before she moved in.

Before she and her son got so enamored with the farmhouse.

A group of cows watched him drive by and for a brief second he wished he were able to live so fully in the moment with no worry for his future. That he could let himself lust after Serena, with no concern for tomorrow or what he wanted for his future.

He'd blown whatever chance he'd had to make his case about how he was the guy to do her renovations by losing his temper. What was he, twelve?

He'd been irritated at himself for reacting to her sensuality and her beauty.

The kicker of it all was that she seemed to appreciate the house. She'd started in on some of the renovations and had done a good job with them. It was clear to him that she was in over her head regarding the bigger modifications that were needed. He was thrilled that she wanted to keep the original lines and character of the house intact; he'd feared she might already have removed any chance of the house staying on the national historic register.

His plan A was shot. Now he'd have to go back and be even nicer to her. He wished he'd gotten out of the Navy ten years ago so that he'd already have the house.

Liar.

The Navy had been his life, still was his life. It was part of him.

Dottie had left him more than enough to satisfy anyone else selling the farmhouse. Except Serena.

Was this Dottie's way of telling him she'd always hoped he'd come home sooner? Give up his Navy life?

He wouldn't give up his naval experience for anything. It was what had made him the man he was today. But damn it, it had also cost him the home of his dreams—the one place he felt like himself. If he'd stayed here and not transferred with the Navy, he might've been living in the house before Dottie died. She'd talked about moving to town, to something easier for her to get around in.

Eight minutes after storming out of the farmhouse he pulled into his driveway and tried not to remember that he'd expected to be the one living in the family homestead by now. He laughed. He'd even planned to get a live Christmas tree and invite his family over—something he never did in the town house due to his deployment schedule and the fact that it was too crowded once all his brothers, their wives or significant others and their children piled in.

What had Dottie been thinking?

He'd known Uncle Todd drank—they all did. But he'd had long periods of sobriety, too. Not many, but enough that Jonas remembered one Christmas when Uncle Todd had come to the house with a sack full of gifts for Jonas and his brothers. Dottie had acted like he was crazy, spoiling her boys. She didn't fool any of them; Jonas knew she'd been thrilled to see her brother sober and as happy as she was during the holidays.

Only after he was older did Jonas come to understand that Dottie had often taken care of Uncle Todd. When he'd been at his worst, she'd always helped him back on his feet, finding him a job or, toward the end, good medical care.

Dottie had taken Uncle Todd's death hard. He'd lingered, survived far longer than his liver should have lasted. Jonas had been on deployment and, just like when Dottie died, unable to get back in time for Uncle Todd's service. But he'd arrived home within a month of Todd's passing and Dottie's grief had shaken him. He thought he'd already seen her at her worst, when his father died unexpectedly of a heart attack years earlier. Jonas had been seventeen and looking forward to going to college on scholarship. Dottie had made him go, even though he'd thought he should stay back a year and help out around the house.

She'd grieved deeply, but after a while she'd picked herself up and taken on more hours at her real estate office. She'd worked part-time while raising him and his brothers, and full-time after he'd left for college.

Dottie was a giver and her entire life had been a testament to her generosity.

Her generosity to a niece-in-DNA-only, however, bordered on insanity.

"What were you thinking, Dottie?" He pushed open his front door and flicked on the hall light. It was only three in the afternoon but sunset wasn't far off. Nightfall came early to Whidbey in the winter months.

He walked into the kitchen and checked his phone—no messages. He usually relied on his cell to keep in touch with his friends and family, but sometimes they called his house.

The lack of messages and the empty house was a sharp contrast to the warmth of the farmhouse.

Warmth that had everything to do with Serena.

Jonas looked in his pantry, then his refrigerator. Nothing but leftover pizza from two nights ago, a box of cereal, a pouch of coffee.

Pathetic.

He'd been back a couple of weeks and still hadn't resumed his regular routine.

From what he saw in his short time there, the farmhouse was filled with Serena's touches. He wanted to hate what she'd done, find fault with her destruction of what had been the heart of his childhood.

He couldn't. She'd rubbed luster back into the wood trim, restoring it to the original cherry finish. All the rugs had been ripped up and the floors finished to a soft honey hue. Wherever she could, she'd breathed life back into the aging timber. Where she couldn't, instead of replacing the wood like the kitchen cabinets, she'd painted them.

Somehow Serena had made the farmhouse a home for her and Pepé, and still maintained the simple beauty of the place.

He cast an assessing glance around his place. He'd bought it as an investment, assuming he'd rent it out once he moved into the farmhouse. As a result he hadn't done much in the way of filling the rooms with furniture or decorating them.

It looked plain when it should look like a palace after the conditions he'd endured on deployment.

It's not the house, or the furniture.

He sank into his leather couch and put his feet on the battered coffee table he'd built years ago. It was in need of refinishing.

No, it wasn't the house. It was the emptiness, the lack of laughter. There wasn't a little boy running around with his dog. And there wasn't a beautiful brunette smiling at him from the kitchen.

"Pepé, there's someone I want you to meet."

He looked up from his plastic building blocks.

"Who, Mama?"

Serena smiled at Pepé. She loved that he still sometimes called her "Mama" when he was in playing zone; it had been the first word he'd spoken.

"Come out to the barn with me."

They made their way to the small structure and she grinned, knowing how fun Pepé's afternoon was about to get. She was also grateful for the distraction from Jonas Scott's anger that radiated off him when he'd left. As she replayed their conversation, there wasn't anything she could have done—his emotions with the house were his.

Yet she'd wanted to reach out to him, to soothe him.

She watched Pepé as his eyes searched around the small barn before his gaze lit upon the two fuzzy, long-necked animals that stood inside the small paddock.

"You got the alpacas! Yes!" He ran toward them, and the shy creatures backed away from the wooden railings.

Ronald barked, his tail wagging, as he trotted next to Pepé.

Serena caught up with him at the fence line. "Like this, *mi hijo*." She held out her hands and cooed to the frightened alpacas.

"Are they boys or girls, Mom?"

"Two girls. Sisters." The alpacas approached them and leaned their cute faces toward Serena and Pepé, their huge eyes blinking.

Pepé held out his hands and the caramel-colored one spit on it.

"Ewww, Mom!"

Serena laughed. "They're checking you out. It'll take some time, but they'll learn to trust us." As she heard her own words, she realized maybe that was all it would take with Jonas. Time to let him learn to trust her, to understand that she hadn't received the farmhouse from Dottie for any reason other than Dottie's whim.

"What are their names, Mom?"

"They don't really have any yet. I thought I'd let you pick the names, *mi hijo*."

"This one is Cami." He pronounced it like a wizard casting a spell.

"Why that name?"

"Because her fur looks like Marine camouflage uniforms. You know, like my G.I. Joe."

Of course. Pepé might not even be making the connection with his dad's uniform, but his heart was.

"What about the white one?"

Pepé looked at the second alpaca, who'd come up and was allowing Serena to stroke her side.

"Snowball!"

They both laughed. "They're not like pets, not like Ronald, but they're part of our family now. Their coats will grow out and then I'll have someone give them a good haircut. Their fiber will be turned into yarn."

"Can you knit me a pair of socks from their yarn?"

"You bet. And a sweater to match." She hoped she'd be able to keep her promise. Owning farm animals was a big leap of faith for her, one more step toward making Whidbey their forever home.

CHAPTER NINE

Whidbey Island
First week of December

"WINNIE, YOUR DECORATIONS are the absolute best!"

Serena clinked her champagne glass against Winnie Ford's and took a sip of the dry Washington State sparkling wine.

Winnie was one of Serena's closest confidantes. Last winter, when Serena had stopped in the shop for some heavier yarn than she was used to, she and Winnie had immediately struck up a rapport that wasn't uncommon with knitters and crocheters.

Pepé's school schedule and Serena's reluctance to get a babysitter so soon after moving to a new place had prevented her from joining the many knitting classes and groups offered at Winnie's shop. But they'd managed to form a bond—especially once they'd ascertained that they shared a bond no two women would ever wish for. They were both military widows.

Winnie's first husband had died in a Navy plane crash several years ago. After that, Winnie had decided to open a yarn shop, which evolved into Whidbey's fiber cooperative, a venture that allowed small-farm owners to participate in fiber production.

Serena had met Winnie that day she'd wandered into Winnie's yarn shop in Coupeville, a small seaside town in the center of Whidbey Island. They'd connected over skeins of alpaca lace yarn, leading to Serena's decision to try raising alpacas at Dottie's family farm. Winnie had told Serena how she'd fallen in love with Max Ford, her second husband.

"I'm so glad you came this year. Last year you were still settling in. And now look at you—a new house and a new venture. I can't tell you how happy I am that you're going to be an official part of the fiber cooperative."

"Me, too. I finally took my friend Emily up on her offer to watch Pepé, and now I'm thinking I should do this more often. I feel like a real adult, not just a mom!"

She needed a night out, and when Winnie had invited her to the Ford family holiday party she knew it was another sign—time to start a social life for herself. She was Pepé's mother and that still came first, but her crazy attraction to Jonas had underscored her need to get out more. If she was around more available men, one guy wouldn't be as likely to turn her head as Jonas had.

"Have you dated since your husband died?" Winnie asked.

Winnie's hand felt warm on her forearm and it didn't occur to Serena to lie. "No. I haven't given it a thought. But lately I've been thinking I should go out a little more."

Winnie smiled. "I understand. I waited an awfully long time myself."

Her gaze drifted to where a tall, handsome man stood with two daughters. "My first foray into a relationship ended up in marriage, as you know."

At Serena's stunned silence, Winnie laughed.

"Don't worry, I'm not suggesting you do the same. Can I give you a piece of advice?"

Serena nodded.

"Relax. There isn't a time limit on grief, or when you'll be ready to be with someone again. But if someone shows up and you find yourself interested? Don't hold back. No guilt."

"I'll try to remember that." Serena watched as Winnie stared at her husband, Max, obviously in love.

"Do you really think I'll be able to handle the alpacas when I'm working full-time?"

"Of course you will. And if you can't, Marcy said she'd take them back."

Serena stifled her doubts. It was going to work; it had to. Pepé had already fallen in love with the two alpacas, sisters from Marcy's herd. Marcy was a fiber friend of Winnie's.

Serena wondered if Jonas had noticed the fresh lumber piled outside the old barn. If he did, he hadn't mentioned it, and besides, why should she care? But his eyes... Those eyes could convince her to do a lot more than she'd thought about doing with a man in a long while....

"Dottie would be surprised that I've refurbished the barn, but I'm excited to take the house and land back to what it was originally. I'm not a farmer by any stretch, but as you know, fiber's in my blood."

Winnie laughed. "Judging by how much yarn you've collected for your stash since you've moved here, yes, it's in your blood."

At what must have been Serena's guilty expression, Winnie giggled and put a comforting hand on Serena's shoulder. "You're not the only one who's hoarding yarn, Serena—how do you think I keep the shop in the black?"

Serena laughed. "Just don't expect me to spin the alpaca fiber. I like my yarn already carded, washed and spun." Serena was content to own and keep two alpacas, but once she resumed her law practice, she'd have little time for anything but the basic knitting that she enjoyed.

"I'll make you catch the spinning bug yet." Winnie winked.

She had all types of fiber classes at her shop, from basic knit and crochet, to how to take freshly shorn wool from the sheep to the skein. This included cleaning, or carding, the fiber before spinning it into unique, high-quality yarn.

"No, I don't think so. Keep your shelves stacked at the store for me."

"No problem."

"I'm grateful for your support, Winnie. It's important to me to make the farmhouse Pepé's and my home, and bringing it back to the way it was when our ancestors built it. It would've been too much for me to have the alpacas if I had to be responsible for the shearing and all."

"Speaking of the farmhouse, have you heard any more grumbling from the Scotts?" Winnie had been a supportive friend and confidante in the aftermath of Dottie's death and Serena's inheritance.

"No, no grumbles, no *nothing,* until the youngest got back from deployment a couple weeks ago." Serena sipped her drink.

"Do you mean Jonas?"

Serena nodded, hoping the heat she felt on her cheeks wasn't too obvious.

"He really had his heart set on getting the house. Apparently Dottie promised it to him. Which makes me feel a bit like a jerk, since Pepé and I are so happy there."

"Don't even go there, Serena. Dottie was her own person. The whole town knew her and adored her, but it doesn't mean she didn't have her own quirky way of doing things. For some reason she changed her mind and willed it to you. Jonas isn't hurting financially, right? He has the means to build a second home if he wants."

Serena looked at Winnie's huge Christmas tree. It was everything a tree should represent—the joy of the holiday, the warmth of a home and the love of a family.

Had she stolen that from Jonas when she'd accepted the house from Dottie?

"I'm not going to be a hypocrite and say that I'm sorry about any of it. The minute Dottie had us over for dinner, I knew I'd come home. Dottie became part of our family. I never expected her to give me the house, of course."

Serena had planned to buy a home once she and Pepé had found their favorite part of the island. That decision was, needless to say, taken out of her hands.

"I don't want to hear one hint that you're feeling badly for Jonas, Serena. He's a big boy and he'll get over it. You've had a lot on your plate these past couple of years—you and Pepé deserve every drop of happiness you can get. Your farmhouse is part of that."

Winnie and Max knew the Scotts from when Jonas's older brother did extensive landscaping on their house and became friends with Max and Winnie.

When Serena had first confided in Winnie, she'd encouraged Serena to accept the house without reservation. She'd also given Serena the gift of insight into Jonas's background—from someone who knew much more about him.

Jonas had been a bit of a wild child, until he found his calling in medicine and the Navy. Dottie's community reputation had been on the line with him several times while he was in high school, but she didn't give up on him, ever.

She also didn't enable him. Dottie had loved Jonas when he needed it most and he'd grown into the successful military professional he was today.

Who loved Jonas like that now that Dottie was gone?

"He came by the house," Serena said. Winnie's eyes widened. "When?"

"Last week. He was very nice. Even charming. Yet he made it clear that he hasn't given up on getting me to sell."

"Typical Jonas. What a jackass thing to do!" Winnie shook her head. "He put Dottie through the wringer with his last girlfriend. It looked like they were going to get married, and the girl had all these dreams of making Dottie's place into a bed-and-breakfast. Can you imagine? She told Dottie all about her plans, acted like it was a fait accompli that Jonas would get the place and, of course, that she'd be with him when he did."

"What happened then?"

"Dottie handled it in her usual straightforward

manner and told Jonas she never wanted to see her family home turned into a hotel."

"No, I mean what happened with his girlfriend?"

Winnie waved her hand in a dismissive gesture. "Just like the others, she broke up with him once she realized his first love is the Navy. She didn't want to wait for him to settle down."

"Is she still here?"

"Yes, she's over there." Winnie nodded toward the fireplace, which was the center of the Ford home. Max stood with their infant daughter in his arms while their two older girls, Winnie's from her first marriage, stood next to him.

All four were mesmerized by a slim blonde who spoke animatedly, her arms floating about her as she emphasized her words.

"Joy Alexander."

"She's beautiful." And everything Serena physically wasn't.

Why did she care?

"Yes, but they weren't good as a couple—it was more of a convenience hookup. She'd been alone a long while, as had he. It was a partnership of the lonely. They just didn't have that spark, you know what I mean?"

"Hmm." Serena didn't want to tell Winnie that she understood all too well what she meant. Seeing Jonas always seemed to send sparks down her spine.

She'd worked with a lot of men in her profession; she wasn't swayed by just any man, no matter how attractive. Jonas Scott was different.

JONAS SAW HER the minute she walked through Max and Winnie's front door. The dark fall of her hair reflected the twinkling lights from the Fords' Christmas tree and made her look more sensuous, more beautiful, than she'd been at her house last week. If that was even possible.

He wasn't a fool. He wasn't a stranger to sudden sexual attraction, infatuation. Add in a long spell without a woman and of course a beauty like Serena would make his need all the more urgent.

It didn't mean any more than that; his body was reacting to a gorgeous woman. He was still alive.

Unlike the kids he'd been unable to save.

He swallowed back the bile spewed by the unwanted memory. He wasn't a pediatric specialist; it wasn't his fault those two siblings had died. They'd been suffering from malnutrition on top of their war wounds—it was unlikely they had the strength to heal from the mortar injuries even if they'd made it to the trauma unit sooner.

Still, he couldn't get their soft brown eyes, filled with pain and fear, out of his mind. Or how sweetly they'd accepted his ministrations, the needles, the meds, without a single whimper.

They'd believed the Americans could save them.

And he hadn't.

Jonas took a swig of his beer. This was his first

Christmas celebration since he'd come home and no one needed his morose regret to smother the twinkling holiday spirit.

"You still moping that you didn't get your farmhouse, Jonas?" Max had waited until Joy walked off before he got to the point, which reminded Jonas why he liked Max as much as he did.

Max always got to the point of any issue. It was one of the reasons Jonas respected him so much.

"It's not the house, Max." Bitterness stoked his guilt. He'd give up his quest for the farmhouse to have those kids back, alive. In a nanosecond.

"Maybe this was all part of Dottie's plan, to get you to learn to share." Max Ford smiled at him, his baby daughter on his hip.

Jonas didn't want to tell Max why he was so upset with himself. Not tonight, at a Christmas party.

"You've gone soft, Max. When I first met you ten years ago, you were as tough as nails. Now look at you—you're married to a woman who has you wrapped around her finger and your baby on your hip."

They both guffawed and Jonas gave Max a playful slap on his shoulder.

"It's been the most humbling, and the best, experience of my life, Jonas. I highly recommend it."

"Humph."

"Now you sound like Scrooge."

"I feel like Scrooge, man, but I'm trying to fight it. This is my first Christmas back home in over five years, between deployments and other tours. For the first time, I'm alone." Max knew about the disastrous Christmas Jonas had spent with Joy. They'd taken a cruise to sunnier weather. Both he and Joy had regretted it—they would've preferred to be with their own families, not together.

"You dating anyone since you came back?"

"Me? Nope. And that's okay—not to say I wouldn't mind a companion, but I'm not ready for the baggage that comes with it." Jonas looked at Max's baby girl.

Max gave him the stink eye.

"Hey, I'm sorry, man. I didn't mean anything by that. You know I'm happy for you."

Max smiled. "I get it, Jonas, more than you realize. But be forewarned—the minute I gave up on ever having a lifelong relationship, gave up on finding the woman of my dreams, she showed up."

"I remember." Jonas nodded.

Max had found out long after the fact that he'd fathered his and Winnie's middle girl during a one-night affair before he'd left on an extended deployment.

"Weren't you angry at Winnie for not telling you sooner, Max?"

"Of course I was. But what can I say? I couldn't change the past. I figured out that if I wanted to live my life to its fullest, I had to let go of whatever had happened before, whatever my expectations had been."

"You're one of the lucky ones."

"Yeah, I'm lucky. But Winnie and I do the groundwork, believe me." Max hoisted his little girl higher in his arms and sniffed. "You need a diaper change, don't you, sweetie pie?"

She giggled, her cherubic cheeks rosy from the warmth of the fire and being in her dad's arms.

Some visceral emotion hit Jonas. He was sure it was just post-deployment letdown. He'd always thought he'd have a family and kids…someday. "Someday" hadn't come yet. Although he had to admit he envied Max's certainty that his family was the source of his happiness.

"Excuse me, Jonas, but this little lady needs to freshen up. Help yourself to the buffet—Winnie went all out and had her friend Ro bake up some of her delicious desserts."

"Will do. Thanks, Max."

Jonas turned around and leaned against the mantel. The heat of the fire made him uncomfortably warm, so he wasn't going to be able to hang out here long, but he wanted to take it all in.

Stop kidding yourself at least.

He wanted to take *her* in.

Serena leaned against a far wall of the great room as she spoke to Winnie, Max's wife. She laughed at something Winnie said and took a sip from her flute of champagne.

Champagne. He'd have to file that away.

Why? Why was he torturing himself like this? He wasn't going to charm her. But he sure as hell could try.

The fact that his need to talk to her right now had nothing to do with the farmhouse was something he'd examine later.

He dropped his empty beer bottle into a pop-up bin placed strategically near the kitchen counter and walked over to Serena.

She looked over Winnie's shoulder and made eye contact with him. The sizzle in their shared glance made him grateful he was a man, grateful he was back on terra firma, U.S.A., grateful he could still feel this kind of interest in another human being.

Winnie smiled as she turned toward him. Was that a wink?

"Hey, Jonas. I'm so glad you made it tonight." She tilted her face toward him and he placed a quick peck on her cheek.

"Thanks for having me."

"Welcome home! I heard you're working in the Peds unit on base?"

He nodded. "Nothing I volunteered for, believe me. My specialty is trauma, as you know. But Peds needs the help and who am I to complain? For the first time in forever I have regular hours."

"With regular grumpy parents and sick kids,"

Serena chimed in, and he couldn't help the grin that spread across his face.

"Touché. Hello, Serena."

She gave him a small smile. "Jonas."

He looked into her eyes a beat longer than he probably needed to before he turned back to their hostess.

"Serena's still sore from overhearing my inappropriate comments at the base clinic. She caught me at my worst, I'm afraid."

Winnie laughed. "Well, I hope we don't see you very often at the hospital, but with the girls being out of school for the holidays and the older two so active with gymnastics practice, we may."

"We're there if you need us. And don't ever hesitate to call me at home if it's after hours and something comes up. Kids are unpredictable."

"Thanks, Jonas. You may live to regret your offer." Winnie glanced past their small group. "Where was Max heading? I saw you talking to him."

"Your little girl needed a diaper change. Max is a great father."

"Yes, he is. Our marriage, the girls—we're so blessed."

Winnie smiled at him, then at Serena. It was painfully clear that "blessed" meant "in love." What was it with the Fords? Why did they see romance everywhere they looked?

"Will you two excuse me? I have to make sure

the beef isn't overcooked." Winnie walked off and Jonas felt like he and Serena were the only two people in the room.

As if she was the only woman in the universe who mattered to him.

CHAPTER TEN

"I DIDN'T KNOW you were friends with the Fords." Serena licked her upper lip after she spoke, spinning the stem of her glass between her fingers.

Did he make her nervous?

Or maybe she was feeling the same sexual crackle he did.

Good.

"We haven't exactly spent time comparing our mutual acquaintances, have we?" He angled his body closer to her warmth, her sizzle.

"No, I suppose we haven't, Jonas." She pursed her lips as if deep in thought and Jonas ignored the urge to tell her she had the most luscious mouth. He shook his head.

"Everyone's friends with the Fords. They're a great couple, a wonderful family. Max and I go way back, and Winnie is friends with my sister-in-law, who's a rabid knitter."

Serena giggled and it produced a feeling of warmth in his chest.

"I like to knit, too, but I don't consider myself 'rabid' about it. I let it go for a while right after...

after Phil died, but lately I've been at it again. Whidbey is the perfect place to knit, and Winnie's shop is fabulous. In fact, she's convinced me to...to—"

She cut herself off abruptly and sipped her drink. "Convinced you to...?"

Guilt, maybe apology, flashed across her expression. "Have my own alpacas."

"Oh. Well, I don't know anything about alpacas, or sheep, but the farm used to have dairy cows, back in the day."

"Yes, I know. I'm not interested in the work cows would need, and I don't want to clear the area needed for sheep, but there are other fiber animals, like alpacas, that could be very happy there. Will be happy there. At the farm. Not that it's a full-fledged farm. I'm not a farmer, per se."

His gut tightened. "Go on."

"I don't suppose you noticed the barn upgrades I had done? The new addition on the other side?"

He had. The piles of lumber and new coat of paint, along with a new door to the stone foundation building, had caught his eye as he left yesterday, but he wasn't about to go back and ask her about it. Not after he'd almost kissed her in the upstairs room.

"Let me guess—not just for show or for aesthetics? You're not planning on using the barn as a storage unit for your hobbies, your yarn?"

She gave him a soft smile. He wondered if

Serena knew how pretty, how damned attractive, she was.

Sexy was more like it.

"Not yarn in *skeins*. I've agreed to keep two alpacas on the property for a trial period. Winnie's helping me, as is her friend I'm purchasing the animals from."

"You're purchasing *trial* animals?" His incredulity at this made him smile. Serena's smile widened into a grin.

"Okay, I've bought the animals, but I can always give them back."

"Like a rental car?"

"All I'm doing is taking care of them. Winnie's friend will handle the shearing and cleaning, and the rest of the fiber processing. It's a good thing for Pepé, too, to give him a sense of belonging, a connection to his roots with the farmhouse. His biological family farmed on Whidbey almost a century before he was born."

"Alpacas, eh?" He didn't give a darn if she put emus in the barn. All he wanted to do was watch her lips form words, see her tongue lick them, sneak looks at her breasts.

He should walk. Away. Now.

"It's my responsibility to restore and maintain the property, Jonas. I'm not going to restore it to the kind of farm it once was, but I do hope to keep it the way my great-grandfather intended—a place to raise a family and provide a small income."

His conscience urged him to open up and tell her what he'd been holding back. Still, he waited.

Not yet.

"Do you ever wonder what this could be like—" he motioned between them "—if you hadn't got Dottie's house, if we weren't related, if we'd just met?"

"First, we're *not* related. Second, I *did* get Dottie's house. Third, I'm not ready to date yet." Serena didn't pretend she didn't know what he was talking about. He liked her direct frankness.

"Aren't you?" He was still mesmerized by her lips. Like a sixteen-year-old with his first girlfriend, he couldn't stop thinking about how soft they must be. How pliant they'd feel under his. And her tongue— He groaned.

Her eyes narrowed. "Are you okay?"

"Fine."

He didn't want to explain his uncontrollable attraction to her.

"Have you been out here before, during the day?"

She nodded. "Yes, but only out front. I usually see Winnie at her shop."

"So you haven't seen their Christmas lights for the kids?"

"No, not yet."

She blinked and he knew he was moving too fast, into territory he had no business entering. But like a riptide, his need to be with her, be *alone* with her, propelled him to make the gutsiest, stupidest, most thrilling decision of the season.

"Let me show you." He clasped her elbow and nodded toward the tall French doors that led to the large deck.

"It's freezing out!"

"We won't be there that long. Drink up the rest of your bubbly and when we're back inside you can get a warm-up."

She did, all the while eyeing him with a suspicious gleam. After she put the empty flute on a side table, she tilted her head toward the doors.

"Make it quick, Jonas."

Jonas nodded and ushered her out onto the deck. The shock of the cold air hit his cheeks and he saw her shiver. Still, he couldn't pull her in his arms.

He shouldn't.

"Is that a tree fort?" She laughed at the sight of the miniature house trimmed with twinkling multicolored lights. Through the tiny window a small Christmas tree winked with white lights.

"Yes, Max goes all out for his girls."

"It's so beautiful here."

She'd wrapped both arms around her, and he watched her profile as she gazed at the darkness, the lights, the stars, the water in the distance, reflecting the crescent moon.

"No matter where I go in the world, when it's time to settle down, be it for a nap or a decent four hours of sleep, I never fail to see Whidbey in my mind."

"This is your home. Of course you should see it in your dreams."

"Is it going to be your home, Serena? How can you be so sure you'll want to stay here with Pepé, that you won't change your mind?"

The moonlight caught her expression and he saw her search for the right words to match her feelings.

When a sharp shiver went through her, he instinctively pulled her against him, rubbing her back to warm her.

She opened her arms and pushed her hands against his chest. Looking up into his face, she opened her mouth, no doubt to protest his bold actions.

Jonas allowed his years of medical and military training to carry him to the next indicated task. He had a beautiful woman in his arms and they both needed to stay warm.

He kissed her.

SERENA KNEW HE was going to kiss her. Knew she was going to let him. Knew, or at least assumed, that she'd like it. Otherwise, she wouldn't have come out here with him.

What she didn't expect was that Jonas's lips on hers was going to release her inner vixen and make her want to jump him right here on the deck, to hell with the partygoers inside.

Her sex life with Phil had been loving, warm, at times exciting. Jonas's kiss was hot, sexy, sinfully wonderful. And his tongue—*Dios mio,* his tongue was doing things to her mouth that immediately made her wish he'd use it on other parts of her anatomy, pronto.

She grasped the back of his neck and pulled his head closer while she angled her hips into his.

Who was she? Where was her composure?

Was that her groan or his?

He lowered his hands to her waist, turned her around and pushed her against the side of the house. The cold wood siding dug into her back through her sweater and grounded her in the moment. The crisp, cold air on her cheeks. Jonas's hot, hot mouth. Her gulps for air when he lifted his lips from hers and buried his face in the side of her neck, his tongue seeking contact with the sensitive skin at the base of her throat.

She grabbed either side of his head and pulled him back up to her lips.

If only she'd kept her eyes closed, the moment might have turned into more.

When she looked up into his eyes, begging him for another kiss, she saw...

Confusion? Guilt?

"What, Jonas?"

One kiss and she was complete mush. She fought through the brain fog her lust had induced.

"Serena, I have to tell you something."

Her skin cooled and the reality of being outside in subfreezing temperatures with Jonas—Jonas, who wanted her to give her house to him—sobered her.

"Oh, God, you're married!"

"No, not married."

She knew he wasn't. Winnie would have said something. So would Dottie.

He put his fingers to her lips. The struggle that played out in his expression wasn't odd to her—he wanted to kiss her again, too. She saw it in the way he stared at her, at her lips, and then licked his own. How could such masculine lips be so sensual?

"Serena, I've bought the land lots next to and behind the farmhouse."

Rejection put an immediate end to her bliss and strangled her newfound sexual attraction to him.

She shivered and tried to steady herself against the cold.

The land lots she'd hoped to eventually purchase, to restore the farmhouse back to its original parameters.

To fulfill her silent promise to Dottie.

"When did you do this?"

"I'd placed bids on the lots while I was still on deployment—I gave my brother power of attorney.

When I first got back I went ahead and signed the initial paperwork. Because of the slow real estate market the Realtor was able to make closing happen quickly."

"It's a done deal?"

"As of four o'clock today, yes."

She lowered her hands from around his neck, leaving them with the lightest touch on his chest.

"Awkward."

She was not going to let him see her disappointment. She still had her pride, for heaven's sake.

"That means this is out of the question, doesn't it?" Thank God for her attorney voice.

"It doesn't have to, Serena. We're both adults."

"I'm not ready for anything like this, Jonas, and certainly not with the man who wants to choke me out of my rightful property."

"Serena—"

She shoved against his chest and he took a step back.

"I'm cold, Jonas."

Serena walked back into the party and headed for the bathroom. She had to sidestep several conversations, but she made it into the powder room off the main foyer without being dragged into any cocktail-party chatter. Fortunately, the bathroom wasn't occupied and she was able to put a closed door between her and Jonas.

She flipped down the lid on the toilet and sat on it. It was covered with a fuzzy snowman's face with a matching rug at the base. Only Winnie would have something so whimsical in her guest bathroom.

Serena felt anything but whimsy as she went over what Jonas had revealed, while trying to ignore her throbbing lips.

So he'd bought the land that surrounded the house? So what? She still had the property that included a good stretch of woods, and the front meadow that rolled down toward the shore almost a mile away.

If he builds, no, when he builds, he'll be in full view of you. Every day. Every time you drive up to your house.

The land had never been built on. It had originally been purchased by Dottie's grandparents when the land was cheap and their dreams big. When Dottie inherited the house from her parents, she'd had to sell off some of the land to buy out her brother for her half of the house. She'd sold it to a local farmer with the promise she'd be able to buy it back when she wanted.

By the time Dottie met Jonas's father, her concerns about the land became less important than raising four boys and enjoying being a mother and wife after years of living alone. She'd mentioned the land one of the times she'd had Serena and Pepé over for Sunday dinner.

Dottie had confided to Serena that she'd hoped to purchase the land once she cashed in some of her stocks in the next year or two. She'd been killed only a month later, before her vision was realized.

Serena blinked back tears and stared at the wall. Did Winnie really have red-and-green printed toilet paper?

The Christmas spirit that had entered her heart when she walked into Winnie's home blew away in a puff of coldhearted truth.

She couldn't bring Dottie back, and now it looked like she might not ever get the land, either. Jonas Scott might be the best kisser. But he played dirty.

She could, too. And it wasn't really dirty. He needed to understand that she and Pepé were the farmhouse's rightful owners.

She and Pepé were also the farmhouse's future, connected to the past by blood. Once she found out more about who her grandparents had been, she'd show Jonas what legacy meant. The first aspect of her research would be the World War II tree ornaments.

Maybe she had some Christmas spirit after all. The ghost of Christmas past.

CHAPTER ELEVEN

Remote island off Thailand
January 1942

FLYING TIGER HENRY Forsyth sucked the juice out of the coconut he'd foraged from the jungle floor hours earlier, before the sun made its daily pilgrimage to the perch that bathed the tiny island in hellish heat. He let the murky liquid wash over his tongue as he lost himself in memories.

Sarah.

Dottie.

He'd see them again. He'd get home. It was only a matter of when.

He was on a dot of land somewhere off the coast of Thailand, his P-40 single-engine propeller aircraft the victim of a Japanese army air force "Oscar" machine gun. That damned Ki-43 had come out of nowhere, just when he'd finished his mission and was on his way back to home base in Burma.

It'd been well over a week since he'd been hit. He sat on the mat he'd made from palm fronds, up against the fuselage and under the starboard wing of his P-40 Warhawk. He squinted against the hot sun as he broke open another coconut. His fingers were rough and scratched his skin when he rubbed his eyes.

Ragged marks into the side of one of the metal tiles on the plane indicated it was his tenth day missing in action. Had he been reported home in a telegram as MIA? Or worse? By his calculations it was January 12, and even if the Japanese surrendered today, it would take the Marines weeks to find him. Followed by another month-long boat transit across the Pacific to Hawaii, where he'd await new orders. He'd never be flown from Hawaii to the States—he was too junior and he wasn't injured badly enough to be discharged. His cuts were healing and the rib he figured he'd cracked in the landing would stop bothering him eventually.

Besides, he didn't want to go home now, when the fight was just starting. He couldn't wait to see Sarah and Dottie again, but he refused to go back without knowing the Japanese had surrendered.

He wanted to return to the fight so badly it made his teeth hurt. Or maybe that was from chewing through too much coconut.

He grinned at the jungle around him. It was tough not having the guys with him to laugh at his crazy thoughts. They were all just as nuts as he.

The tendons at his wrist still complained when

he went to move his left hand, but the swelling had receded from the softball-size lump.

"I haven't lost all my luck. I'm still alive." He might find himself gone cuckoo if he kept having these conversations with himself.

The pile of gnarly dried branches he'd collected caught his attention. He'd picked them up on his walks to and from the beachfront. Without a working radio, and out of range even if his batteries hadn't failed, he had no way, other than the stars, to be sure of where he was. His vision got clearer every night, at the same rate that the pounding in the back of his head and sides of his temples subsided. From the amount of dried blood on the back of his cockpit seat when he'd awakened, he must have taken a doozy of a crack to his noggin.

He wanted to have the comfort of a fire at night but even with a foggy brain he knew it could get him captured. It wasn't worth it.

Sarah. Visions of her, naked on their bed, would give him all the consolation he needed.

Christmas. He'd missed it. Their first Christmas apart. He'd been granted a week of leave after his flight training, right before he got on the boat to Burma. He and Sarah had tried to make it a good week, like Christmas, but it wasn't the same. It couldn't be.

He didn't have a gift for her this year, hadn't sent her or Dottie anything, but he could make them one.

After his afternoon snooze he'd get himself a solid branch and create something using the knife that had made the trip in his flight vest.

HE ENJOYED MORE than a nap—when he awoke it was dark. The nights out here were darker than any he remembered. He knew that wasn't really true but it was lonely out here. Whidbey Island got dark in the winter but as long as he could see the stars or the moon he never felt alone. Reality was that his solitude and vulnerability were closing in on him. He missed home.

Whidbey Island.

Funny how quickly Whidbey had gotten into his blood. At first he thought it was because of Sarah, as did his family back in West Texas. They thought he'd get tired of the long gray seasons and bring his wife back to the town he'd been raised in.

It hadn't happened. After five years as a resident of Oak Harbor he belonged in the Pacific Northwest as much as he belonged with Sarah. Once Dottie came along, their family was complete, and he had no doubt they'd give Dottie a little brother or sister.

It had to wait until after the war, but he was going to see Sarah's belly swollen with his baby again.

He *would* get back to them.

He wrapped his fingers around his pocket-knife and he itched to make something for them *now*. Even if they never got it, just making it would bring them closer. At least it would feel that way....

Finally the sand reflected a silvery glow. The moonlight was the only light he could trust. Moving around wasn't an option, either, as he didn't know enough about where he'd landed to make traveling in the dark worth the risk of being captured or falling prey to wildlife. There could be wild cats and poisonous snakes, but he hadn't heard any animal noises that concerned him.

He was too close to the beach. He should have moved farther inland. His instincts had told him to get to the trees, where he could hide better, which he did after he'd crashed in a grove not more than five hundred yards from the sand. His hunger made his stomach growl so loudly. Which was more of a risk—having his stomach noises heard by the enemy or risking capture if he went out to the beach to catch a crab?

Blue light glowed over the ocean water as he checked out the beach through the forest of palm trees. He ignored the feel of dozens of insects crawling over him, and the sound of their buzzing. His skin was getting bitten to hell, but at least he was still alive, and he didn't feel feverish or sick. Both very good things.

His memory lit on the image of Sarah's face when she'd held Dottie for the first time. Dottie had been as wrinkled as a tiny prune, her clenched fists fighting their way out of the yellow blanket Sarah had knit for her.

Sarah's face had been like an angel's, radiant with her love for their newborn. The smile she gave him when she looked up at him from their bed at the farmhouse, after all the pain she'd been through, had left him breathless. Sarah was his partner for life, and Dottie his dear daughter.

He had to make it back home to Whidbey. Sarah and Dottie were counting on him.

SARAH LEANED OVER HIM, blocking his view of the blinding sun.

"Don't forget me, Henry."

Her breath fanned his face and his erection demanded satisfaction.

"Did you hear me, Henry?"

She kissed him and he tried to pull her closer, but his hands, his arms, wouldn't move. He had to accept her kiss as she gave it, his consuming need for her blotting out his worry that he couldn't move his limbs.

"Sarah—ooof." Pain shot through his shoulder and his mobility returned at the same moment he thought his arm was falling off.

"Hey, stop it!" His yell was lost in the mayhem that surrounded him. Three Japanese soldiers stood around him, one with the butt of his rifle coming down again, this time in the middle of his gut.

They'd found him.

He'd get away. He had to.

But escape with a dislocated shoulder and most likely internal bleeding wasn't going to happen. Not today, not on this godforsaken island at the edge of Southeast Asia.

They kept screaming at him in Japanese. He managed to stumble to his feet, his left hand clutching his right breast pocket.

He had the mini P-40 he'd carved for Dottie. Its sharp edges poked through his flight suit's fabric. If these jerks kept hitting him, the Santa Claus he'd carved in the cockpit was going to break off.

More yelling, more shoving, as they forced him to the beach. He remembered destroying his navigation and communication equipment and maps. He allowed satisfaction to warm his cold prospects. The enemy wouldn't get any information from him.

He stumbled onto the deep sand and saw where they were taking him—to a small launch that didn't look much bigger than his father's lake boat. Farther out on the horizon he recognized the silhouette of one of the Japanese imperial fleet's many transport ships. He'd bet his life that it had the word *Maru* stenciled on it, an indicator of the Japanese cargo class. He'd flown a mission over one just weeks ago.

It was a floating death trap. The Allied submarines were going to take all of them out.

So this was what it came down to? He'd survived being shot down, being captured, to be set afloat in a Japanese tin can that would see the bottom of the Pacific before it got anywhere?

More yelling. He was almost relieved he didn't know Japanese. He'd probably kill at least one of his captors with his bare hands before they drove their bayonets through him.

The swift crack of something hard on his skull drove him to his knees, bright spots floating in front of him above the hot sand that burned his skin.

He saw the carved toy airplane fall out of his front pocket, onto the sweltering ground.

"No!" His hand reached for his one link to home, all he had left for Sarah and Dottie. The wooden carving disappeared as the butt of a rifle crushed first the miniature P-40, and then came down a second time to crush Henry's hand.

Pain made him gasp for breath and his logic fought with the primal anger that enveloped him.

"If you get taken, stay calm. We'll come get you. Don't give anyone a reason to kill you."

The words of one of his instructors spoke as if from the grave.

The only thing he had to hang on to was the one place in his heart they'd never destroy.

Sarah. Dottie.

Family.

Philippines
April 1942

"THEY'RE GOING TO make us all walk to the end."
Bill Payton from Alabama was behind Henry, his
words floating up to Henry from time to time
as they crossed the Philippine jungle. Henry still
couldn't believe he'd survived the hellish transit
from Thailand to the PI in that floating piece of
crap. Once they landed he'd been relieved to be
shoved into a group of seemingly thousands of
Americans and Filipinos. Until he realized that
the Americans had surrendered and the Japanese
were intent on getting them all to one camp miles
away.

Henry had only known the Philippines as a point
on the globe before. Now, he felt that the Filipinos, along with all their Allies were his brothers.
He'd seen what the Japanese had done to the na-
tives when the tank ship they'd transported him
on arrived to the PI. They'd slaughtered them by
the hundreds, right before his eyes. He and his
fellow prisoners knew it was a warning to them.
Comply or die.

Screw them. He'd outlive these bastards who
held him captive. He'd get back home to Whidbey. In one piece.

"They need our labor. They can't afford to let
all of us die."

He muttered the words over his shoulder to

his buddy, hoping the sound of their feet dragging through the overgrown jungle would muffle their sound.

Thwack.

The pain never got easier. He'd have thought by now that he'd be numb to whatever the bastards wanted to do to him. Then he'd witness or experience another form of torture heretofore unimaginable.

Trickling dampness that flowed thicker than the perspiration that covered him from head to toe told him that his back had been sliced open. Henry knew he had to keep going, keep walking, as if he hadn't been struck a potentially fatal blow in the dank, humid jungle.

Infection was omnipresent without running water and soap to clean up wounds.

"How much longer?" he dared whisper to the Filipino, Tommy, who marched next to him. Tommy spoke English and Japanese, but their captors hadn't caught on that he knew the enemy's language.

"They said something about Camp O'Donnell." Tommy's voice was sober, tinged with fear.

"I heard that, too." He could make out the English words spoken by his captors amid the static of their language.

"It's fifty more miles."

Henry didn't reply. One of their four guards had walked up next to them, staring at him with dark, angry eyes. Henry was willing to die for his country but no sense giving this loser a reason to take him out before his time.

Sarah.

He stumbled, the soldier's shirt in front of him brushing his nose. The cloth was rough against his sunburned skin, and Henry imagined his face was dripping blood instead of the sweat that had been a constant companion since he crash-landed his P-40.

He kept his faith, given no other choice.

He believed he'd live to see more days.

THE THIRD DAY Henry noticed he wasn't sweating any longer. You couldn't sweat when you weren't taking in any water. They weren't allowed anything for their thirst. Stopping for a leaf, a flower, in the hope of finding a drop or two of liquid, was reason for instant execution. The most common form Henry had witnessed was decapitation.

Local Filipinos had tried to aid some of them at their own peril. Two rows of men in front of Henry, Tommy and Bill had been either bayoneted or beheaded when they broke ranks to run down to a tiny stream that paralleled their path.

Henry was surprised to see blood flow from their wounds. Who had anything left inside?

More yelling, more groans. He'd had to let his bowels go sometime during the afternoon and continue to walk on. Otherwise, he'd never get back home.

Would home still be there for any of them?

AFTER SIX DAYS they reached not where Tommy had said they were going, Camp O'Donnell, but a place called San Fernando. Henry didn't care anymore.

He'd walked through hell and seen images he knew would haunt him for the rest of his life.

Maimed, dismembered bodies. Men and women beheaded, cut down in the midst of a breath. Women's bodies littered the road in some spots and had clearly been raped before their deaths. How could people do this to one another?

He was afraid to bring his memories of Sarah and Dottie to his awareness. Afraid of tainting them with the evil he walked through. Without them, he feared for his survival.

AT HIS FIRST sight of the cargo train, Henry wanted to cry with relief. Finally, a better mode of travel. No more walking through the thick heat. They'd get to the camp sooner, wouldn't they?

His relief lasted until he was shoved into a car, not knowing if the air could reach them once the Japanese shut the metal doors. If there'd be enough air for all of them. How many would live until the end of the train ride?

HENRY SPLIT THE pile of rocks one by one, never looking up from his task. No talking allowed. He and his fellow prisoners had to wait until nighttime to attempt communication or risk death.

His back muscles screamed but he was past the point of letting the pain stop him. Instead, it drove him, proved he was still alive.

He still had hope—hope he'd make it back to Sarah.

Camp O'Donnell had the American sign on it, but the flag with the rising sun flew over what had been American soil only days earlier.

Where the hell was MacArthur?

By Henry's count they'd left the port with at least ninety to one hundred men. Thirty of them stumbled into Camp O'Donnell. Maybe a few more had survived, but the train journey had shoved together men from different groups.

He'd never been in a place so crowded, not even during training exercises on the ground back in California. He and thousands of his closest allies were summarily hosed down and left to dry. Exhaustion seeped from every pore, and the stink of his skin should have made him vomit on the spot. In some macabre way he was adjusting to the constant rank smells, the sight of the sore-riddled faces of his brothers-in-arms.

Henry watched his captors as they ordered him from one impossible labor task to another. Did they have families? How could anyone with a mother treat a fellow human being this way?

His stomach sank as he comprehended the awful truth. He'd probably have years to contemplate that question. If his body held out.

Watching his brothers fight alongside him, he learned that it wasn't his body's failure that would get him in the end. It would be the death of his spirit.

His loss of hope that he'd ever see Sarah or Dottie again.

CHAPTER TWELVE

Whidbey Island
Second week of December

AFTER A WEEK of unusual cold for early December, the clouds parted and sunshine bathed Whidbey Island in a soft white light. Because the days were short, Jonas had been ready and was halfway to Mount Baker before the sun rose. His skis had sat in the garage for too long and it was time to take advantage of being only two hours from a snow-covered mountain.

The quiet of the slopes soothed his anxiety as to when, or if, he'd ever feel like himself again.

How could he be, when he'd watched such horror unfold in his ER in Afghanistan? When he couldn't save those children, couldn't give them a chance at a peace like this?

It had been a war zone. It was beyond his control. He'd saved so many lives. That wasn't enough to erase his guilt, his sorrow.

Usually he'd either have hooked back up with an old girlfriend by now, for laughs, or found a new one. Someone he could stay warm with through the chilly nights.

Instead, he had to contend with a woman who, until two weeks ago, had been a complete stranger to him. She lived in the house he'd grown up in.

His house.

No, not anymore.

It was Dottie's to give to whomever she wished.

Still, what had changed her mind? She'd promised him the house long ago. They'd all joked about it, after his brothers had moved on and found their own places, and his Navy career had brought him back to Whidbey through no small effort on his part. He'd agreed to deploy this last time so he'd have his pick for his next tour—and he got it. Whidbey Island.

Yet he was still in the town house he'd lived in or rented out for the past fifteen years. He'd bought it as an investment after he was commissioned in the navy medical corps. It was his way of showing Dottie he planned on a future here in Puget Sound. This was his home.

Dottie knew that. And yet, she'd willed her house to a woman she'd barely met, biological niece or not.

What did any of them really know about Serena?

He ignored the self-recrimination that told him to give Serena a break. It was clear that she was the real deal. She wasn't some kind of treasure-seeker.

The ski lift made light work of the slope he'd taken twenty minutes to descend, and within minutes he was back at the crest of the mountain, ready to hit the trail again.

Jonas paused at the edge and took in what he could see of Snoqualmie Valley. It was partially obstructed from his view by low clouds, but the sun shone off the Skagit River as it snaked through the fields that would be abloom with tulips come April. There, in the far distance, under what looked like a huge puff of cotton candy, sat Whidbey Island.

Home.

Did it really matter what house he lived in? The Pacific Northwest was as much a part of him as nursing was. Whidbey healed him the way he hoped he helped his patients heal.

It *did* matter, damn it. That was all he had left of Dottie—her house. Their family home.

Jonas pushed off and started to zigzag down the mountainside, taking it easy and breathing in the crisp cold air through his balaclava.

Dottie had knitted it for him years ago—he loved it. The newer microfibers were probably just as warm, but they weren't made by Dottie.

"Why did you do it, Dottie?" He spoke to himself as he swished around a bend, narrowly avoiding a group of fir trees weighed down with globs of fresh snow. The snow sat so perfectly on each branch, it looked like the Grinch's house could be around the next bend.

Dottie didn't answer his question, which he thought was a good sign for his mental health. What he was certain she would've advised against was going too fast, putting pressure on Serena. Good things take time and patience, she'd tell him, like his medical degrees had.

Instead, he'd barreled his way into Serena's life. Not to mention her son's.

Jonas hadn't been at his best at the Fords' party.

When he'd seen her walk into the place, looking like the woman of his dreams, the logical part of his brain had stopped functioning.

But hey, he was an adult. Why couldn't he have taken a moment to get himself together and act like one? No, instead he'd reacted as if he were a teenager.

It wasn't the kiss—which had been pretty damned fantastic—that annoyed him but his crappy timing. He should've told her right away that he had the options on the lots surrounding the house.

Then when he kissed her he wouldn't have felt like such a fake.

He slowed his pace, coming to a stop at the edge of the path where the view once again opened up to the valley below. The run was at the halfway mark, and he needed to take it easy if he planned to stay up here all morning. His deployment had been at a lower altitude, and his cardio limited to the machines in the base gym. That had been predicated by the heat. If it was too hot, no workout. Simply existing in the hellish conditions had been its own workout.

After the two Afghani siblings had died, he'd wished he could get on a pair of skis and head for the Himalayas, never to return to the real world.

War was like that. It made a man want to take off forever.

You've made it back.

He had. There wasn't another mission pressing down on him, no rush of mortally wounded victims coming through the ER at NAS Whidbey. Sure, disaster could always strike, but if the past two weeks had been any indication, his life was going to be decidedly routine for the next few years.

Exactly what he'd asked for, thinking he'd be rehabbing and living in the farmhouse.

So why couldn't he build a house on the adjacent land? The land had originally been in the Forsyth family for that very reason—to provide places for succeeding generations to build on. Homes would need to get bigger, more modern. Dottie knew that, but she'd never lived to see her dream of owning all the land, recreating the original property, come true.

Still, he could make it happen.

Serena was his only obstacle to achieving Dottie's goal. Jonas had all the time in the world. Maybe if he kept telling himself that, he'd start to believe it. He really wanted to convince Serena that it was in her best interest to give the house up.

Kissing her had been stupid, but it had also been unavoidable. All that heat between them had to go somewhere. Now that they both knew how hot their chemistry was, they could either agree to a physical relationship with no strings, or they could avoid each other entirely.

Jonas grunted.

No way in hell would Serena take him into her bed. Not with her son around, and not while she knew he had one basic motive—to get his house back.

He'd have to appeal to her intellect and her good nature. Maybe she wanted to stay on Whidbey—fine. But it didn't have to be in *his* farmhouse. And if he offered to buy it from her at a price that could guarantee Pepé's college education as well as her own security for the foreseeable future, how could she refuse him?

She said she's financially secure.

There was that.

As he descended the remaining part of the mountain, Jonas focused on the trail in front of him and tried to knock all thoughts of Serena Delgado from his mind. His mind wasn't the problem, however.

The problem was he could still taste that damned kiss.

"THANKS FOR MAKING time for me, Paul."

"Trust me, it's my privilege. After you." Paul Scott, Jonas's oldest brother, motioned for Serena to go ahead of him into the large conference room. A long oak table occupied the center of the space, with ten executive chairs around it. A full sheet of glass window served as one of the walls, and Serena noted that her heels sank into the rich carpet.

"Have a seat."

She chose the first chair on one side while Paul sat at the head of the table.

"I'm thrilled you're considering us, Serena. Your résumé is impressive, and with your expertise as a Gold Star spouse, you can relate to so many of our families on the island."

She smiled. "It's not a professional skill I ever wanted to have, but yes, you're right. I know that I've learned how to navigate military red tape, which is something survivors as well as active-duty family members need to do."

"Can I ask what made you decide to come in now?" Paul's eyes were the same blue as Jonas's. She had to make a conscious effort to stop the comparisons. This was *her* interview, Pepé's and her future.

Jonas had nothing to do with it.

"I'm feeling settled. Not that I didn't before, but when Dottie died…well, you know."

He nodded.

Paul did know—he'd been her attorney when Dottie died. It could have been a conflict of interest as she'd warned him, but he'd insisted on representing her, on the recommendation of her boss at the time, Drew Brett. Drew was the physical therapist with whom she'd found her initial job. Paul had offered to represent her not just because of Drew, but because "Dottie loved you and this is what she'd want."

He'd quickly ascertained that Serena wasn't a suspect in the view of the Island County Sheriff's Department, and she'd been grateful. Dealing with Dottie's loss had seemed insurmountable at the time, since it was so soon after she'd adjusted as well as she could to losing Phil. She'd worried about Pepé's reaction to their second loss in two years, but he'd taken it better than she'd expected.

She wished she had some of his youthful bounce-back ability.

"As I told you before, Serena, you don't have to take on any more cases than you want to. That said, we have a good number of clients who would benefit greatly from your skills."

"The only glitch I'm concerned about, frankly, is your brother. He still wants Dottie's house. Will that be a problem for you and your family if you hire me?"

Paul's eyes flashed with intensity and Serena stiffened.

His laughter rumbled across the room. It was deep and sincere. She'd never heard Jonas laugh like this—did he ever indulge in a real belly laugh?

"Serena, Jonas is a dreamer. He's the one who had to get off island, go see the world. The rest of us have been very happy here and none of us expected to get anything from either of our parents. Dottie was the best of all stepmothers. We couldn't have asked for more."

"But the house—you all have memories there. Jonas most of all, being the youngest."

Paul's brows rose and he gazed out the huge window at the water that was at least fifty feet below the edge of land where the firm's building perched.

"Yes, but we also knew Dottie. We trusted her. She was the best judge of character I've ever known. And she trusted *you*. As far as I'm concerned, that's that." He returned his gaze to her. "Will Jonas be pissed that I hired you? He could be, but he'll get over it."

Serena didn't think so, and she wasn't sure how much Paul knew about Jonas's recent real estate purchases. She assumed Paul was the brother he'd given power of attorney to. Paul probably knew everything, but she couldn't break client-attorney privilege to ask. Anyway, it would be rude to put him on the spot.

"Thank you, Paul. I appreciate your support."

"No problem. Now, let's go meet the team."

Serena stood up to follow Paul out to the offices. She, too, could have an office here if she wanted.

One of her first loves—the law—was closer than it had been in years.

SERENA WALKED OUT of Paul Scott's law firm and headed for downtown Oak Harbor, her heart heavy. The interview had gone well and Paul had offered her the job on the spot; her skills in family law were needed and would be well-compensated.

Exhilaration at knowing she was still in the game bubbled up from deep inside. She'd been suffering from doubts about her career viability after being home with Pepé for the past couple of years.

But the enthusiasm she had been feeling when she walked in the door had been chased away by anxiety the minute she saw the other lawyers. They'd all stepped out of their offices to greet her, and it was the friendliest interview she'd ever had. But they'd been in continuous practice. She'd taken a long break. How could she catch up? *Would* she? Washington State laws differed from Texas. She had a lot to learn, as her courses for the Washington State exam had revealed.

And the other problem that gnawed at her... Had she gotten through the past few years, settled in a new place, only to go back to a high-paying legal career that would leave her exhausted at the end of the week, wondering if she'd made a difference or not?

True, the lawyers at the firm didn't look overworked or stressed. Paul had insisted she'd name her own caseload—no questions asked, no repercussions. She was free to earn as much as she needed to support herself and Pepé, but also able to take off time to be there for him. She'd never have to miss a school function or a soccer match.

Could she let go of the competitive attorney she'd once been? Could she settle for "good enough"? Losing Phil had certainly realigned her expectations. She hadn't been able to go back to work as quickly as she'd hoped, not with the heavy load of grief and dealing with Pepé's adjustment. It had been her choice to move out to Whidbey, and the fact remained that she was a single mother, which meant Pepé's needs had to come before many of her own wishes and desires.

She parked in the public lot near the beach and started walking.

The coffee shop one block down had a nice view of City Beach. A cappuccino sounded like the perfect mood-booster. She tightened the belt on her cream wool coat and was grateful she'd worn her tall leather boots. The heels weren't made for long hikes, but the boots were much warmer than her patent-leather heels would have been in this wind.

They didn't call it Windy Whidbey for nothing.

The bell over the door jingled when she opened it and it felt as though all eyes in the place turned to focus on her.

You're just imagining it.

It was hard at first, after Dottie's death, to ignore the constant stares and whispers. She'd never been under serious suspicion. But the fact that she'd worked at the clinic where Dottie was murdered and was there when the murder actually occurred, that she was a stranger to town and had presented herself as a long-lost relative of the deceased—it had all made for intense gossip fodder.

"Hey, Serena!" Emily Bowman waved at her from a small table where she sat with her laptop open and knitting in her lap.

Serena walked over, removing her cap and gloves.

"Hi, Emily. Multitasking?"

Emily smiled and Serena noticed that the laugh lines had returned to her face. Like Serena, Emily was a widow, but her husband had died almost a decade ago from cancer, only a year into their marriage. Serena and Emily had met in Winnie's yarn shop and become friends while taking a Fair Isle knitting class at the same time.

Emily worked as a nurse in the base hospital's

labor and delivery unit, but was also a budding knitting designer.

"I have a deadline for my pattern book that's coming out next year, and the dye lots on some of my merino blend need to be straightened out. When I get tired of the spreadsheets, I knit a few rows. What are you doing today?"

"I'm coming from my job interview. Pepé's in school, and I didn't want to go home to the farmhouse quite yet. I'm feeling a little sore from taking down wallpaper in the back laundry room for the past two days."

"Get a coffee and come and tell me about it. Unless you need some time alone?" Emily was the epitome of grace. Serena placed her at about the same age she was, but Emily didn't have a child. Yet, judging by the way she warmed up around Pepé, she'd like one of her own someday. Still, Emily never complained, which Serena respected. Her mother and family in Texas had never really learned how to be like that. Everything from family gatherings to major life events always had to measure up to her mother's expectations. Emily, on the other hand, accepted things as they came. It was a quality Serena hoped to emulate.

"I'd love to. If I'd been thinking about it I would have planned it this way. Do you want anything? I owe you for watching Pepé the other night."

"You owe me nothing. I'm glad you had a good time. But I'll take a cappuccino." Emily grinned.

After Serena got their cappuccinos and was seated in front of Emily, she didn't know where to begin.

She kept it to business to start with.

"My alpacas are doing well."

"Are they? Great. I knew you'd enjoy them once you got used to their routine."

"What routine? They're worse than puppies. They act as if they're starved for attention every time we go out there."

"They have that lovely pasture to enjoy! I really like what you've done with the newer parts of the barn, too."

"That pasture is not as big as I'd first thought it might be."

"Oh?"

Serena explained to Emily how she'd hoped to purchase the land around Dottie's homestead but that someone had beaten her to it. She was reluctant to reveal the new landowner's name, for reasons she didn't want to examine just yet.

"That's not a problem for the alpacas. But is it going to bother you every time you walk out there, knowing you'd hoped to have all of that area, clear down to the cliffs?"

Not as much as it bothered Jonas that she had Dottie's house.

"I can live with it, for now. As long as the owner doesn't build anything that gets in the way of the view."

Emily nodded, knitting as she listened. "It always seems great to have a huge chunk of land with no neighbors, but we're social animals at heart. We need other people. Have you met the owner yet?"

Serena couldn't keep this up. "It's Jonas Scott."

Emily's eyes widened and she put her cardigan down. "Now that's very interesting. Have you had a chance to talk to him, spend any time around him?"

Serena knew her cheeks were red and prayed Emily would blame it on windburn. They hadn't had an opportunity to sit and talk in ages. When Emily had watched Pepé the other night, she'd insisted Serena get right out the door to have more time to herself.

"He came by to introduce himself right after Thanksgiving. We actually met in the base clinic before that." She filled Emily in on the details, including seeing him at Winnie's party.

Emily looked at her. "You didn't mention that when you came home the other night."

"Um, no." She'd still been absorbing her ranges of emotion from the kiss to the kick-in-the gut disappointment when Jonas told her about his land purchase.

"What do you think of him?"

As usual, Emily wasn't cutting her any slack.

"He's articulate—a medical professional who appears to care about his patients. He was great with Pepé that day in the clinic and then later, at the house."

"Cut to the chase, Serena. Do you think he's hot?"

"Hot? He's…handsome. To a point. But a bit pushy when he wants something." She wasn't going to tell Emily about that kiss. She wasn't ready to share it with anyone else.

"Wants something like his house back."

"It was *Dottie's* house," Serena insisted.

"Hey, you're not telling me anything new. But I've known his family for a while, and I run into him at work every now and then, when's he's stationed here."

"And?"

"And I think he'd be a wonderful neighbor."

Emily's smile indicated she meant more than the traditional connotation of "neighbor."

"If you think he's so attractive, why don't *you* ask him out?"

Emily shook her head. "He's not my type."

"How would you know? And who are you to encourage me to date when you're still single after how many years?"

Emily picked her knitting up again. "I'm single because it's who I am. You have a child, and you're the marrying type. You scream 'homemaker.' Me, I scream 'crazy cat lady.'"

Serena laughed. Emily had eight cats on her

property, three of them living inside her house. The rest had comfortable space in her heated garage.

"Will I see you and Pepé at the Christmas tree farm?"

Emily played Mrs. Claus at the Oak Harbor venue.

"Yes, you will. Pepé can't wait."

SMACK.

The ball sprang from Jonas's racket to the wall and was hit by Doc, all within a few seconds.

"Ready for it today, I see." Doc wasn't trying to distract Jonas, yet Jonas still had to focus to keep his head in the game.

"Always. Bring it."

He relished the vibration up the shaft of the racket as he slammed the ball back at the wall, forcing Doc to reach in a long lunge for the return. Their voices echoed strangely in the confined space at the base gym.

"How's it going with Pepé's mom?"

Doc had taken to calling Serena by her parental role, Jonas noted. As if mentioning her name would bother him.

"Damn it!" He missed the return and shook his head. Sweat was starting to drip between his shoulder blades and his glasses had fogged.

Doc Franklin looked as if he'd hardly broken a sweat.

"That well, huh?"

Jonas palmed the small racquetball and tried to force a grin that didn't want to happen.

"I blew it. I happen to find her very attractive, but she's off-limits. She has my house, and I intend to get it back."

"Here." Doc held up his hand to catch the ball and start the game again.

After several back and forth jumps across the box of a room, Doc spoke again.

"You catch more flies with honey than vinegar, Jonas. As the old saying goes..."

"Yeah, well, this bod's not for sale."

Doc laughed as he jammed on the ball, making Jonas jump for the return.

"I'm not saying to get involved with her like that, man. She's new to the island, her only relative here—your stepmom—died. She and her son have to be lonely at times. Fill in the gaps. Let her see you're a nice guy. Give her a reason to *want* to sell the house back to you. She cared about Dottie and Dottie obviously adored her— enough to leave her the house. Use it to your advantage."

Jonas grunted as he kept his eye on the ball. "I'm not one for games. You know me, Doc."

"Yes, I do, and I know you can charm just about anyone. You're always the go-to guy for the patients who give us the most trouble with their treatments. Use that talent on this woman. Show her you belong in the house. Her son's getting older and he'll want to be closer to town, closer to kids his age. It would be easier on her, too, if he was on a bus route."

"I never thought about the bus route. How do you know about it?"

Doc grinned. "I bought some land a mile over as an investment, in the same zoning area. All the parents of school-age children drive them into town each morning and then back home in the afternoons. They have a carpool going, but still, it's a lot of work for a single parent. Does she have a new job yet?"

Thump.

Jonas hadn't hit that one hard enough and made it an easy target for Doc to strike, forcing Jonas to his knees to save the point.

"She's a lawyer, but she claims she doesn't need to work, not right away. My brother Paul wants to hire her." From what he'd gleaned of Serena's intelligence, she'd need to go back to work sooner rather than later. Staying home didn't seem to fit her, and it had to be lonely at Dottie's place while Pepé was at school.

Dottie's place.

It wasn't Dottie's place anymore. It wasn't his, either. Not yet....

"Can you at least pretend to give a hoot about the ball, Jonas?"

Jonas blinked. Doc Franklin rarely called him by his first name.

"Sorry. Daydreaming."

Doc bounced the ball and looked at Jonas with the same expression Jonas had seen when one of the junior staff was missing an obvious symptom.

"Of course, you might not need to scheme and charm the house away from her. Are you sure you wouldn't mind taking on more than the house?"

Realization shot through Jonas's crown to the base of his skull.

No. Way.

Like he'd already told Doc, Serena Delgado was off-limits. A: She was in his house because of her deceased aunt's overgenerous spirit. B: She had a kid. C: Jonas wasn't ready to get married.

When will you be ready to marry?

"Best of three. Loser buys." Jonas was talking about beers at the O Club's happy hour on Friday night as he started a new game and pushed thoughts of Serena out of his mind.

Images of her smile weren't as easy to shut down....

"ONE WEEK OF these antibiotics and the strep throat will be a memory. She should start to feel better within a day or so." Jonas typed in the 'scrip for the sick ten-year-old who sat in the examination room as he spoke to her mother, an active-duty sailor.

"Thanks, Commander. She's been miserable since last night. It'll be good to have my happy girl back." The mother smiled at her daughter, who smiled back.

Just like Serena and Pepé did, all the time.

"Okay, you're good to go. Stop by the pharmacy and pick up the prescription. Call me if she's not feeling better by Monday."

"Will do. Thanks again."

Jonas watched them leave, his mind still on Serena and Pepé. He tried to control his obsession by telling himself it was all because of the house.

"Jonas?" Emily Bowman, a nurse in the obstetric ward, stood at the door.

"Hi, Em. How's it going? Everything all right down there?"

"It's quiet. We haven't had a delivery in a few days, if you can believe it."

Jonas smiled. "That's bound to change—you'll have five all at once."

"You're probably right," Emily said with a laugh. She looked away, then back at him. "That's not why I'm here."

"Oh?"

"It's about Serena. And Pepé."

Jonas grew still. "Are they okay?"

"They're fine. In fact, I have it on good authority that they may be on the hunt for a Christmas tree tomorrow, and I know Serena's too proud to ask for help."

Jonas let his shoulders relax. "What kind of help?"

Emily filled him in.

CHAPTER THIRTEEN

Whidbey Island
Three weekends before Christmas

SERENA COULDN'T BELIEVE their luck. Not only had they been dusted with snow overnight, but when she and Pepé pulled up to the Christmas tree farm, the snow was still falling. The steam rising from the hot apple cider Mrs. Santa was brewing rose in fluffy wisps from the large slow cooker. Even the Claus family benefitted from modern technology.

She also knew that Mrs. Claus was none other than Emily, who said she got the biggest kick out of watching all the families and children come and haul away their own tree each year. Serena didn't buy it—she knew that Emily was doing a job few others could spare the time for.

"Mom, there's Santa!"

Pepé pointed to the small three-sided "cabin" where Santa sat on a large willow-bark rocking chair, posing with kids for their family Santa photo.

"Oh, wow, what a treat! Maybe you can tell him what you want for Christmas, Pepé."

"He didn't bring it last year, Mom."

Serena tried to ignore her regret. "It helps if you stick to toys, Pepé."

Last year, to her horror and the shopping mall's Santa's dismay, Pepé had asked for a father to come and stay "with me and my mom, like my dad did before he died."

Phil had been gone for three Christmases by then, between being on deployment and then his death, and that was when Pepé decided to ask for him.

"It would be nice to have a dad, Mom."

"I know, honey." She couldn't say more, wouldn't. It wasn't her priority to find Pepé a dad. That dad would have to be a man she'd be willing to spend her life with. Which meant she'd have to get to know him first. Actually go on a date.

That kiss with Jonas had opened up the room in her heart she'd sealed off since Phil died. She hadn't worried about finding someone until she realized how much she'd been missing—all that warmth, not to mention sizzle.

The man could kiss, she'd give him that.

"Come on, honey, let's go pick out our Christmas tree."

Pepé clambered down from the high seat and allowed Serena to tighten his scarf and close the snaps over his jacket's zipper. On school mornings he often wiggled out from under her hands, fighting her attention. Today was different. Today was Christmas-tree day. Santa day.

"Mom, can I go pet the reindeer?"

"Why don't we pick out our tree first, then we can come back and spend as much time as we want in Santa's village."

Pepé looked first right, then left, before he sent her a big smile.

"Okay. Good idea, Mom."

Serena laughed—until she heard someone speak not far from her.

"Need some help chopping down a tree, neighbors?" She'd know Jonas's voice anywhere.

It should alarm her, how quickly he'd eased himself into her psyche.

"Jonas!"

"Jonas." The trill of excitement in her belly wasn't for him, or the surprise of him showing up on her holiday celebration with Pepé. It was because of the holiday itself. Christmas was an exciting time.

"Are you getting a tree, too?" Pepé gazed up at Jonas as if he were Thor, Pepé's favorite mythic hero. Serena had to admit to herself that, except for his short haircut, Jonas would make an excellent Thor. He certainly kissed like a god.

Stop it.

"Why, as a matter of fact, I am, but I'm going to buy a small one. My place doesn't need a big huge tree. Not like yours."

At least he'd referred to the house as theirs and not Dottie's or his family's.

Suspicion erased Serena's polite smile. "What brings you here today, Jonas, at this particular hour?"

"A tree, like I said." His grin was like a blowtorch to the icicles with which she'd carefully surrounded her heart.

"We don't happen to have a mutual acquaintance in Mrs. Claus, do we?"

She suspected Emily had "run into" Jonas at the hospital and let him know that she and Pepé were going to be here. She really needed to talk to Emily about matchmaking. Serena wasn't ready, and certainly not for Jonas.

He overwhelmed her.

"Oh, Serena, ye of little faith. Why can't you accept that I'm here of my own accord? That I really want to be friends? Not to mention a tree."

Because she was a lawyer, she knew people often had deeper motives, or different ones, than they proclaimed. Because she had a child to protect from anyone who wanted to become "friends" and then leave when he'd attained his goal. Because she was living in the house he still thought was his, no matter how gracious he was being at the moment.

"Hmm."

"Want to help us find our tree, Jonas?" Pepé asked eagerly.

"Sure. Do you need a saw?" He looked inquiringly at Serena.

"I was going to have Santa's helpers do it for us."

"No need. If you'll allow me, I have a handy-dandy Christmas-tree saw right here." He held up a grocery bag with the handle of a small tree cutter sticking out.

"How fortuitous."

Jonas laughed. "Your mom has a wonderful vocabulary, Pepé. I'll bet she's the best lawyer ever."

Pepé wasn't listening—he'd taken off down the path that cut through the rows and rows of trees.

"Pepé!"

"Let him go. The precut trees go about halfway down the lot, and then he'll get to where the live ones are. We won't lose sight of him."

Serena looked at Jonas as they walked together, their boots making the cold snow crunch in the squeaky way she loved.

"I rarely saw snow as a kid. Sometimes I feel like I'm only six years old, too."

"Did you grow up entirely in Texas?"

"Yes." She hesitated, then allowed the words to come. "My mother raised me on her own until she met my stepfather, another store owner in our small town. She still owns the best tortilla bakery in south Texas. It kept her and us in a good lifestyle."

"Did you ever want to find out about your biological father?"

"I didn't know about him until after Phil died. It was only then, when I was in a pit of depression and my mother was afraid I wouldn't climb out of it, that she told me she'd had to raise a kid on her own, too. Me."

They'd caught up to where the live trees grew in neat rows. Pepé was weaving around each tree in the row, taking his time to pick the right one.

"She married my stepfather when I was four. They had two daughters and twin boys of their own. Yet I never thought of my siblings as half anything. We were all a family, together." Serena realized she hadn't told anyone that much about her family since she'd shared her past with Dottie.

"You must have been angry when she told you about your father...my uncle Todd."

"I was devastated. Especially when I found out he'd passed away. Thank God for Dottie— she reached out and told me I'd always have family here."

She turned to Jonas, who stood with his gaze on Pepé.

"Why are you asking about this?"

"I'll admit I wasn't thrilled about your showing up, not with all the stories you hear about seniors being taken advantage of nowadays. But now I know you're legit, and I want to know what made you both move all the way out here."

"That's a longer story than we have time for at the moment," Serena said. "The quick answer is that I needed to start over and give Pepé and me a new life. Something different from what we'd known." And away from the constant reminders of their loss.

"Mom! This one!" Pepé's excited shouts reached them and they laughed. Jonas's blue eyes sparkled with warmth as he looked at her and Serena felt that jolt again.

Knowing. Recognition. Soul-level attraction.

"I think he may have found a tree to saw down. Come on, let's go help your son." Jonas grabbed her mittened hand in his gloved one. Serena glanced at their hands together, then up at him.

He gave her a quick tug.

"Come on, Serena. Let go. Have some fun."

What would it hurt to let go for a few hours?

She answered by grasping his fingers more tightly and walking with him toward the tree Pepé had deemed Christmas worthy.

JONAS HAD TO keep his grin either aimed at Pepé or to himself. He lay on the crunchy snow, staring up at pine-needle branches, his saw and Pepé's wide eyes, shining with boyish excitement. Pepé got it—that they were on a quest to find the best tree for him and his mom. And he'd succeeded in achieving their target.

Jonas only had to make sure they cut the tree down without Pepé's getting crushed or nicked.

Neither would place him on Serena's good list, which was his goal.

Her faux fur–trimmed snow boots were in his peripheral vision, reminding him of her feminine presence.

He was doing this to show her his more human side, per Doc Franklin's suggestion. Doc was an ace at career survival and dealing with the slickest, highest-ranking officers. That he was single and not so lucky in love didn't matter to Jonas.

This wasn't about relationships or love, he reminded himself yet again; it was about getting Dottie's house back. And convincing Serena that she and Pepé would be just as happy in a new place closer to Oak Harbor.

"That's it, Pepé, move back a bit so you're not in range of the wood chips and put your hand on the handle here."

Pepé's small hand in its red mitten fit firmly around the saw's handle. It was going to take a little longer as Jonas didn't want to crush the kid's fingers, but he admired Pepé's spunk. Nothing fazed this kid.

"Okay, let's start sawing. Ready?"

"Ready!"

Jonas kept his focus on the saw and Pepé's fingers. Even though he couldn't help being aware of Serena, hovering a few feet away from them...

"This is a tough one, Jonas." Pepé's eyes watched the teeth of the saw and the flecks of wood that spit out as they worked together. His face was scrunched up behind his safety goggles and Jonas laughed at the adult expression on such a young face.

"What's so funny?"

"We are, Pepé. We think it's hard to chop this tree down, but just imagine how hard it was for the tree to grow!"

"Will Santa still be there when we're done?"

"He'll still be there, honey. Just get the tree down so that we can get it onto our car." Serena's voice broke through Jonas's concentration and he paused in his sawing motion. He looked up to see her gaze steady on both of them as she crouched beside the tree.

"Stay behind us, Serena, or risk being pummeled by this green beast."

"I'm fine, Jonas, don't worry."

It took several more minutes but finally the tree was about to fall.

"I'll hold it from the top." Serena's face disappeared and Jonas felt her boots against his back as she grasped the main trunk.

"Got it!"

"Pepé, let's slide out nice and easy. Once you're on your feet, get behind your mom."

Pepé did and managed to unwittingly kick a bootful of snow in Jonas's face.

"Oomph." He would have laughed if the cold hadn't shocked him so much. Pepé was right;

where was the Santa village? He needed some hot cider. Maybe he'd luck out and Santa would have hot coffee.

Once up and on his feet, Jonas stood behind Serena and reached into the center of the tree. Her backside fit nicely against him, and he allowed himself to inhale the warmth of hair that fell from under her snow cap.

"What are you doing?" Her whisper was supposed to chastise him, but tell that to his groin.

"I'm enjoying myself. How about you?"

Her brown eyes turned their sharp intelligence on him and Jonas wanted to kiss her, push her down into the snowy ground, reach up under her jacket...

"I've got the tree. You and Pepé go over there and watch it fall."

"Oh!" Her eyes were still on his, the awareness crackling between them. She stared at his mouth, and Jonas bit the inside of his cheek to keep from moving in closer.

"I've got my camera!" Serena slid out from under him and he had to stare at the snow-covered tree for a second to will his erection into merely semi-uncomfortable.

"Come on, Pepé, let's go stand where it's safe. We'll get a great picture of our tree falling down."

"Hurry, Mom!" Pepé ran out in front of her and Jonas couldn't have stopped the laugh that rumbled out of his belly if he'd wanted to. The pure joy on Pepé's face was worth every bit of discomfort.

"Ready?" He could stand here all day when Serena was up next to him, but in the cold he became aware of the weight of the tree and the way his muscles were starting to protest from lying on the cold ground for so long.

"Hang on, I need to get this focused properly."

"Take your time." He really wanted to say "Snap the picture already!"

"Okay, Pepé?" He saw her bend her head toward her son. As Pepé grinned up at Serena, the similarity in their profiles struck him as endearing.

Endearing?

Had he taken a crack to his skull while under the tree?

"Okay!"

"Timber!" Jonas bellowed the word more to get his mind off his uninvited emotions than for any dramatic effect. Pepé jumped up and down as the tree tipped and took its final bow before becoming a Christmas decoration. White puffs of powdery snow flew up as the boughs hit the ground, the definite *thud* validating Jonas's concern for his and Pepé's safety while under the tree.

"Okay, let's haul her in." He was glad he'd worn his leather work gloves instead of his ski gloves, but the cold bit at his fingertips. A warm cup of coffee or cider was on his mind as he slid the tree onto the plastic sled he'd brought, courtesy of his brother's overstocked garage, and pulled it up the path back to Santa's village.

"Keep an eye on the back of our caravan here, Pepé, and make sure the tree doesn't jump off the sled."

"Okay!" Empowered by the order, Pepé ran behind the sled as if his entire Christmas gift pile depended upon it.

"You didn't forget one detail for this, did you?" Serena's brown eyes narrowed as she walked beside him, her face turned toward him.

"Why so suspicious? Can't a guy help out?"

"It's not the helping that bothers me. I'm very grateful that you were here. Otherwise, I would've asked one of the workers to get the tree for us and haul it back. This way Pepé was able to fully participate. Thank you, Jonas."

"You're very welcome."

"I'm not sixteen, and there aren't any stars in my eyes, however. It's been my experience that men are this helpful for one of two reasons."

"Go on."

"In your case...you're either feeling guilty about purchasing the land around Dottie's house and want to ease that guilt by doing a good deed for Pepé and me. Or you want something."

"Such as?"

"Dottie's house. Don't be obtuse, Jonas. Do you

think I believe for one minute that you've given up on getting back what you feel is rightfully yours?"

He stopped in the snow. Santa's village was another two hundred yards down the path.

"You'd suck the sugar right out of a candy cane, wouldn't you, Serena? Is there anything wrong with a little Christmas spirit?"

"Do you blame me?"

"No, but I'm going to give you a chance to feel like I didn't take this whole day right out of your hands. Here, use your energy for something other than trying to figure me out. I'll meet you at the snack shed."

He handed her the rope handles to the sled. Her mouth fell open and he saw a fleeting shot of regret before she gritted her teeth and started to pull the tree.

It was petty, but the grunt that came out of her mouth with her first few steps gave him tremendous satisfaction.

"Pepé, your mom has command of the tree. Keep an eye on the stern for me!"

"Aye-aye, Jonas!"

"Good boy."

He turned back to Serena. "It gets easier once you have the momentum of the tree's weight sliding on the snow with you."

He didn't wait to hear her retort as he jogged up ahead of them toward Santa and a warm cup of joe.

SERENA HAD SEVERAL minutes to her thoughts as she clomped through the snow. It wasn't hard to imagine she was out on the tundra with the cold wind hitting her square in the face and the heavy weight of the tree making the trip to warmth feel like it was miles away.

Except that in the tundra she'd have sled dogs pulling the tree for her, wouldn't she? She didn't have the energy to laugh, or she would have. She absolutely deserved this. She'd been rude to Jonas after he'd made their tree search more fun and certainly less laborious for her.

Until now.

"All clear in the rear, Mom!" Pepé chortled at his rhyme and Serena smiled. He was having the time of his life.

He needed positive male attention and role models. It wasn't his fault that his dad had died, nor was it hers. Still, she worried about a child's ability to cope. When they'd visited Beyond the Stars two summers ago, she'd discovered that what had helped her get through her grief more than anything was learning to accept life on its own terms. But Pepé was so young and as much as he took things at face value more than she did, it was also easier for him to escape into an imaginary world.

After Phil died, Pepé had retreated so far into his private fantasy world that he didn't speak to any adults other than Serena. Even his beloved *abuela* was hard-pressed to get a word out of him.

Only after the counselor at the resort for Gold Star families had helped Pepé get over his new fear of jumping into the deep end of the pool had Pepé started to talk again.

That counselor, Lucas, had been male and Serena didn't miss the significance.

As much as Pepé was a well-adjusted kid, thriving in his new environment, Serena knew he had a hole in his heart. He craved a father. How could he not? Phil had been there for him 100 percent of the time when he wasn't deployed downrange. They'd bonded as a solid father-and-son unit. Right after Phil died Serena had a hard time separating her grief at losing her husband from the sheer torture of watching her little boy grieve for the father he'd called "Bud." Pepé had been "little buddy."

"That was then, this is now." She murmured the reminder to herself; it was advice from her grief counseling sessions. She didn't have to carry the guilt and the grief for both of them any longer.

Serena wiped a stray tear from her cheek and felt a bloom of gratitude she hadn't experienced in a long while. Here they were, she and Pepé, hauling in the first Christmas tree they'd handled all by themselves, from picking it out to cutting it down, and now they had the decorating to look forward to.

Jonas helped you.

He had. And she'd been a complete jerk to him.

"I GUESSED YOU'D want the hot cider—just drop the ropes there." Jonas handed her the steaming cup as he nodded toward the ground where she gladly let go of the sled handles.

"All clear, Jonas!" Pepé sprang over the trunk of the pine and smiled up at his hero. Serena wanted to warn him to not get too close; it could lead to a broken heart. Instead, she sipped her cider and tried to focus on the gratitude she'd discovered moments earlier.

"Hot chocolate for you, Pepé. I wasn't sure if you liked marshmallows, so I didn't get them, but if you want some, Mrs. Claus said you can go to the front of the line and have them added."

"Be right back, Mom!"

Serena watched him walk the short distance to Emily, and ask for the marshmallows.

"Thank you, Jonas. I was a Scrooge to you and I'm sorry. You've done so much for Pepé and me today, and I do really appreciate it. I'm not the best at expressing my emotions."

"Oh, I think you're pretty good at letting your heart show."

The gleam in his eyes made her think of the many barbs she'd thrown his way in their short acquaintance and she grimaced.

"I'm overbearing when it comes to Pepé making new relationships with adults. I know that."

"As you should be. The world's not the place it

was when we were growing up. I'd be protective of him, too."

They enjoyed their drinks in quiet. Serena kept her eye on Pepé but let her thoughts wander to… nothing. That astonished her. This kind of serenity was so unusual. Her heart was still, her thoughts weren't racing. She wasn't holding her breath waiting for the next tragedy to befall them.

Everything was okay, for the moment.

"What's the smile about?" Jonas hadn't missed her elation.

"Call me corny but I think the Christmas spirit just got to me."

"Nothing corny about enjoying this time of year."

She saw the shadow pass over his face.

"Are you enjoying it?"

"Am I what?" At her silence, he relented his pretense. "I'm not the happiest I've ever been, no. It takes time to readjust after deployment."

"More so after a wartime deployment, though. You weren't on a ship, removed from the action, either. You were in camp, right?"

He looked past her, to where Pepé had walked over to study the reindeer.

"Yes. We treated a lot of civilians, more than I ever have before. Except for natural disasters. Earthquakes, hurricanes—that's always more of a civilian situation. My first two deployments to Iraq and Afghanistan involved almost exclusively military casualties. This time, the Taliban had done a number on several different villages. So many civilian casualties poured in. It never ended."

"Does it make you mad to see how much we take for granted here?"

"Sometimes. Oak Harbor's not too bad—we have so many military families here and the civilians have always embraced us as their own. They know the struggles we go through. What bothers me most is seeing how healthy and naturally happy our kids are—the way all kids should be—while so many children overseas aren't. Every kid deserves the chance to be happy."

She stayed silent. His voice mesmerized her with his heartfelt confession.

"Now who sounds all corny and sentimental?" He shook his head.

"It's the truth. Thank you for sharing that with me, Jonas."

He didn't reply as he walked around her and bent down to grab the sled's rope handles.

"Let's bring your tree over to the tree shaker. Pepé's going to love this."

"Pepé!" She called him over from petting the reindeer and made a mental note to see that he washed his hands well before he ate dinner.

He scrambled toward them, his cheeks flushed with happiness.

"Are we going to decorate the tree now?"

Serena laughed with delight at his enthusiasm. "Not yet. First we have to shake it, then it has to rest on the porch."

Pepé seemed confused and turned to Jonas for confirmation.

"We're going to shake the tree?"

"Your mom's right, Pepé. We have to make sure there aren't any loose needles to mess up your house."

"How are we going to do that?"

"We're not—the machine over there is."

They gave the tree to the attendant, who handed them a slip to go and pay for the tree. Once Serena had paid and returned with the receipt, the tree was put into a rudimentary machine that shook it for several minutes. Needles and pinecones dropped to the snow. Pepé watched in amazement as the tree was then placed in a nylon net that bound it into a very compact size for transport home.

"Mom, is that hurting the tree?"

"I don't think so, honey. It's probably like being wrapped up in a warm blanket."

When Jonas met her eyes, she felt as though she was mentally communicating with him. The question in his eyes—*do you like to be wrapped up warm and tight?*—made her think of long nights with him in her bed, cozy under the blankets. Did he see the answer in hers?

Heat burned her ears, although she'd thought

they were numb from the cold. She made herself look away before she said or did something stupid, like give Jonas a catlike smile.

Or think that starting a physical relationship with Jonas was feasible.

"Let's get the tree onto your car." Jonas's voice vibrated across the short space between them and it was as arousing as if he'd touched her. Was there anything about this man that didn't turn her on?

He wanted to kick her and Pepé out of their house. Their home.

It should have been an easy turnoff, but it wasn't as lust-dousing as she'd hoped.

She was in trouble.

"Don't even think about it."

Jonas's voice was too familiar, too comfortable. And, at the moment, too annoying. Serena couldn't put her reaction into words.

She stepped back from the side of her SUV and lowered her arms, her hands holding the bungee chord she'd unhooked from around the tree and ski rack. Jonas didn't take a step back and he was so close, so tempting.

"I can get the tree off the top of my car, Jonas."

"I have no doubt. You can also scratch the heck out of your car and risk breaking some tree limbs in the process."

"Isn't that why the tree's wrapped like this?"

"It's to make it easier to transport but there's no

guarantee the netting will protect it. Are you always this averse to help from a neighbor?"

Neighbor.

"When do you think your house will be built?"

The sparkle in his eyes dimmed and the grim lines she'd first noticed in the clinic the day they'd met threatened to resurface under his day's growth of beard.

"Ground will break in the spring, after the storms blow through. Why?"

Why indeed.

"Just wondering."

"Mom, can Jonas stay for dinner?" Pepé poked his head between them, one arm on each of their legs.

This was getting too cozy.

"Not tonight, honey." She never took her gaze from Jonas's. Was that a challenge in his stormy blue eyes?

She swallowed. "We'd love to have you for our tree-decorating party in a few days. Can you come?"

She knew he wanted to say "no." She could tell from his stiffness and the grim line of his mouth.

"Jonas, it'll be fun! Mom makes the best chili, and we can frost cookies."

Finally he broke their stare to shift his focus to Pepé. "Sounds wonderful. As long as I don't have to work late at the hospital, I'd be delighted to join you, Pepé."

Serena wanted to be irritated that he'd weaseled

his way into their family tradition. But how could she when *she'd* invited him?

"We usually eat around six o'clock—is that too early for you?"

Were his eyes always this sexy when he looked at a woman?

"It's fine. I'll call you if I end up working."

"Great." She forced a smile but didn't have to force the warm tingles that danced on the surface of her skin and continued to her midsection, inviting more of her to wake up and join the fun.

"Let's set this tree up on the porch."

In one smooth motion Jonas hoisted the tree onto the ground and began to pull it up the walkway toward the porch.

"We always kept it on the front porch for a few days in a bucket of water. Do you have a different place for it?"

"No, I have the bucket out, the green one to the left of the door."

"Roger."

"Pepé, can you go open the door and let Ronald out?"

"Roger!" Pepé grabbed her keys and shot toward his mission.

"He loves being around military jargon." She spoke her thoughts aloud, trying to remember she needed to protect Pepé from forming bonds with men who weren't going to be permanent in his life. He'd had enough loss.

"I did, too, as a kid. G.I. Joes were my favorite toys." Jonas didn't glance at her as he complimented Pepé, his breath in great clouds in front of him as he hauled the heavy tree up the three steps to the wooden porch that ran the length of the house.

"He's always been that way. Right after Phil died, I worried about him so much—he withdrew into himself in a way I'd only ever seen in adults. It was scary when he stopped talking to everyone except me. But we got through it, and he's thriving."

"I saw in his chart you took him to BTS." His easy reference to the Beyond the Stars resort for Gold Star families didn't surprise her. No doubt he'd referred patients from the hospital there.

"You read his entire chart?"

Jonas set the tree down and leaned it against the side of the house. He turned to face her and smiled.

His smile must have encouraged a lot of women to get undressed....

"I make a point of going over every patient's chart thoroughly. It makes diagnosis easier, and hopefully more accurate." He raised her chin with his finger.

"I wasn't prying, Serena. It was in the comments from his last yearly checkup—that he'd greatly improved since his week at BTS."

Trust me.

He didn't have to say it; it was in his expression, in the clear blue sincerity of his eyes.

"Oh." Embarrassment reddened her cheeks. She prayed Jonas would chalk up her blush to the cold.

"You have the most beautiful eyes," he said. "Pepé has them, too."

Jonas's tone was clinical in his appraisal but his eyes were lit with a warmth that had already started a fire in Serena's belly.

When he bent toward her, she heard the inner voice that warned her to step back, to avoid any connection with this man. She heard it and ignored it as she closed her eyes. His breath was warm over her lips and she smelled mint, cinnamon and his scent—the scent she'd had difficulty getting out of her memory after their searing kiss at the Fords' Christmas party.

"Ronald!" Pepé's yell was followed by the vibration of Ronald's four paws hitting the deck. He ran through the front door and launched himself into the yard, grateful for the chance to relieve himself after being home alone all afternoon.

Serena opened her eyes to find Jonas had dropped his hand from her face and turned to watch the antics of a boy and his dog.

When he faced her again, Jonas grinned.

"We're not done here. Anticipation can be fun, though, can't it?"

CHAPTER FOURTEEN

Camp O'Donnell, Philippines
Early 1944

DAYS NO LONGER had meaning, but they were a means to an end for Henry. A way to get back to Sarah.

Tommy had been paroled to his Filipino family only three months after they'd arrived at Camp O'Donnell. Bill had died last year, in the middle of monsoon season. It wasn't cold, but the constant dampness, be it from rain or sweat, had been the death of many of his fellow prisoners.

Henry wasn't sure why he'd made it this far. It had to be because he was going to see Sarah again. Soon. He felt that he was going to be on the move again, and trusted his gut. He only prayed it was back to the States.

When the guards rounded them up and forced them to walk out of the camp together, Henry realized they were going to kill them. Why else allow them to leave their well-controlled prison?

The view of the ocean and the Japanese container ships gave him hope and dread in equally painful amounts. Not again. Odds were against him that he'd survive a second trip in one of the tin cans.

Where were the Allies?

By the end of the day he was in the bottom of one of the dreaded Japanese merchant cargo ships. He could hardly breathe and had to fight the anxiety and fear that threatened to close his throat or stop his heart. Until now he'd been able to look past the pain, to see that if he was still breathing it was a good day.

Not any longer. This was hell on earth, no matter that it was at sea.

He'd thought the acrid stench of human feces, sweat and fear after the march from Bataan was horrible. This was excruciatingly worse. Nearly every prisoner threw up the little they had in their stomachs as the lack of windows and fresh air mixed into the most potent cocktail for seasickness. Raw bile and sewage covered their bodies as they stood pressed against one another, holding each other up over the long tortuous ocean crossing.

Their captors had to be taking them to Japan. This was a good sign, he thought. The Allies must be moving in, coming back to the Philippines to save them all.

So of course the enemy soldiers were taking their labor force to safety.

Just kill us now.

It was getting harder to ignore the insistent possibility of freedom from the interminable suffering. Long hours passed when Henry could no longer conjure up Sarah's or Dottie's faces.

"God save us!" Jersey's voice reached him in the darkness. "Henry?"

His friend's call shook him from his purgatory. "I'm here, Jersey."

"We're going to be dead, man. We're not going to get out of here alive."

Groans turned to grumbles as his fellow sufferers agreed.

Henry didn't reply. Anger and complaining were signs of life. He worried about the men who weren't making any noise. Worried about when he'd become one of the quiet ones. When he, too, would let his spirit go.

Sarah. He closed his eyes tight, trying to see her face, smell the scent of her skin. He couldn't—as if his heart didn't want to mark her with where he was, in this pit of hell.

And Dottie, his dear little girl. What kind of world had they borne her into, that allowed this?

September 1945
Japanese prison camp

IT TOOK THE prison guard three hits with the handle of his baton to Henry's backside before Henry's vision cleared and he remembered where he was.

The vision of climbing over Fort Casey with Sarah vanished. He cried out at the anguish of losing her, if only his memory of her.

Reality had become too hard.

The guard yelled at him and Henry didn't try to make out the Japanese. He'd given up on that months ago. At first he'd taught himself the language, little by little, as he put together what the guards said to them.

He looked at where the guard pointed.

Buck lay on his side, his eyes unseeing. One of the last men he'd come to this hellhole with two years ago had died.

Lucky bastard.

No.

He owed it to Buck and every other G.I. who'd died in this labor camp to get back to Whidbey. To live the life he'd set out to have with Sarah a decade ago.

A world, a lifetime, away.

He wordlessly picked up the small spade the guard pointed at and carried it over to his colleague. His brother-in-arms. Jersey hobbled over with a woven bamboo tarp of sorts. Together they lifted Buck's thin, lifeless form onto the makeshift litter, trying to keep as much dignity in what they did while the Japanese guard yelled at them and no doubt shouted obscenities at them the entire time.

They made a slow funereal walk to the outer parts of the camp, where their captors had forced them to bury one friend after another. No thinking was involved. If Henry stopped to think, he'd die. Thinking brought too much despair.

He dug the shallow grave. Shallow was all that was possible in the rocky soil with such a poor tool and his failing strength.

Would Sarah reject him when she saw him? Would Dottie run in fear?

No thinking.

Only surviving.

He focused on the spade, the pitiful amounts of dirt each motion moved.

He breathed.

"IT'S TOO HARD." Jersey's whispered observation reached Hank's ears as the two lay side by side on the dirt floor that had been their sleeping area for the past year.

"No. Hang on. They're getting more and more desperate. We have to be close."

"Maybe."

"Did you see the guard's eyes today?"

"I try not to look at the bastards."

"He's afraid. They're hungry, too. They're losing. Our boys will be here any day now."

"Do you really believe that, Henry?"

"I do." He had to.

"You have a wife, a family. It helps."

"You have your girl, Jersey."

"We were engaged. I can't expect her to still be waiting for me."

"Why not? There aren't any other men at home. Everyone's off fighting."

"Maybe. Maybe."

They lay in the darkness, staring at the meager roof over their heads, shivering in the cold night.

When Henry first heard the rumble, he thought it might be one of the Japanese vehicles that carried the guards from point to point around the large compound. Or maybe Jersey was having a bad case of diarrhea.

But they hadn't eaten in days and their bodies had nothing to eliminate.

Only after a boom shook the ground did Henry allow himself to start to believe.

"There's our boys, Jersey."

"Do you really think so?" Jersey's normally gruff voice was faint, his eyes closed. Henry saw his expression with the light from the moon that spilled through the slivers of open roof.

"I know so, man. Stay here, Jersey. Don't go. Hang in there."

"My girl, she's probably with another man by now. I don't blame her."

"You don't know that. And so what if she is? You'll find another girl."

As Henry forced those words of comfort through his chapped lips, a sharp pang of compassion went through Henry. Sarah could have found someone else, too. Did she even think he was still alive?

He couldn't begin to imagine his Sarah with another man. Another father for Dottie?

No.

He had to get out of this hell.

THE NEXT MORNING Henry was awake before the guards came. He'd made a game of waking before they did. He hadn't slept that well, thanks to the cold. No matter how many nights he got through, he didn't take one for granted. And he'd never adjusted to the harsh temperature swings in this country. The summers were like Dante's fires, especially since their captors didn't see a need to provide them with regular water breaks. As a boy in Texas he'd thought he knew what it meant to be thirsty. He'd never felt real thirst before the Japanese had interned him.

Only winter brought relief, at first, from the unbearable heat. Until the thin uniforms they wore weren't warm enough, and they were lucky to earn a paper blanket to try to conserve their body heat.

The cold did more damage to them than the heat. As if their bodies recognized the long, dark frigid days were going to be too much to bear they started to shut down, catching dysentery or other illnesses without any strength to fight them.

Henry looked over at Jersey, whose chest

was still rising and falling. He'd made it another night, too.

"Hey, Henry!" Tom Osbourne, a Brit who'd been brought in as early as Henry almost three years ago, crouched next to the plank he and Jersey shared.

"Are you trying to piss them off and make them even madder, Tom?"

"They can get as mad as they want. The Americans are closing in. We're going to be liberated."

"How can you be so sure of that?"

"Bugsy climbed into the south guard tower last night. Says he saw our boys with their equipment on the way in."

The guard who manned the south tower was known to enjoy his sake a bit more than he should. The past several months he'd taken to drinking until he passed out. The prisoners whispered among themselves, planning escape after escape, even though they all knew it was for naught.

"Don't you want to wake up Jersey and tell him?"

"Naw, let him sleep while he can. He's fighting it."

"Fighting it" was code for fighting against the inevitable death that awaited all of them if the damn war didn't end soon. As long as the Japanese continued to work them to death, there was no hope. Without a forced Allied liberation of the camp, they were dead. In the event of a Japanese surrender, Henry knew in his gut that their captors would conduct vengeful executions of all of them, anyway.

"Tell him to fight it for a few more days. They're waiting to make their strike, I know it."

"I hope you're right."

Henry went through the rest of the day fighting his own demons. Visions of Sarah and Dottie had started to appear to him when he was in the midst of breaking stones with the primitive tools they'd been given. He had to be alert to avoid the wrath of the guards, but he couldn't stop his mind from wandering. His mind had grown muddled from years of hunger and thirst, years of not knowing which of his colleagues would be the next murdered. When was it going to be his turn?

But his wavering thoughts had never been this unpredictable. He kept Sarah and Dottie in a quiet, safe room in his heart and took them out only when the horror of his life was least likely to intrude upon them.

His growing mental weakness couldn't be a good sign.

Was this the start of *his* giving up?

CHAPTER FIFTEEN

Whidbey Island
Two weeks before Christmas

"WHEN I SUGGESTED you be nicer to her I didn't mean a full-on seduction. That's not fair to you, her or her son. With your anti-marriage stance, it can only lead to disaster for both of you."

Jonas listened to Doc Franklin berate him as he eyed Jonas over the mug of coffee he'd poured from the office pot. The doctor lifted the carafe toward him.

"Want a cup?"

"Sure." Jonas grabbed a mug emblazoned with the NAS Whidbey insignia off the cart and held it out.

"I could get used to this, Doc. You make a good waitress."

"Watch it." Doc Franklin put the carafe back on its burner and sank into his executive office chair.

Jonas laughed as he lowered himself into one of two matching sling chairs across from Doc Franklin's large oak desk.

"Back to you and Señora Delgado."

"Yeah." Jonas sipped the brew and grimaced at the spicy flavor. "What's in this?"

"It's called 'Christmas Spirit.' The new owner of the coffee stop near the gate is selling it. I like it—cloves, nutmeg, maybe some star anise."

Jonas shook his head. "I never pegged you as a coffee connoisseur."

"I have my nuances."

Both men laughed.

"I'm not avoiding your question, Doc. There isn't an answer—there's nothing serious between me and Serena. I want my house back. You told me to play nice about it. That doesn't mean I'm going to stop trying to convince her that what's best for her and Pepé is to get a newer place that won't require as much upkeep. She's a lawyer and once she gets busy with her career again she'll figure it out."

"Maybe I was wrong." Doc Franklin had a smug gleam in his eyes that went perfectly with his smirk.

"About what?"

"Would it be so bad if things got interesting between you and Serena? Let's say you're perfect for each other. Why not check that avenue out? You might end up with the house, after all. Maybe that's what your stepmother planned all along."

Jonas gripped the mug as tight as he could without worrying about smashing it to bits in his hands.

"She has a son. He can't be toyed with, Doc."

"Who's toying? If you're willing to think about something more than a passing fling with his mother…"

Was he?

Jonas had enjoyed his bachelor freedom more than most. There had been a serious fling here or there, and of course his most recent un-relationship with Joy Alexander. Great lady, but not for him.

Lately the only woman he thought about was Serena.

For him, settling down had meant living in the farmhouse, working on Whidbey as a civilian once he retired, taking overseas assignments on contract for the government if he felt the urge to travel abroad again.

A permanent relationship with a woman hadn't entered the picture, not ever.

A woman and a child, that was entirely outside his scope.

"She'll never see me as anything other than the man who wants to take her home away from her."

"Unless she falls for you. And you for her, of course."

"Have you been talking to Emily in labor and delivery?" Serena's friend had been really obvious when she'd dropped the hint that Serena and Pepé were going to be at the tree farm.

"Who?" Doc was either playing stupid or thought Jonas was.

"Never mind."

"You won't know until you give it a try, Jonas."

DOC FRANKLIN'S WORDS rang in his mind all through his shift that day. Was Jonas falling for a woman he'd only met in person less than a month ago?

As he set a six-year-old's broken arm, he thought of Pepé and knew how upset the parents were that their child was injured. When a sullen teenage girl came in with her frazzled mother, he wondered what kind of teenager Pepé would be, and how it would affect Serena. He couldn't imagine her beauty marred by the trials of adolescence, but in his observation and experience no parents went unscathed when puberty hit their child.

His last case of the day was the child of a man whose active-duty spouse had been killed in a helicopter crash in Kandahar Province only weeks earlier. Jonas had been on his way home when the accident happened; otherwise, he'd have been in the trauma unit when the casualties arrived. As he looked into the young father's haunted, grief-stricken face he knew that the antibiotics he prescribed for the strep throat both he and his daughter had could only cure their sore throats and body aches.

Jonas couldn't bring back the widower's wife or the girl's mother.

He felt his gut clench at the hell Serena and Pepé had lived through.

As he sat at his desk doing paperwork after his clinicals, his fingers stopped midstroke.

Doc Franklin might be right.

Jonas didn't consider himself obtuse, and as much as he avoided dealing with his emotions, just like the next man, he found it impossible to ignore the fact that he might be falling.

For the first time in his life, Jonas faced the fact that his heart was taking precedence over his methodical, logical brain.

Whidbey Island
Ten days before Christmas

JONAS STILL COULDN'T believe he'd managed to get Serena to agree that she and Pepé would come to his brother's house for their pre-Christmas cookie baking and house-decorating party. Every year Paul and Mary had the whole clan over the second or third weekend in December. This year they were having it on a Sunday, since their twin girls had ice hockey practice and a game on Saturday.

"Are you sure it's okay that we're bringing Ronald with us?" Serena sat in the passenger seat of his Jeep Wrangler as if this was the hundredth time they'd gone anywhere together and not the first. The sense of familiarity between them was undeniable.

She might think it's a date.

After the conversation with Doc, he admitted to himself that he was in over his head with Serena. But he wasn't going to start a serious relationship with her, or use their attraction to each other to get the house. He had to play fairer than that.

He'd get her to love his family. Once she grew to know them as Dottie had, she'd see why the house needed to stay with the only family Dottie had raised.

"It's no problem having Ronald along. Their dog, Sadie, loves other dogs, and they'll tire each other out."

God, she didn't think he was trying to date her, did she? She was the one who'd made it clear that she wasn't interested in a relationship at the moment. Even if she was, he'd be the last person she'd trust.

And she'd be right. His entire reason for getting to know her and Pepé better was really for her to get to know him and his family. To make giving him back the house irresistible.

And if he was going to date a woman with a child, he wouldn't take her out on a date with her son. He'd take her to a great restaurant, order a nice bottle of wine, drive to one of the many lookout vistas on West Beach and watch the surf with her. He'd kiss her senseless....

He risked a glance at Serena. He didn't want her to misinterpret his interest as anything more than friendly. His goal was to have her accept him as a good neighbor first, then she'd warm up to him as a friend and see her mistake in taking the house from his family.

He had it all figured out.

"Pepé's quiet." Interesting how quickly he'd gotten used to the little guy's constant chatter. The silence bothered him—and that raised the hairs on the back of his neck.

Getting in deeper than he'd anticipated was worth the risk, to a point. The house belonged to him—he felt it every time he walked inside. Serena had made all those changes and, contrary to what he'd expected, it didn't feel alien, only updated.

"He's out cold." Her voice could melt Mount Baker's glacier. "If we drive more than ten minutes he falls sound asleep. When he was tiny he used to get carsick. I think this is how he keeps himself from feeling icky."

"I envy being able to fall asleep like that." He slowed down on the main highway as a family of deer were crossing.

"They're so small compared to real deer." Serena smiled as she referred to the Whidbey Island deer. "Have you ever seen mule deer? They make these look like miniature poodles."

"I've only been to Texas when I was sent to San Antonio for training at the air force hospital there.

They have the best burn unit in the world, as I'm sure you're probably aware."

"Yes, a few of the men from Phil's unit were transferred there."

Just like that, silence swooped in over the front seat, too. Phil hadn't had a chance to make it to San Antonio. Damn it. He hadn't meant to bring up her husband.

He reached over to her before he had time to consider the consequences.

"I'm sorry, Serena. This is supposed to be a fun day for you and Pepé. I didn't mean to bring up anything uncomfortable."

She didn't pull her hand out from under his and he ignored the relief he felt. He couldn't ignore her soft skin or the warmth that grew where their hands joined.

"It's okay, really. I honestly prefer to talk about it, to be more open about it. I don't ever want it to be the 'we don't talk about it' taboo so many people make the loss of a loved one. Pepé's not going to remember Phil very well and that's a tough thing to accept, but then again he's not suffering the pain of loss like an older kid would."

"From what you told me and what I read in his medical chart, Pepé had a hell of a time at first."

Serena nodded.

"He did. Those months when he stopped talking—they were horrible." Her voice wavered and he squeezed her hand. The deer had cleared the road and he released her hand as he put the car back into Drive.

"You've been such a good mother to him, Serena. It's obvious that he's well-adjusted and enjoying the life you've made for yourselves."

Guilt gnawed at his stomach. He shouldn't be praising her move into Dottie's house, not if he wanted to convince her to leave it. He wasn't really, he told himself; he was referring to her demeanor and the emotional support she gave Pepé.

"I didn't have a choice." She wiped the condensation off her window and looked out at the bare fields as they drove south on the island before turning back to him.

"It's not a matter of doing what's right or wrong when tragedy hits. At least, for me it wasn't."

"Why do you think your mother didn't tell you about your biological father before Phil died?" If she had, he might have met Serena when they were both younger.

Pepé could've been his kid.

He swerved the Jeep as the shock of that thought made him jerk. "Sorry about that. Too much coffee."

Serena wasn't paying attention to his anxiety.

"You'd have to understand my mother and her family. My mother is the child of a Mexican cook for a huge ranch, and her father was the son of the ranch owner. When my grandparents married it was at a different time—their marriage was considered "mixed" and my grandfather was disowned by his family. They came around when my mother was born, however. So when my mother found herself pregnant by a man who'd said he'd loved her, but then admitted he wouldn't stop drinking, she wouldn't marry him, and they closed ranks. They protected her and helped her with raising me until she met my stepfather, who, by the way, is a wonderful man. Like Dottie was a mother to you, Red is a father to me."

Her profile was regal as she stared out the windshield and relayed her thoughts to him.

"When I married Phil after law school and we moved away to his first duty station in North Carolina, my family had a hard time with it, especially my mother. Then we got orders back to Texas. We weren't that close in El Paso, but at least we were in the same state. Pepé came along, and it was great to have my family nearby. Phil's family is from the same area. He and I met in Austin when we were in college—me in law and him in international relations. He was there on an Army scholarship. He never got his commission, though. They ran out of spots and he enlisted. He was that dedicated."

She stopped so suddenly he shot a glance at her.

Her profile was beautiful. Raven hair flowed around her large brown eyes and high cheekbones, flaring out where her lips curved. Full, moist lips. She'd taken the time to put lipstick on; he'd never noticed the bright red stain before. Had she wanted to impress his family or taunt him with her seductive mouth?

Jonas wasn't the effusive type when it came to describing women; he categorized them as attractive or not when they evolved into dating prospects. Dottie had taught him and his brothers that every woman has her own beauty, and he knew that was true. None had drawn him the way she did.

He wanted to believe that it was only a physical attraction. That would make all of this so much easier. Instead, Serena outshone the previous women in his life. The women he'd cared for the most had all been intelligent and they'd all possessed a keen sense of humor.

Serena had those qualities as well as a compassionate heart and remarkable level-headedness, especially considering everything she'd been through.

He'd bet she gave her clients superlative legal counsel.

"We don't need to talk about Texas, or your previous life." He took the turnoff to Paul's.

"I don't want to talk about it, Jonas. It's not as painful as it was twelve or even six months before. I simply don't want to bore or burden you. That's my past, Pepé's past. We've started a new life out here, a life we've grown into. I've learned that taking this journey one day at a time works best for me."

"You sound like you're in a twelve-step program or something."

She laughed. "No, I'm not, but it's a good philosophy, isn't it?"

He didn't answer as they drew closer to Paul's house. It lay in the midst of a sprawling meadow, bordered by tall fir trees on one side and more sturdy maples and oaks on the other. Puget Sound and the mainland were to the east of the property.

"This is huge. Was it always here, or did Paul put it in?" Her gaze took in the meandering gardens and thickets of evergreen trees.

"My brother John did it for him."

"He does landscaping, right?"

"Landscape design. His company is Eagle Scapes."

"That's who I paid to come out and level the land for the alpaca barn. They put in some rhododendrons for me, too."

"You didn't know it was my family's business?"

"No, not right away, but then I put it together. Dottie had told me about everyone, and of course she managed to get us together once before she died. After the funeral your family invited Pepé and me to a few things but I felt they were being polite. I didn't want to put any of us through more grief than we were already experiencing." She shook her head as if clearing out sad memories.

"It seems like your family's all over the island. What else do they own?"

Jonas laughed. "It's not that bad. You'll only run into me at the base hospital, and John if you have more landscaping done. And of course you're going to be working with Paul. You haven't needed a therapist or social worker, have you? My sisters-in-law can help you there."

SERENA DIDN'T SET Jonas straight on the position with Paul's firm. She hadn't decided yet whether she'd take the job, and if she did, how she was going to limit her work hours. She'd never been good at that; once a case piqued her interest she allowed it to consume her until she had it settled.

That was before she'd become a widow, before she became a single mother and had to worry about being away from Pepé for too long.

"Wake up, Pepé." She twisted in her seat to gently shake his leg as it dangled from his booster seat. Ronald barked and Serena hopped out of the Wrangler as soon as it came to a stop.

"'Kay, Mom."

She turned back to Jonas. "Ronald needs to go potty. He never barks unless he does."

"You can let him run here."

"I'm afraid I'd never get him back. If he spots a deer or rabbit I'm out of luck." She clipped his leash onto his collar before she undid his doggy seat-belt harness.

"I still can't believe you have a seat belt for your dog."

"Anything that isn't buckled down is a flying missile in a crash." She ignored the way her hands shook. Her awareness of Jonas as more than Dottie's stepson or her future neighbor was getting ridiculous. They'd shared that one stupid kiss on the Fords' back deck and she'd been unable to erase it from her memory.

"Come on, Pepé, I'll show you around while your Mom takes Ronald to do his business."

Serena watched them walk away. Jonas was a full-dimensional guy. One minute he appeared as the modern bachelor, complete with all the sexy moves to prove it. The next, he was using a quaint turn of phrase she hadn't heard since she'd been a girl in Texas and her mother reminded her to take their dog out to do its "business."

Pepé bounced next to Jonas as they walked up the paved path that wound around several flower beds and up to the front door of a huge cedar-shingled home.

Paul's firm must be doing very, very well. Not that she cared other than for employment purposes. Observing the house also provided a good distraction from how sweet Pepé looked as he walked with Jonas.

She blinked back all-too-familiar tears. Pepé had unfairly lost his father to war. There was nothing she could do about it, and fantasies of Jonas becoming a father figure to Pepé were poison. They'd destroy *both* her and Pepé.

Ronald made quick work of his "business" and Serena steeled herself to go into the world of Jonas's family. She breathed in the Whidbey air and allowed the early-winter pastel hues that streaked across the western sky to calm her heart. Jonas was being nice, and Paul had always been accepting of her.

Serena had met Jonas's sisters-in-law when she and Pepé had stayed at BTS. Both women volunteered at the nonprofit. She'd met them only briefly, but the setting and purpose of the resort for Gold Star families was so intimate that most of the people there felt more like family. They'd known she was Dottie's biological niece and had been welcoming.

But Jonas's brother John and Jackie's husband, Jim, were unknowns.

A vision of Dottie, laughing at something funny Pepé had done, overwhelmed her. Dottie. That was why she was here. To reinforce the tie of love Dottie had woven around all of them.

If Serena ever lived as long as her aunt had, she hoped she'd have a fraction of Dottie's grace and sense of purpose.

"Let's go, Ronald."

She let herself into a magnificent foyer that was decorated with portraits of Paul's family. Front and center was one of Paul, Mary and their twins on the beach, all dressed in white tops and blue jeans. Shiny red Christmas garland draped around each frame.

Serena felt a tug of envy. She'd planned to have a family photo done when Phil got back from the war, the three of them in blue denim shirts, jeans and cowboy boots. Against the backdrop of the Texas hills.

With a start she realized her envy was more a regret. Not the overpowering grief it would've been a couple of years ago.

Had she reached another level of healing?

She heard laughter and followed the sound into an expansive great room complete with a fancy center island. Black granite flecked with gold specks covered the area around which Paul's wife, Mary, John's wife, Jackie, and the twin teenage girls stood. Mounds of dough, bags of flour and sugar and dozens of cookie cutters were scattered across the worktop.

"Mary and Jackie, nice to see you again. I'm not sure if you remember Pepé and me?"

"I'd never forget you two. These are our girls, Megan and Morgan."

"Hi." The lanky teens spoke in unison, then giggled.

"Nice to meet you. What grade are you in?"

"We're freshmen in high school."

"Fifteen?"

"Not yet—but they think they're sixteen already." Mary gave her girls a stern look.

"Mom, we were on our property!"

"Dad taught us how to start the pickup!"

Jackie grinned. "They took Paul's truck for a bit of a jaunt last night."

"Aunt Jackie!"

"Jackie!"

Both the twins and Mary expressed their horror.

Serena laughed. "I don't need to know the details. I grew up on a ranch—I was driving when I was thirteen."

"Really?" Both girls' eyes grew wide.

"Well, maybe it was fourteen." Serena shrugged.

Mary shifted into cookie-baking mode. "Girls, get Pepé started with the cutouts. Pepé, there's a huge gingerbread boy that you can be in charge of, okay?"

She turned to Serena. "Here's an apron. We'll work on making the dough for the peanut-butter cup cookies. Did you go to BTS for Thanksgiving?"

Mary's smile lit up features that were framed by a chic blond bob. Serena didn't miss her deliberate change of topic and silently had to give her points for not letting her irritation at her daughters spill over into the rest of the conversation.

"Yes, we did. It was lovely."

"Was there a good crowd? We were all here."

Jackie poured them each a cup of coffee from Mary's Christmas-themed thermal carafe.

"Thanks. Yes, there were about twenty people around the table, and it was wonderful to see how much everyone's changed and moved on. They were happy to see Pepé."

Serena held the snowflake-patterned mug between both hands and took a deep sip.

"Mmm, is this chocolate mint? Where did you get it?"

Jackie laughed and looked at Mary, who had a definite blush on her cheeks.

"It's, um, kind of 'vintage.' I froze a few packages last year when the drive-through coffee place I liked went out of business. It's still good, though, isn't it?"

Serena was a little shocked by that. The coffee drive-through had been owned by the psychopath who'd murdered Dottie. "Yes." Serena thought for a moment. "By the way, the coffee stand's open again."

It was Mary and Jackie's turn to look shocked.

"No, not that drive-through. Do you really think we'd… Oh, dear." Mary shook her head. "It's from a place near here, closer to Langley."

"Oh, that's a relief."

"You really loved Dottie, didn't you?" Jackie encouraged Serena to talk, but Serena didn't want to discuss Dottie with Jonas's family. It came too close to what mattered to her—and to his family. Dottie's legacy.

Her biological roots, which Jonas no doubt wished had never been disclosed. At least not until after he'd gotten the house.

And then there was the matter of her working with Dottie the day of Dottie's death....

"Serena, I'm sorry. We're sorry. We know you didn't have anything to do with what happened to Dottie. It was such a blow to us at the time, so we probably came off as horribly rude at the funeral. But we never blamed you, not for a minute."

"Thank you. I know that—you've been so kind, and you've invited me and Pepé to so many things. I'm sorry I didn't take you all up on it sooner."

"We're glad you're here today, Serena." Mary walked over and gave her a hug. Serena hugged Mary back, and for the first time since Dottie had died, she felt like a door had reopened to her new family.

JONAS WATCHED SERENA working at the counter with his sisters-in-law and had the same feeling he'd had whenever the missile-warning siren went off in Kandahar.

Panic.

He was heading into deep water here, and he had no one to blame but himself.

She looked so natural, as if she and Pepé had been part of his family forever.

In a way, she had. Through Dottie.

Grief clutched at his heart and he zoned out of his brother's banter about the Seattle Seahawks football game on the oversize flat screen above the fireplace mantel. They'd all been here the past six months; they'd had a chance to get used to Dottie's not being around. Hell, his stomach still sank any time he pulled up to the house and realized Dottie wasn't inside baking him some of her trademark oatmeal chocolate-chip cookies.

He couldn't deny the anticipation of seeing Serena walk through the doorway, however.

"Earth to Jonas." John stared at him with a combination of annoyance, humor and understanding. "Women troubles on your mind, buddy?"

Jonas shook his head. "I'd need a woman to have those kinds of troubles. Unlike the rest of you boys, I've got a life free of encumbrances."

"Yeah, it looks like it today, pal." Jim elbowed Paul and cast a meaningful look toward the kitchen.

They were right. He'd brought a woman, her boy and their dog.

To his family's get-together.

"Hey, you all know the deal here." He deliberately kept his voice low, not wanting it to carry over to the cookie elves. They were so busy laughing, rolling dough and cutting out cookies that he doubted they'd notice if he jumped up on the coffee table and shouted. It didn't hurt to be careful, though.

"We know what you *think* you're doing, if that's what you mean." John kept his face straight, but the glint in his eyes told Jonas that John wasn't being accusatory. Annoying, yes.

"Don't make this any more than it is. Dottie knew and loved all of us. And I know she'd be pleased that I brought Serena and Pepé here."

"Maybe not for the reasons you think." Paul's gaze remained on the game, since he was a die-hard football fan, but his quiet comment carried more weight than the others' teasing.

"What reason do you have in mind, counselor?" Jonas kept his tone light. No sense getting his brothers in a tizzy over what they seemed to think was his overinvolvement with Serena. Or maybe they thought he didn't have a snowball's chance in hell of getting the house.

Or Serena.

Where had that come from? He wasn't trying to get Serena!

Paul shouted at a fumble before he directed his attention to Jonas.

Jonas was thirty-five and Paul was forty-three, but Jonas still felt like the little brother he'd been whenever Paul had caught him doing something wrong.

Jonas was at once in awe and wary of his brother.

"Dottie was a romantic at heart. Maybe she saw

something in Serena she thought would be good for you."

"Doubtful." His response was immediate. So was his physical reaction. He clenched his hands, itching to pound the quiet, knowing look off Paul's face.

"Ooooo, the lady doth protest too much." Jim could be an annoying ass when he wanted to.

"She's hot, all right, but isn't she practically related? I think any relationship between you two would be bad for your offspring." John never missed a chance for a one-liner.

Jonas fought to keep his jaw from clenching and smiled at his brothers. Judging how stiff his cheeks felt, he was probably sneering. He couldn't control everything.

"She's not related to us at all. Dottie wasn't related to us, except that Dad married her. Not that any of it matters—Serena's a friend, and I'm trying to be *her* friend. I'm not going to get the house back with strong-arm tactics, so why shouldn't I go after it in a nicer way for everyone?"

He expected his brothers to sling more punch lines at him, to ridicule his actions. It was what they did; it was how they handled emotional hot-button issues they didn't want to talk about openly. It was a childhood position they went back to even as grown men.

Yet Paul, Jim and John remained quiet.

"What, you don't have an answer to the most sensible way to get what is rightfully mine?"

Paul's gaze was back on the game, but his lips twitched as if one of the players had turned into Peter from *Family Guy*. Jim had his stoic "don't ask me" expression firmly in place. John stared at the floor, not meeting Jonas's eyes.

The prickle he felt at his nape whenever Serena was around prodded him.

No.

Yes.

"I'm heading out to walk Ronald for a bit. Do you think it's okay if Pepé hangs out in the house while I go?" Serena stood at the end of the couch, her face calm but her eyes throwing sparks that threatened to ignite Jonas's humiliation.

Why should he care if she overheard?

Because you sounded like a complete idiot.

CHAPTER SIXTEEN

SERENA MADE A hasty retreat with Ronald along the path she'd seen from the kitchen window of Paul's house, leading out to the cliffs. She craved the solace of the woods that lay between the house and the rocky cliffs. Jonas's family didn't need to see her come unglued.

Since when had she started thinking of the Scotts as Jonas's family and not Dottie's?

She knew all along that Jonas's niceness stemmed from ulterior motives. He'd made it clear that he wanted "his" house back.

It still hurt every time he confirmed his motives. And in front of his brothers!

A bramble whipped her cheek and she swore at its sting.

Her heart, too, felt as though it'd been flayed by thorns. Jonas wanted the house; he'd never considered it anything less than Dottie's wish for him to have the place. Even Dottie's amended will, signed six months before she died, wasn't enough to convince him.

But Jonas's desire to get the house he'd dreamed

about for the past two deployments wasn't what angered her. It was her stupid, girlish response to him. She knew full well what he was about. Yet she'd let that little flame of hope stay lit.

"Serena, wait!"

Quick footsteps followed the shout, and when she whipped around she almost crashed into Jonas.

She took a step back.

"Pepé?"

"He's eating some real food after those cookies. The pizza and wings were delivered right after you ran out."

"I didn't 'run' out." Well, it wasn't actually a *run*. "I needed to get moving after standing around eating all that sugar."

"Serena, I'm sorry. What you overheard in there wasn't anything more than guy talk."

"Spare me, Jonas. You've made it clear from the start that you want Dottie's house. No matter what." Anger simmered and mixed with her awareness of him. The tang of Puget Sound hit her, along with the cedar scent of the forest—all ancient, primal, inciting her basest instincts.

"Yes, I have. Before I got to know you and Pepé it was easier, believe me. I thought that buying the land around yours would convince you."

"It hasn't and it won't. Dottie wanted that land to go to me and Pepé. Pepé is what's at stake here, Jonas. It's his legacy as much as mine. You've got a lot to learn if you think getting between me and my son's future is going to be a winning proposition for you."

As she stared at him, she saw frustration in his eyes and in the way he pursed his lips as if he was biting his tongue. His jaw was clenched and she shifted her gaze to his neck, his chest.

But that wasn't smart, because Jonas's body was her idea of ideal masculinity, which only made her more frustrated with herself. Where was the woman who used to be able to manage her life, control where it was going?

That woman died with Phil.

Serena lifted her eyes to meet Jonas's, bracing herself for his intensity. His gaze was intense, yes, but they also reflected her own frustration, and a good measure of...compassion.

"Oh, no. We're not doing this. Don't feel sorry for me, Jonas."

She'd survived a lot in her life—young widowhood, single motherhood and Dottie's murder. One man was *not* going to keep her from putting down new roots here.

"Pity? You think that's what I'm feeling?" His brows drew together and he looked away, drawing her eyes to his proud, strong profile against the late-afternoon sky. Her fingers tingled to reach up and smooth the short hair on his forehead, mussed by the wind. His hands were in his jacket pockets and his jeans fit him perfectly. The fading light bathed his face in a golden glow.

He turned back to her—she didn't remember seeing him like this before. His military bearing was nowhere in sight. This was Jonas straight-up, with his unique combination of integrity, strength and drive all aimed at her.

"I'd never try to hurt you or Pepé, Serena." Jonas's voice vibrated with sincerity. "I want you to be able to trust me. I've never hidden my desire to get the house back. But I don't want to do it in a way that causes you any stress."

"That leaves us at an impasse, Jonas. Pepé and I have made a home here—at the farmhouse."

She cursed the emotions roiling in her gut. Especially the one labeled "Jonas deserves the house."

"I never expected us to get along so well." His statement pulled her back from her despair. She smiled—she couldn't help it.

"You call this 'getting along'?"

The compassion she'd seen in his eyes became something more potent, even dangerous.

"No, this is what I call it." She watched his lips form the words and that instant connection she'd felt before he kissed her the last time zipped through her, igniting her baffling need for him.

He was going to kiss her and she was going to let him. It was broad daylight, without the dark of night they'd enjoyed on the Fords' deck. This wasn't a surprise meeting of their lips.

They both knew what they were doing. They both wanted to do it.

He hesitated before he leaned in, leaving a tiny gap between them. She dragged her gaze from his lips and looked back up at him. He watched her, waiting. He wasn't going to make this easy for her. It had to be her choice, too.

"Kiss me, Jonas."

He moved in, and her entire body reacted when his lips touched hers. The kiss was at once familiar and new and she thrilled to every nuance. When he teased her by sucking on her lower lip, she gave up trying to keep her hands at her sides and wrapped one around his neck, the other around his waist—still holding Ronald's leash.

She wanted to blame the way she felt on the fact that she hadn't had sex in a long, long time. Or to assume it was because she'd been so focused on Pepé's well-being over the past two years. She wished she could convince herself that this would feel as good with any man.

Her heart knew better.

Jonas moved his lips to her neck and she felt the soft bite of his teeth as he gently nipped at her and kissed her and made her dizzy with lust.

Her reaction had everything to do with Jonas.

She reached up and kissed his neck, as much as she could with his thermal shirt and pullover sweater in the way. The feel of his skin, its slightly salty taste and his distinctly male scent only served as a catalyst to her arousal.

She groaned when he lifted his head from hers. His chest heaved as he allowed a few inches between them.

"I'd say we get along well."

They laughed together and it was almost more intimate than their kiss had been.

As they stood quietly together for a few more moments Serena used every tool she knew to keep her hands off Jonas, to keep from insisting he make love to her right here in the trees outside his brother's house.

Paul's house. Her almost-boss's home.

"Crap, Jonas. Did we really just, um, almost lose it?"

Jonas flashed her a grim smile. "Yes, we did."

"Not the smartest thing I've ever done."

"There's nothing smart or stupid about physical attraction. It just is." Jonas's statement did what thinking about a cold shower couldn't. He doused her desire with a single sentence.

That was all it was for him. Physical attraction.

"We need to cool it. We still have no idea how we're going to work this out, Jonas. I don't want to give up the house. You don't want to believe I won't change my mind. I'm not thrilled about the idea of you building a house so close to my land, even though you own that land now. And then your family— Pepé and I shouldn't have accepted your invitation today. It's just going to make it harder in the end."

Ronald barked and brought Serena back to the reason she'd come out here. She walked away from Jonas, half expecting him to return to the house, but he fell in step with her.

"I've screwed this up, Serena, and I'm sorry. I'd really like a chance to be a friend to you and Pepé. No ulterior motives, no talk about the house."

"That sounds nice, Jonas, but every time you and I are together and Pepé's not with us, we end up getting into trouble."

"Whoa, you're calling my kisses *trouble?*"

"You know what I mean." She refrained from nudging him with her hip. Despite everything, she felt an easy comfort with Jonas. Even when he infuriated her.

"Pepé isn't an adult. He won't understand when you stop being our friend and he doesn't see you anymore."

"Friendship doesn't end like a romance, Serena. It can last a lifetime."

Jonas might as well have shot a lightning bolt through her. She wasn't looking for a lifetime *anything,* not with anyone and especially not with the man who wanted her house.

"I think we're better off being acquaintances, don't you?"

"We're past that. If you think about it, we've always had the Dottie connection." His eyes were serious and full of determination. Serena had seen the same look in Dottie's eyes. Jonas might not have been her biological son but for all practical purposes she'd made him hers.

"You have me there." She sighed. "I wish we knew why Dottie did this. Why didn't she give me and Pepé something else, if she was so driven to give us anything?"

"We might never find out. But Dottie had a reason—maybe to teach us to fight for what we want?"

"For you that makes sense. You want your boyhood home back."

"And you want to keep your biological legacy."

She didn't reply. They were nearing the house and Serena was ready to go home. Jonas's hand on her arm made her stop.

"I'm not your blood relative or Pepé's, but I'm a link for Pepé, for him to know about his grandfather. For you to know about your father."

"I don't need to know about my father. I found out what I had to from Dottie, for medical history purposes." She wasn't about to explain her sense of anger and loss when her mother had told her about the man who'd left before she was born.

"Uncle Todd wasn't the friendliest guy by far. But he did his best. Now that I know he had a child that he never claimed or supported, I understand his bitterness. It was with himself. I still don't understand why Dottie didn't urge him to go back and at least meet you and get to know you."

"What I figured out from Dottie is that he didn't tell her until right before he died. By then he thought it was too late. He gave her my mother's name. It took Dottie a while as my mom doesn't use her maiden name, but she found us. Dottie told my mother she planned to contact me within the month if she didn't hear from me first. That's what forced my mother's hand—she had to tell me or face my anger when I found out from a stranger."

She shook her head, closed her eyes and focused on the cold wind flowing through her hair. The wind lifted it away from her face and she breathed in the clean air that was Whidbey's trademark. Ronald stood next to her, leaning against her leg as if to indicate he was taking it all in, too.

"Your husband was killed at the same time?"

"The same week."

Jonas quietly whistled. "That's harsh."

"Life often is." She opened her eyes and met his. "I don't plan on making it any more chaotic than it needs to be, though. There's not a hell of a lot I have control over, but I have the ability to choose where and how I'll raise my child."

"I admire that about you."

"Do you? Really? Because it's why I'm not budging on the house, Jonas. It's mine, and it's Pepé's. He'll have the chance to decide whether he wants to raise his own family here."

He looked away from her and out toward the sinking sun as it disappeared in slices over the mainland. Serena knew she could come to care for this man.

Too much.

"THANKS FOR A nice afternoon, Jonas. Even with our…forest interlude." She offered him her best lawyer smile. He stood on the porch and she deliberately didn't invite him inside. Pepé was already in the house and Ronald contentedly sniffed the perimeter of their yard, happy to be back on his own turf.

"It was my pleasure. I only hope I didn't make it harder on you than it should've been. My family likes both you and Pepé, you know."

She did know that. She also knew that their opinion of her, while favorable, didn't matter as much as she'd once believed it did.

"It's been a long day, Jonas. Pepé needs me—it's bath time."

"Friends hug goodbye." He held his arms open, waiting.

"Of course."

She took a step toward him so she could give him a quick, friendly hug. Ignoring her lips and the fact that they wanted to do a lot more than smile at Jonas wasn't easy, but she was an adult. She could do this.

He offered her a similarly light, nonsexual hug.

I am not disappointed.

Well, maybe she was a little bit bummed. Maybe a lot. Maybe she still needed that cold shower.

"Bye, Jonas."

"Good night, Serena."

She shut the door and because it had beveled glass windows in the frame she stood back and waited until she heard his vehicle start up and drive away. Then she fell against the door and sank to the ground.

Life on Whidbey was supposed to be her gateway to the simple life. Not the complicated, heart-twisting adventure she was on at the moment.

"Mom! Can we read *Captain Underpants* after my bath?" Pepé skidded into the hall in front of her, in his socks.

"How about something else tonight? What about one of your Christmas books?"

"Can we read *The Smallest Christmas Tree?*"

She nodded; the book by Linda Cardillo had become one of their favorites. "Sure. Why don't you go get your pajamas and I'll bring Ronald inside. Then we'll draw your bath."

"Great!" He scooted back down the hall toward his room. Tears welled up as Serena allowed herself to embrace the reality of Pepé's life. He was a happy six-year-old. No more emotional angst over his daddy's passing, no missing his family in Texas, since he'd been so young when she'd moved them out here.

She was about to accept her dream position at the top firm on island. They had no financial worries, and a house that was truly their home.

It was everything she'd dared to hope for.

She would not let any regrets over what Jonas Scott wanted interfere with their happiness.

SERENA WOKE TO the sound of the gale-force winds rocking the house. The eaves and roof shingles made a constant rippling noise that reminded her of dominoes falling in perfect cadence.

"Ronald?"

Ronald lay at the foot of her bed, curled up into a ball—the way he preferred to sleep during cold weather—but his head was erect and his ears were pricked. It was still a week before Christmas and not officially winter yet, but the arctic air that was dipping down into the Northwest made it feel like they lived in Alaska.

The house shuddered and sighed in the wind. It wasn't the first gale-force storm they'd had since she'd moved here, but it appeared to be the worst to date. According to the weather reports, it might last through tomorrow afternoon at least.

Pepé hadn't run into her room, so she sent up a silent prayer of thanks that he was sleeping soundly.

Still, she went through the checklist in her head for the house prep needed for subzero temperatures. She'd unfastened the two garden hoses, left the kitchen cabinet doors under the sink open for the pipes to stay warm and moved her SUV into the garage.

Ronald issued a low growl and Serena blinked.

The alpacas! She'd forgotten to make sure that Snowball and Cami were okay in their small barn.

"We've got some quick work to do, Ronald."

Ronald jumped off the bed and she made short work of shoving on her fleece warm-up suit. She peeked in on Pepé to see him snoring softly under his *Frozen* comforter, his arm above his head in total repose.

Once she was at the back kitchen door, she jammed her feet into her work boots, grateful for the wool socks she'd stocked up on at an end-of-season sale last year.

Ronald alerted her. His low-throated growl and raised hackles as he looked at the back door unnerved her.

"It's the wind, puppy. You stay here and protect Pepé. Got it?"

Ronald stilled, but continued his warning noises, no doubt expecting to go outside with her.

Serena felt completely safe on the island, and especially in their small area of Whidbey, which was protected from the major highway by acres of trees and meadows. It would take an intruder extra effort to come out here, and she'd have ample warning with her long drive the only way up to the house.

But she knew that strange things could happen, so she grabbed the baseball bat she kept near her bed.

The alpacas had to be checked and she wasn't going to go out there and leave Pepé alone in the house, even though it was only a couple of hundred yards away, unless Ronald stayed with Pepé. In the house. Still, she felt a twinge as she made the quick walk to the new barn.

Inside she was relieved to find her two alpacas huddled near each other, blinking at her with their cartoonishly large eyes as she interrupted their humming. Pepé loved to hear them hum at night, but no way was she waking him now. Besides, school hadn't been canceled for tomorrow. Not yet.

Confident the alpacas were comfortably settled, she shut off the light and left the barn. She locked the main door and turned around to see a large male figure not two feet away from her.

Serena screamed.

CHAPTER SEVENTEEN

Whidbey Island
Nine days before Christmas

JONAS TOSSED AND turned like a teenager with his first crush on a girl. He wanted to blame it on the storm but couldn't muster the energy to try to fool himself.

Serena was the reason he was awake. There was more to her, more to his attraction to her, than the damn house.

He wasn't ready for a major involvement with anyone. She'd made it clear she wasn't the casual-sex type, which he'd known from the minute she and Pepé walked into the clinic a month ago.

Was it only a month ago? Barely. Was it possible to fall for someone after such a short time? The woman had a child, for Pete's sake. And the kicker was that Jonas liked Pepé. A lot. He was a good kid. He deserved all the love Serena gave him and more.

The kid deserved a dad.

Jonas groaned. He was not father material. He loved his nieces and was happy to see how much joy the girls brought Paul and Mary. Jonas had been mobile for too long, always going to the next crisis on the globe for the past two decades. Although he planned to serve out his time on Whidbey until he retired in five years or so, he still didn't think he was a good candidate for parenthood. Not to mention marriage.

He groaned and sat up in bed, swinging his feet over the side. What was he, seventeen?

"Maybe twenty years ago," he muttered.

A trip to the shelter in Coupeville next weekend might be in order. A dog would get his mind off things he couldn't have, shouldn't entertain.

Serena.

When he kissed her she enjoyed it as much as he did. It was in her subtle reactions as well as her boldness—the way her fingers dug into him, the way her tongue fiercely matched his explorations.

He'd blown it tonight. It had been going well, and she'd been relaxing and even laughing at his stupid jokes. But he couldn't keep his hands, or his tongue, to himself. The town house shook from the force of the wind and he paused. If it was this bad here in town, it was twice as rough out on the finger of land the farmhouse sat on. When the wind blew, the power always went, and the cold could be unbearable until the woodstove was going.

Did Serena know how to light the woodstove? And then the pipes—they'd burst a couple of times. It happened in the lower part of the farm-house, the part that had been added on in the eighties.

Serena was an adult. She'd managed in the house for six months. Besides, who said she'd lost power?

"I'm not her caretaker." As a nurse practitio-ner, his automatic response was figuring out how to take care of someone. He had to work at not thinking that everyone's well-being was his re-sponsibility.

It was the very reason he wasn't good marriage material. He got palpitations at the thought of hav-ing to worry about a spouse day in and day out. And then kids…

His throat tightened and his anxiety shifted from a slow jog to a run.

"I'm not in the med unit. I'm back home."

Thankfully his post-deployment nightmares had been few, and this was the first real anxi-ety he'd experienced since he'd returned. Intel-lectually he knew that he was in good shape; he certainly wasn't suffering like so many of his col-leagues.

And his anxiety hadn't stirred until…

Serena.

The bedside clock glared 3:00 a.m. and he knew sleep was going to be at least several hours away. He'd be lucky to grab an hour before he had to get ready for work.

His bare feet were cold on the kitchen tiles as he moved about the dark room. He hit the switch for the under-cabinet light and flicked on his electric teakettle. As he grabbed a mug from the cabinet, his glance landed on the kitchen faucet.

He looked at the clock over the stove to confirm the time before he picked up his cell phone.

Serena didn't answer. She hadn't let her battery run out, had she? They were probably without power. He'd bet asses to doughnuts that she didn't know how to work the generator stored in the oldest shed on the property, farthest from the house.

"Come on, Serena, pick up."

When her voice came on and told him to leave a message, Jonas unplugged the teakettle.

"It's OKAY! NOTHING to worry about here, lady." The man sneered at her in the dark, his face unrecognizable in the glow of the motion detector light over the barn. She'd never seen him before.

Serena's heart pounded and she cursed herself for resting the bat against the side of the barn when she went in. She grasped at it but it was out of reach. She wished she had a shovel or a hoe in her hand. Anything. She was completely defenseless and she sensed this stranger knew it. He was here, though, and not at the house, thank God. She'd only been gone a few minutes—and he couldn't have gotten into her house. Ronald would attack any stranger who entered.

"Who are you?"

"A friendly soul who needs a dry place for the night. That's all. You wouldn't have found me if you hadn't been so nosy."

As he spoke his spittle shot out in front of him and mixed with the icy snowflakes that were beginning to fall. The wind drove the snow into her eyes and she blinked to keep her vision from blurring. His eyes appeared bloodshot, glassy.

What was he high on?

A shiver ran through her as she recalled recent news reports about the area meth rings. And about the heroin addicts who stole prescription narcotics to support their habit. All the headlines screamed at her in a cluster of scary possibilities.

Keep him talking. That was what she knew how to do.

"How did you get here?" she asked.

Her teeth were chattering but she had to hold her ground, keep him far away from Pepé. Oh, God, what if he had more addicts with him? Surreptitiously she groped in her pocket for her cell phone and came up empty.

Damn it, she'd left it on her nightstand.

"My car tuckered out. I walked in from the road."

He swayed on his feet and it was clear he was under the influence of something. She didn't smell booze on his breath, only a sweetly rancid scent, one she usually associated with sickness or death.

Think, think, think. Keep him talking.

Every instinct, everything she'd ever learned in any case study, raced through her mind and she fought to stay focused. Pepé's life might depend upon it.

"I don't have any narcotics in the house."

"I'm not going to hurt you." He grabbed a length of her hair. His height and his physical advantage over her kept her standing in place. As soon as he swayed again, she'd give him a shove and get past him.

"What do you want?" She used her attorney voice and thought of the many ways she would prosecute this derelict who dared to come on her property and threaten her, her home, her *child*.

He didn't know about Pepé. He couldn't.

"I just need a little help, honey. You can help me. You've got some painkillers up in that house, don't you?"

He slowly blinked and bent his head toward hers as if he were moving in a dream.

Serena kneed him in the groin and shoved against his chest as hard as she could. She saw his eyes roll back as his head hit the side of the small barn, but his weight shifted again and he fell against her leg. Stars flared under her eyelids as his chin slammed into her face and knocked the back of her head against the wall.

"Ahhh!" Pain radiated through her cheekbone

and she fought to stay conscious. She had to get back to the house, to Pepé.

JONAS'S GUT RARELY failed him and when he saw the beat-up car at the end of Serena's driveway he knew his need to get to the house was warranted.

His military training had him peering at the license plate. He memorized the number. *California.* It could be anyone, but someone legitimately visiting Serena and Pepé wouldn't have stopped here—they would have made the half-mile drive up to the house.

Shutting off his headlights, Jonas relied on the thousands of other times he'd gone up the driveway, since it was all but pitch-dark and the blowing wind had started to include snow.

His stomach dropped when he saw the house lights, including those in the small barn extension Serena had installed for those yarn-making animals she'd raved about.

It took him thirty seconds flat to park, get out of the car and run to the front door where he pounded loudly. Ronald's barking was all he heard past the roar of the wind. He ran around to the back door and peered through the kitchen windows as he tried the door. It opened and Ronald sprang out at him, teeth bared. Jonas raised his arms for protection, but Ronald wasn't interested in him as he raced off into the dark.

Toward the barn.

Jonas dashed behind him, wishing he had his nine-millimeter handgun. He didn't know what he was going to find when he got to wherever Ronald was running, but he knew it might be very ugly.

He'd seen villages, soldiers and civilians ripped apart physically and mentally by numerous battles. Nothing prepared him to see a huge man hulking against the barn wall, next to what he instinctively knew was Serena's prone body. Ronald had his teeth bared and he growled ferociously a foot in front of the assailant. Jonas wasn't ready for his emotional response but his Navy training kicked in and with minimal, almost surgical moves he took out the criminal, not stopping until the guy was flat on his back with Ronald growling over him.

"Good dog."

Jonas heard Serena moaning, so he risked the few seconds it took to dial 9-1-1, then threw his phone onto the ground, leaving it on speaker while he tended to her.

He gave the emergency operator directions and informed her of his assessment of Serena as he went through his exam, one he'd done too many times in a war zone.

Anger threatened to break through his professional bearing more than once as he noted an egg-size lump on her forehead, a definitely broken nose and a swollen lip. He wanted to kill the monster with his bare hands.

He kept his eyes on Serena's and refrained from doing anything that would take him from her side.

"Pepé," she whispered between the sobs that were starting to rack her frame. He heard the sirens and squeezed her hands.

"I'm sure he's okay, honey. I'll go check on him as soon as the paramedics get here."

"The police…"

"They're coming, too."

"Pepé."

He felt tension in his gut. A sure signal that he, too, needed to know how Pepé was. But he couldn't leave Serena, and he wasn't going to give the creep an opportunity to take off, not even with Ronald standing vigilant watch over him.

Fortunately, the first police cruiser rounded the last bend of Serena's driveway and Jonas didn't have to make a choice.

CHAPTER EIGHTEEN

U.S. ship LST-19, Pacific Ocean
September 1945

"How are you doing today, Henry?"

Henry opened his eyes to the familiar voice. Charles Dempsey, a Navy sailor on the ship that was taking him far away from Japan, sat on an upside-down crate next to Henry's cot.

"Same."

"I brought you some paper and a pen. I thought you'd want to write a letter to Sarah. I can mail it for you when I go back to the States."

"Do you really think you'll beat me back home, Charles?"

"I'm going to try, you bet."

Charles smiled at that. Henry hadn't paid attention to people's smiles in a long time, but Charles's grin was so full of life. And Charles looked so healthy—his skin glowed and he had good muscle tone.

I used to look like that.

"I don't think I could make it much farther than this cot, truth be told."

"Aw, you'll be up and at it before you know it. It's not going to be long now. Just keep eating the food the nurses are bringing, and as soon as you can, get out on the deck for some air. It'll do wonders for you."

Henry knew it would, but his legs had grown too weak for him to walk farther than the distance to the head, the naval term for the john. "Where are we going, have we heard yet?"

"Yes, we're dropping you and your buddies off at the hospital in the Marianas. We'll pick up some of the men who are ready to go home and take them to Hawaii, maybe back to the mainland." Charles winked at him. "I'm a Waterman First Class. I'm not on the 'need-to-know' list, if you follow me."

Henry tried to smile but it took too much effort. Would his energy ever return? Now that he'd survived the war, and the war was over, he should be doing handsprings on this ship's deck. Instead, he was practically bedridden, his bones and skin all that was left of the man he'd been.

"The Marianas, they'll be like Hawaii, right? Tropical?"

"Everything out here is tropical!"

Charles laughed from his belly and Henry envied it. He wanted to be able to laugh like that again. As if he really believed life was good, and that he had everything to look forward to.

"Will you help me write the letter to Sarah? My hands are still shaky."

"Sure thing. Here, let me help you up."

"No, I'll just lie on my side and we'll do it like this." Henry rolled to his right side and took the paper and pen that Charles offered.

"Here's a magazine." Charles slid it under the letterhead stationery, giving Henry a firmer surface to write on. "You're left-handed, are you?"

Henry nodded. "Yes."

He wanted to talk more freely with Charles, and supposed that maybe he would as his strength returned. It was such a godforsaken slow process, getting better.

"Will you help me if I can't do the words?" He sounded like a schoolboy. Probably looked like one, too.

"Sure thing."

Charles sat and whistled a jaunty melody, gazing off into space.

Henry appreciated the attempt to give him privacy in such cramped quarters. Compared to what he'd lived through, though, his cot on the LST was like a featherbed in the Taj Mahal.

It took a while for his hands to obey his thoughts, but eventually he was able to write his letter to Sarah.

Whidbey Island
Present Day, nine days before Christmas

"YOU DID THE best you could, Mrs. Delgado. No one expects to find a stranger on their property in the middle of an arctic freeze." Detective Cole Ramsey had sent most of his team back to Coupeville and the EMTs had left an hour ago. They were in her living room, part of the great room that included the kitchen and dining area.

"Still, if I'd had the dog with me, none of this would have happened."

Jonas knew she'd beat herself up for this, but it wasn't her fault. Pepé was still sound asleep in his room—Jonas had checked on him and made sure his window was locked tight before he came back downstairs to stay with Serena.

Serena sat on her couch after being looked at by the EMTs and Jonas. She'd promised to go see a doctor on base tomorrow but Jonas didn't think she had more than a broken nose.

The loser was locked up and would spend his holiday behind bars. He was a known troublemaker on the island and Detective Ramsey had made it clear that he would not bother Serena or anyone else again.

Jonas wished he'd been comforted by the fact that the pipes under the kitchen sink would have burst if he hadn't arrived and put the space heater in place next to the counter.

No matter what he told himself, his unease and his instincts had been all about Serena and Pepé, as well. They'd had nothing to do with the condition of the house or its fate during the storm. The house had been his way back to her.

Thank God.

"In all the time we lived out here, we only had one transient. Dottie found him on the property down by the stream and had the police out here before the guy woke up."

Detective Ramsey from the Island County Sheriff's Department chuckled.

"Yes, I remember hearing about that when we were still in high school."

Jonas and Cole Ramsey had played on the school basketball team together, before they'd gone their separate ways after graduation.

"You're back after deployment, aren't you?"

Jonas nodded. "Yes. It's great to be home."

"How long will you be here?"

"For the duration, I hope. I'm planning on finishing out my Navy years here, then settling down."

"You'll work after you're done with the Navy?"

"Of course—I'll only be forty-two. Not too old, at any rate."

Ramsey laughed. "If you need a contact at the hospital in Coupeville, let me know. My wife is a nurse there."

"Thanks, Cole. Will do."

Ramsey turned back to Serena. "Are you okay, Mrs. Delgado?"

"Serena. It's Serena. And yes, I'm fine."

"Do you have a family member or friend who can come and stay with you? It's never easy to go alone right after someone's trespassed on your property, not to mention the fact that you've been assaulted."

"I'm staying. She won't be alone." Jonas spoke up, ignoring the glare Serena shot him. Even with cotton shoved up her nose she was beautiful.

"That's not necessary."

Cole Ramsey sized up Serena. Jonas knew he was thinking what any man would. She was a beautiful woman. The possessiveness that sprang up in him didn't surprise Jonas but it didn't make him feel any better.

"I'd take him up on it, Serena. Besides, with this cold weather, it's going to be rocky for the next few days. The power's out in town, too." Cole didn't miss a thing. He'd observed Serena's house while the police went through to confirm that the intruder hadn't made it that far.

Jonas sent up a silent prayer of thanks. Serena would heal in a week or so. Her swelling and the fact that she hadn't blacked out indicated she didn't have a concussion. If anything had happened to Pepé, they'd be dealing with something far worse.

"We're done here." Cole turned to Jonas. "Want to walk me out?"

"Sure." He squeezed Serena's hand. "I'll be back in a minute. Sit tight and don't get up until I'm with you. Got it?"

"Since when are Navy guys meaner than Marines?" She watched him with her steady gaze.

"It's not mean, it's for your safety. You need to take it easy. Otherwise, I'll have Cole drop you off at the base clinic while I stay here with Pepé."

As her eyes filled with tears, his gut tightened. He'd spoken without thought, and yet he meant every word. He'd been worried about Pepé, too.

"That's okay," she said. "I'll wait here."

Jonas walked out to Cole's small car with him. The last squad car was driving away, its red taillights growing smaller as it wound through the woods toward the road.

"Good seeing you again, Jonas. It's none of my business, but are you involved with her?"

"In a way. As you know, she inherited my stepmom Dottie's house. Dottie was her biological aunt. Why do you ask?"

Cole paused. "I found myself involved with a widow not too long ago."

"Are you warning me to stay away, Cole?"

Cole shook his head. "More like the opposite. There's a series of break-ins in this area over the past two months. They seem to be escalating in violence. Serena's lucky you showed up."

"She was halfway to the house and had kneed the bastard in the nuts. She was doing just fine on her own." Jonas's fists still itched to strike out.

"*Hmph.* It seems that this jerk likes to break into homes and steal prescription narcotics. Vicodin, OxyContin and other painkillers. They sell them to the local high school kids and use the money to buy heroin."

"I'm sure that's not unique to Whidbey, is it, Cole?"

"No, it isn't. But I like to keep Whidbey as safe as it was when we were kids—the place our parents and grandparents made it when they settled here. At any rate, keep an eye on her if you can. This guy's going to be locked up for a long time with the assault-and-battery charge the district attorney will slap on him, but it won't keep him from telling his buds that she's out here alone."

"Should she move into town for a while?"

"No, as long as you or another friend is with her, and she keeps her dog close, she'll be fine. These aren't hardened criminals with weapons on them—yet. The only reason the dirtbag targeted her house in the first place is because he's in heroin withdrawal. It's an ugly symptom of a devastating disease. Anyway, they normally hit houses that are empty, when the owners are out and about. But if she's here alone with her kid, she appears vulnerable. I'd hate to see her bothered again."

"I'll see to it that she's safe, Cole."

"Good. I'll send patrol cars out regularly. And we'll get this group of troublemakers rounded up by Christmas."

"I hope you're right."

They clasped hands in a brief but friendly handshake.

"Thanks for everything, man," Jonas said. "Hey, Cole?"

"Yes?"

"What happened to the widow you got involved with?"

Cole laughed. "I'm married to her."

Cole climbed into his car and drove off as Jonas watched. How the hell would he convince Serena that he was going to stay with her and Pepé as a friend, without any ulterior motive?

SERENA WOKE WITH Pepé's face next to hers.

"Mom, they've canceled school!"

Her head throbbing, she looked at her clock radio and groaned. She never slept in this late.

"How do you know, Pepé? Just because there's snow doesn't mean there aren't any classes."

"The school left a message on your cell phone, and I checked online. Pepé's right."

"Mom, what happened to your face?"

Two male voices, one sweet and high, and one low and reassuring.

"You stayed," she murmured.

"Jonas said he came to help us with the iced pipes in the kitchen."

Jonas chuckled, and the warmth of such a masculine expression of humor caught her off guard. Her lips tilted up in a smile.

"Ouch."

"You've got quite the swollen lip. How do you feel?"

"Fine." She looked at Pepé, who stared at her with unabashed fascination. "I slipped outside, honey, and hit my face on the ground." She was strategic in her reply. A six-year-old boy didn't need to know everything.

"When were you outside?"

"Last night, when the wind started howling, right before the big snowflakes fell. I was checking on the alpacas." She ruffled his hair. "Is it the sticky kind of snow that will make a good snowman?"

"I want to make an igloo."

"Hmm."

"Pepé, why don't you go get your mom one of the muffins I baked, and bring it in here?"

"Sure!" He shot off her bed and down the hall before she could blink.

"You baked muffins?"

Jonas shrugged. "I do have some hidden talents."

Sore bones, aching muscles, a pounding head and a swollen lip couldn't keep her from reacting to his comment, even though he'd meant it in the most platonic way.

Didn't he?

"That's very nice of you." She slowly sat farther up in bed.

"I'm much better than we thought—it was more the emotional shake-up than anything. You can go home now."

Jonas smiled before he sat down on the edge of the bed.

"Nice try. Let me take a look at you."

She sat while he checked her face, asking her how many fingers he held up and the usual vision questions.

It wasn't more than a few minutes but for Serena it felt like an hour with his fingers on her cheekbones, her temples, her jaw.

Dressed in a white T-shirt under a wool pullover, Jonas looked rugged yet approachable—with his nurse persona well in place.

"Do you feel dizzy at all? What about a headache?"

"My head's pounding, but it's the kind of headache I usually get when a large weather system comes in. You know, sinus stuff. My lip feels more stiff than painful. Honestly, I'm okay. Pepé and I will be fine. Next time I'll make sure I take Ronald with me if I have to go out at night."

"No, you won't—that would leave Pepé vulnerable. You can't kid a kidder, Serena."

"Don't you feel a little awkward being here? We hardly know each other."

He stared at her and to his credit didn't bring up their kisses.

"What finer way to spend time together during a storm? We both have a vested interest in the house and the property. We're going to have to get to know each other better at some point."

"I've already explained that Pepé doesn't need this, Jonas. It'll be too much for him when... when..."

"Pepé needs positive male role models. Our families are permanently intertwined thanks to Dottie, no matter how you and I feel about each other and the house. It's in Pepé's interest for all of us to get to know one another. My family is his family, and if he grows up here, my nieces will be an immeasurable support to him at school. They'll be his safety net."

He had a point. Or maybe her head was too fuzzy to argue with him.

"Mom, you're going to love this muffin."

Pepé squeezed in front of Jonas on the side of the bed and deposited a large berry muffin on Serena's chest. Ronald came over to sniff the treat and Jonas stood up.

At least he didn't try to clean the crumbs from where they'd landed on her breasts.

"I think you need a napkin, and I'll get you some coffee."

"Coffee sounds like heaven."

"How do you take yours?" She met his eyes, which radiated concern. And interest.

In her.

"A splash of light cream, that's it."

"A gal after my own heart."

She couldn't help it; her eyes wandered past his shoulders, his waist and down to his butt as he walked out of the room.

"Try the muffin, Mom."

"Mmm, this is very good. You're right, *mi hijo.*"

Who knew the nurse could bake, too?

JONAS WAS HAPPY to help Serena and Pepé as the storm raged outside and their power flickered on and off. Dottie had put in gas heat several years ago, but the draft from the gale kept blowing the pilot light out, so Jonas turned the gas off and had the woodstove cranking out blessed warmth.

He'd forgotten how cold it got when the polar air currents dipped low into Puget Sound.

Serena sat in a recliner with the footrest up, her long fingers moving rhythmically as she knitted what looked like some type of ski hat. He caught her dozing every now and again. He felt a sense of satisfaction from knowing that she was relaxed enough with him to rest. It was the beginning of trust.

Trust.

"I've got you, dog!"

Pepé wrestled with Ronald on the living room rug in front of the stove.

"Watch yourself there, buddy. The stove will burn you if you touch it."

"It's never burned me before."

"Have you used it before?" He hid a grin at the puzzled look on Pepé's face.

"No. That's Mom's knitting space."

"I had to move that big basket of yarn to the corner of the room or it would've caught fire. The woodstove is filled with logs and sticks, burning to keep us warm."

"So the pipes won't ice?"

"You mean 'freeze.' Yes, so the water in the pipes doesn't freeze and make the pipes crack."

"Oh." Pepé looked at Jonas, the woodstove and the kitchen sink. Then he went back to playing tug of war with Ronald.

Jonas's amusement kept him watching the two of them for a few more minutes. Pepé had asked myriad questions as Jonas hooked up the space heater and set it in front of the open cabinets under the sink. He'd listened as Jonas explained why it was so important to keep the pipes warm.

Jonas remembered his father giving him a description of everything he did around the house. As if he knew he'd leave Jonas as a seventeen-year-old high school senior, far before he should have.

The pain of losing his father so young had never

lessened, but it had become bearable over the years. Dottie had played a big part in that.

What would she think about his being here, with Serena and Pepé, trying to be helpful instead of figuring out how to manipulate Serena into giving up the house?

He looked over at Serena. Her hands were still as her brown eyes searched his.

"He'll be okay, Jonas. He and Ronald play rough, but they don't get too crazy."

"I'm sure Ronald's the wiser of the two."

She laughed and he noticed the empty coffee mug on the end table next to her chair.

"Let me warm that up for you."

He poured the freshly brewed coffee into Serena's mug, which Pepé had painted at the pottery shop in downtown Oak Harbor. Pepé had proclaimed it "her favorite" when they'd fixed her first cup of coffee hours earlier.

A splash of half-and-half, and he walked it over to her.

"Here you go."

"You're spoiling me. I can get my own coffee."

"Tell me that when I start to stink." He was still wearing the same clothes he'd put on in the middle of the night.

"Did you get a shower earlier?"

"I did, yes, when you were sleeping. I hope you don't mind that I used the upstairs bathroom." She had a bathroom off her bedroom, but he didn't want to wake her, so he'd found the one upstairs. It was obviously Pepé's.

"Did the dinosaurs scare you?" The shower curtain was emblazoned with several different species.

"No, but I darn near had a cow when I stepped on a squeaky toy."

Serena laughed. The sound was getting too familiar, getting to be something he craved. He missed it when she didn't have anything to laugh about.

"Even though he's a big boy, Pepé still likes toys that squeak and squirt in the bathtub."

"Mom! Stop!" Pepé ordered.

"I have toys in my shower, too, Pepé." Jonas smiled at him.

"You do?"

"Sure. I have a waterproof radio so I can listen to the news or a Seahawks game, and I have a long-handled brush to scrub my back."

Pepé wrinkled his nose. "A brush isn't a toy."

"It's a grown-up toy, Pepé." Serena replied for him and smiled, but when her eyes met Jonas's her smile faded. Blatant sensuality and unabashed lust flowed between them. He wondered if she could see the visions in his mind—of scrubbing her naked body with his bare hands, soaping her shoulders, her back, her ass, then reaching around her small waist to her breasts. Her nipples would be erect and—

Thud.

The front windowpane reverberated from the impact.

"What was that?" Serena was up and out of her recliner, her coffee sloshed on the carpet.

Jonas looked at the snow that had spattered against the picture window.

"My money's on a hawk or an eagle. Probably lost its way in the wind and snow."

Serena walked over to the large expanse of glass and peered at the snow print. "I think you're right. See how the snowflakes hold the outline of the beak, Pepé? And the wings." Pepé ran up next to her and Ronald stood behind him on the braided rug, tail wagging.

"Neat! Is the bird okay, Mom?"

Serena looked carefully out the window. "I don't see any sign of it, so my guess is that it bumped the house and flew away."

Pepé nodded, apparently losing interest. "Mom, I'm hungry."

"I've got some peanut butter and jelly sandwiches with your name on them, buddy." Jonas didn't want Serena doing anything today. If she could get one day of complete rest, her bruises and aching muscles would heal that much sooner.

"That sounds great for me, too." She offered him a sheepish grin. "I suppose you saw the inside of our refrigerator."

Jonas grinned back.

Her fridge was stocked to the max with half-empty jars of sauces, pickles and yogurt containers.

"Don't look so embarrassed. It's nothing compared to mine when I'm working long hours at the clinic. I saw you have the fixings for lasagna, but I couldn't find the tomato sauce."

"It's in what I think you used to call the sun porch. I had it closed in to give the stuff from Dottie's attic a safe storage place and to give Pepé and me a decent pantry."

"Smart thinking on your part." He hesitated. Exactly what attic "stuff" of Dottie's did Serena have?

She held up her hand. "Before you get worried, all I have of Dottie's are her Christmas decorations. Mostly old plastic ones from the sixties and seventies. Like I told you, your brothers came and got whatever they wanted, but they insisted I keep the decorations she'd bought specifically for the house."

"Some of those go back to her parents, her grandparents, even."

Serena nodded. "I know, Paul explained that. I still have a lot of sorting to do but eventually I hope to salvage whatever I can and I'll use it to decorate the house again."

"Tell him about the airplane, Mom!"

Pepé stood next to her, holding a large jar of peanut butter.

"Put that back on the kitchen counter, Pepé, and don't interrupt."

When she looked back at him he saw the wariness in her eyes. Was she hiding something?

"What airplane, Serena?"

CHAPTER NINETEEN

SERENA COULDN'T BELIEVE Jonas had stayed the night.

Well, she could, considering she'd had a bad shake-up and he was a military man. A medical man used to helping others. It made sense when she looked at it that way.

How he was looking at her was another matter. His gaze set her skin on fire and made her forget that they'd known each other for less than a month. What did they really have in common, anyway, except for a house that she wasn't going to give up and that he'd never get over losing—to her?

She followed him into the storage room.

"You showed me this before, but I didn't realize all those bins were filled with Dottie's Christmas ornaments."

Serena laughed at that. "What, did you think I had some kind of rock collection?"

Jonas stood beside her in front of the shelves that held her numbered plastic bins.

"I didn't know, honestly. I'm impressed with how well-organized you are. I had no trouble finding anything in your kitchen. Where did you learn to be so neat?"

"My mother's a stickler for tidiness, and law school taught me that the answer is always available in the law, somewhere. You just have to be able to find it. Once I became a Marine wife, my obsession with organizing took over our household goods, too."

"The movers must have loved you." Jonas smiled.

Serena smiled back, not fazed by the reference to her military life with Phil.

Her heart didn't squeeze shut every time a memory came up, nor was she reminded of what she and Pepé had lost.

Your heart has healed.

She gave a quick shake of her head. "I don't know about that."

She removed the clipboard she'd hung on a nail and handed it to him. "Here's the list of what I've found, but it's preliminary. I don't know which lights are still working, for example, or if they're safe enough to be plugged in. Some of the strings are from the forties, if you can believe it."

"Oh, I believe it," he said. "Dottie inherited her parents' Depression-era habits of saving everything that had the remotest chance of being useful in the future. At one point when I was young, my father had to convince her that she didn't need to save twist-ties anymore."

"My mother's frugality was the same. She's eased up as the years have gone by, but it's hard to shake the lessons learned in poverty, when a family's in pure survival mode."

"Dottie was a product not only of the Depression but of World War II. I think that's why it took her years to let go of her tendency to make everything from scratch and accepting that modern conveniences aren't all a waste of money."

"Yes," Serena agreed with a laugh, "but she still insisted on preparing homemade meals for Pepé and me, and she never failed to bake him cookies and cupcakes."

Jonas nodded absently, studying each page of her inventory, stopping at items as they jogged his memory.

"The star! Red lights on a tin shape, right?"

Serena nodded. "Yes. It was definitely handmade."

"By Dottie's grandfather. It was made for her mother when she was a girl."

"Most of the lights look like they're probably burned out but you can buy those new vintagestyle lights now, and I thought I'd get some, try to string them around it. Do you know where they hung it?"

"Over the highest roof point. There's a ladder back in the big shed."

"I saw it."

"I'm sure you have that inventoried, too." He

glanced up from the clipboard and stared at her. "Is there anything you're *not* good at?"

Serena's stomach grew hot and her lips twitched, which made her grimace.

"You have to keep your lips covered with the ointment so they'll heal more quickly. Your cheek took the worst of it, but your lips have to be feeling raw." He'd found all her first-aid supplies and added some from the medical kit he kept in his car. The healing balm for her lips was a godsend.

"I know." She swallowed. "I'll never be able to repay you for all your help last night and today."

He placed his hand on her shoulder. "Stop. I didn't do anything but show up. You would've made your way back to the house." He raised her chin so that she had to look at him. His eyes reflected sincerity, warmth and something more. Something she didn't want to face, not now, not with Jonas.

"You kept Pepé safe, and let's face it, this is normally one of the safest places on the planet. It's remote enough that even Whidbey locals don't know about it. It's a fluke that the drug addict showed up here."

"I realize that, in my head. The odds of losing someone in the war were supposed to be on my side, too, but, well, look where that got me."

"You've had some rough knocks. But this will pass, Serena."

Who was this Jonas standing in front of her?

Where was her nemesis, the man who wanted her house?

Did he mean all of this would pass when she agreed to sell the house to him?

"It will. Hey, I'm a lawyer, and family law has its risks, too. I've been threatened by my clients' ex-husbands when I've had to get restraining orders against them, and I've had more than my share of unhappy survivors who didn't get what they expected from a family estate."

"Like me?"

"I didn't mean it that way, Jonas. Sure, you're not happy, but I'm not afraid you're going to do anything nefarious to get the house back. Except… you did purchase the surrounding land."

"Yes, I did."

"Feeling guilty?"

"Not one bit."

Her familiar annoyance at his arrogance returned and none too soon. Jonas's effect on her was intense, and it would be easy to convince herself that she'd been wrong about him, about their chances of starting a relationship.

"What was the airplane Pepé mentioned?"

She glanced at the small worktable where she'd left the bin in which they'd found the stocking and ornament.

"We came across a hand-carved plane that I think is a Flying Tiger from World War II. It's next to my laptop in the dining room. I'll show it to you when we go back inside."

Jonas stood while he thought aloud. "It could very well be a P-40 Warhawk. I know Dottie's father was a pilot in the war, but she said he didn't talk much about it once he came home. She was five or six when he left for flight training. He didn't come back until she was nine or ten."

"Pepé's age. When her father went to war, I mean."

"Yes."

Did he think she'd used Pepé as another means to manipulate Dottie? Didn't he see that it was all a coincidence? Dottie hadn't told her anything about her father fighting in World War II. She'd had no control over when her mother was going to tell her about her biological father.

"Did you ever meet Dottie's dad?"

"No, he'd passed on before Dottie met my dad."

"Was she a lot older than your father?"

Jonas smiled. "By twelve years."

"Really!"

"Yeah, but you know, she and my dad were perfect for each other. She was a beauty, a real product of the summer of love, the whole hippie thing. She was in her forties when she and Dad met. I never looked at her as older. She was a stunning woman in her day—just look at some of the photos in Paul's house. I think my dad needed someone like her—a real live wire. Dad was quieter—an engineer. He'd come here to work on weapons systems at the base and to train the aircrew. He'd lost my mother to a drunk driver right after I was born. He deserved a break. Dottie was it."

Compassion surged in her chest for the little boy Jonas had been when he met Dottie. Had his eyes widened at her full-throttle laugh like Pepé's had?

"I only knew her as an older woman," Serena told him, "but she looked at least twenty years younger than she was, and acted forty years younger." She paused, not sure if Jonas wanted to hear what she had to say. When he stayed silent, his expression relaxed, she continued.

"We communicated by email at first. My mother gave me Todd's name and told me he was from Washington State, from some island. Between the internet and my legal connections, it didn't take long to track him down. He was deceased by then, but I found out he had a sister. Dottie."

She shoved her hands into her hoodie's pocket.

"I had no idea what to expect. But as soon as I talked to her on the phone, I knew we had a connection, something more than blood. I brought Pepé out with me to meet her, before we went to BTS. Our weekend trip ended up being our house-hunting trip. It felt right. Pepé and I had stayed in the same place for a year after Phil died and it was time to move on."

"Your family couldn't have been too pleased about you leaving your home state."

"My siblings understood, I think. I'm the oldest, the oddball, as they're all my half siblings. My mother married their father, Red, when I was very young."

"Yet you needed to find out about a man who'd been nothing more than a sperm donor."

"I really hate that expression. From what Dottie told me he suffered horribly because of his addiction and never felt he deserved a family."

"My uncle was a good guy, despite his heavy drinking. I can't believe he knew about you—it wasn't in him to ignore family."

"I don't know what to think anymore." She looked at the floor, the shelves, anywhere but at Jonas. "It doesn't matter anymore. I'm grateful that I found Dottie and was able to give Pepé a sense of his family history."

"Like I said, Uncle Todd was a great uncle when he was sober. We were all he had, really. He put in his time at his job on base, and went home to hole up with a bottle all weekend."

"You remember him like that?"

"Not specifically. I remember him as the uncle who brought us the biggest chocolate Easter bunnies, who gave us the most money in our birthday cards."

"What about Christmas?"

"He used to really piss Dottie off!" Jonas grinned. "He'd bring us whatever the latest and greatest toy was—you know, the one that was advertised on television and cost too much. Dottie would yell at him and tell him to save his money."

"What did he do when she yelled at him?"

"He'd laugh and tell her he wasn't going to live long enough to spend it all."

"He was right."

Jonas sobered. "Yeah, he was right. He did himself in with booze and cigarettes, the classic combo."

He must have noticed her silence. "Are you feeling okay, Serena? You've been on your feet for a while now and it's a good idea to take it easy for a couple of days."

"I'll go crazy if I sit anymore. Besides, it's time to get dinner started."

"Nope. Not happening. I'm making dinner for you."

"You need to go home, Jonas."

"I don't need to go anywhere. The roads are a mess and the base is closed. It's emergencies-only at the base hospital, and I'm not on call. Doc Franklin knows I'm here."

"Did you tell him what happened?"

"Not all the details, no. You know the assault and arrest will make it to the police blotter, right?"

"Yes. I can't tell you how many of these reports I've read over the years, or how many cases like this I've handled. Mostly, I made sure the victims' medical bills were paid if they didn't have insurance."

"But now it's your life. You've been the victim of a crime."

She nodded. "I know it could be a lot worse, and it's going to pass, this feeling of helplessness. It's strange, that's all. A home is where you're supposed to feel the safest."

"Come here."

She didn't fight him. Strong arms and a warm, solid chest under her cheek were the best medicine Jonas had offered all day.

"It's okay, Serena. You can let go. It's not always your job to be the tough girl."

She allowed him to massage her shoulders, her back. His hands on her waist and shoulders were the definition of solace. He placed a firm kiss on her forehead, the side opposite her bruise.

"You're an impressive woman, Serena."

"You're too nice."

"No, only a casual observer."

Their embrace was a heck of a lot more than casual. It should have scared her, this overwhelming need for him. Instead, she wanted more.

Jonas woke her needs and not in a soft, gentle way. He brought them roaring to life with his constant, steady presence, which compelled her to notice him, notice how they were when they were together.

But they hadn't been together—not completely.

Was it only a matter of time?

Shivers ran down her neck, her spine.

"Cold?"

"No."

His body stiffened and his chest stilled as she heard him take a quick inhalation. He got her meaning, another indication of the invisible yet tangible connection they shared.

"Serena, I want to kiss you but I don't want to hurt your lips."

"Mmm." She was willing to stay in his arms all day.

His kisses started on her face. Gentle touches of his lips to her skin, his tongue darting out to taste her when he got to her earlobe, her throat, skin between her neck and her shoulder.

Her hands moved up under his shirt and her fingers seemed to burn from the heat that radiated off his chest. The man was built, his muscles sinewy after his deployments.

"You work out a lot."

"Not really. It's the quality, not the quantity, you know." His hands swept up from her waist to her breasts, softly kneading them through her shirt. Her nipples strained against her bra and she leaned her forehead on his shoulder.

"Jonas…"

"I know. Pepé, the dog, dinner. It can wait, can't it? We can smooch here for a bit, can't we?"

"Smooch? Is that what this is?"

"Mmm…" He nuzzled her neck as his hands drifted to her bottom and pressed her into his hips. His arousal was obvious and insistent and Serena bit her lip, ignoring the sharp pain from her bruises.

"Ow!"

Jonas pulled his head back. "What? Does this hurt?" He maintained eye contact as he pressed her into him again, making her close her eyes and groan.

"No."

"I want you, Serena."

"I know. But not now, not here. Pepé…"

Jonas pulled away again, keeping his hands on her shoulders. She was grateful; he'd made her knees go weak, the sexy man.

"Not now, but soon, Serena. We owe it to ourselves to explore this attraction."

"When I'm the owner of the house you think is yours?"

He dropped his hands to his sides and the flicker of desire in his eyes snuffed out as quickly as if she'd slapped him.

Verbally, she *had* slapped him.

"I've learned that everything in life is negotiable."

"I'M GOING TO take the job at Paul Scott's firm." Serena spoke breathlessly, carefully picking her way up the cliff-side path she was hiking.

"Wonderful! You won't regret it. It's time for you to take your career back." Emily's words weren't as punctuated by intermittent breaths as Serena's. With no family, Emily had more time to exercise and was in the kind of shape normally seen in college athletes.

"Yes, it is." They'd climbed up the treacherous rock wall and were rewarded with one of the best views on Whidbey Island. The sun shone on the familiar hump of Camano Island in the distance, and glistened off the white peak of Mount Baker in the Cascade Mountain Range, about a two-hour drive from where they stood.

"This is a big part of what's kept me here." Serena let the wind hit her cheeks while pulling her hat lower, over her ears. She and Emily didn't have the protection of the cliff anymore, and the ambient temperature dropped even with the bright sun.

"I've tried to contemplate moving several times." Emily laughed. "It's been so damn lonely since I lost Peter, and my odds of finding someone else would be better in so many other, less remote, places. But part of me is married to Whidbey, I suppose."

"You've never told me all about it, Em."

Emily's hazel eyes reflected golden rays as she looked off at their vista.

"What's there to say? I had three wonderful years with Peter, one of them married. We thought we had all the time in the world. Everything was going to happen for us, eventually. The house, the kids, the settling down."

"You did settle here." Emily had been a Navy nurse and her husband was a naval flight officer. They'd hoped to move all over the globe together. Until Peter got sick and died within eight months, a terrible loss for anyone.

More so, Serena thought, for a medical professional like Emily.

Did Jonas suffer from having lost anyone close to him? Did he grieve for lost patients? She was certain he must, but it wasn't anything he'd shared with her yet.

"Yes, I stayed on. I think Peter and I would have, too. The only thing that would send me back east is my parents, but they're still healthy and now they're in a senior community that offers step-up care. I can go there for months at a time if I'm ever needed."

Emily faced Serena. "So far I haven't been needed. I'm happy here, too. I enjoy my work at the base clinic. And now I'm going to be an author!"

"Do you wish you'd had kids?" She'd seen how Emily looked at Pepé as if she could devour him.

"Sure. I wish Peter and I had decided to have kids sooner." Emily took a swig from her water bottle. "We could've frozen his sperm, but he was already so sick, and each day we delayed chemo would've shortened his time here. As it was, we're lucky we had as long as we did to say goodbye."

"I don't think eight months is a long time."

Emily shook her head. "When you see the patients I have, who never had even a day to say goodbye, you realize it's a blessing to have that time. My only regret is the pain Peter was in toward the very end."

Serena's gut was in a knot. Dottie hadn't had any time to say goodbye, either.

"It's such a cliché, one we hear every day—'life is short.' But it's true, Serena. Grab your happiness where you can. You said you're going to take the job? When will you start?"

"I start right after Christmas. I wanted to wait until Pepé's begun the second part of the school year, for a smooth transition."

"Are your hours flexible?"

"According to Paul, yes. I can work as much or as little as I like."

"We both know what that means. You'll be doing sixty-hour weeks before you blink."

Serena laughed ruefully. "The old me would, for sure, when I had Phil at home from deployment, or my own family right there, for support. Not now. I've been through too much to make that mistake. Pepé needs me, and I need him. It's important for both of us to maintain our routine."

"Yes, it is." They stood quietly for a few minutes, absorbing the beauty.

"What about Jonas?"

"What about him?"

"The fact that you haven't brought him up makes me think there's more going on here than a man who wants your house. Is he still staying with you?"

"No, I convinced him to go home after a couple of nights. The power came back on, and I promised to text him every night before I go to sleep."

"That's cozy. When are you going to admit there *is* more going on?"

"There might be. There could be. But it's a nonstarter. He's not looking for anything permanent and since I'm going to be working for his brother, and Pepé's made connections with his adopted cousins, I can't get involved. It's not worth the potential heartache later for Pepé."

"For Pepé?"

Serena looked at her friend. "For me, too. I know I need to date, or at least think about it. But bringing a man into the mix…I'm not ready for it yet. Not with Pepé."

"How does he kiss?"

Serena blushed. "Adequately."

Emily giggled and nudged her arm. "I *knew* you'd made out with him."

"What did I do that gave it away?"

"You haven't done anything. It's Jonas. When I see him at work he has the look of a man completely lost in his thoughts. Men don't do that for passing flings, Serena."

"It hasn't gone that far." Not yet.

"Do you ever see him alone, without Pepé there?"

"No. And there's no need to. It'll only lead to trouble." Serena turned and started to walk on the long, slowly descending path that would take them back to where they'd parked their cars.

"What about you, Emily? How's your love life?"

"Touché. It's nonexistent at the moment, but I can always be hopeful."

"No prospects at the hospital?"

"Are you kidding me? Most of the men there are still boys or they're married. I've got no interest in a Navy man since I don't want to move."

"You'd move for the right relationship," Serena said confidently.

Emily blew one of her corkscrew curls out of her face. They were halfway down the path, and the woods offered protection from the wind. Serena enjoyed the crunch of the leaves under her hiking boots, the snap of twigs as they traversed an overlooked path.

"Maybe."

The scent of burning wood—no, make that marijuana—hit her nostrils before Serena identified a group of three men in the depths of the woods.

"Em, look." She spoke quietly.

Emily stopped, too, and took in the smokers. "They haven't seen us yet. Let's keep moving, quickly." Serena didn't answer, but she and Emily upped their pace and made a beeline for the other path, where they'd passed groups of hikers.

"We're okay, Serena. It's just some teens out for the day."

They got back to the main path before Serena spoke.

"It's just scary." Serena shook with what she had to assume was residual fear after the intruder's visit to the barn.

"I know, hon. That's why we walked together and not by ourselves!" Emily smiled and patted her shoulder.

"Em, if Jonas hadn't shown up when he did…"

"You would've made it to the house before the loser even got up, and the police would have taken him in."

"Pepé could have been hurt."

"He wasn't. You made sure of that. But he could

be hurt getting on the school bus, or playing soccer on City Beach. Life's a risk, Serena."

"I know that. Of course I know that—I'm a
damned lawyer. But living alone in the middle of
nowhere, it's…different. Riskier."

Emily waved her hand at Serena in a gesture
of calm.

"You're doing fine, Serena. You'll get more and
more used to being out there, and you'll settle in.
The alpacas made it through the night fine—now
you know you don't have to run out to see them
whenever it gets cold."

CHAPTER TWENTY

Whidbey Island
Late October 1945

SARAH HEARD THE dogs barking and she looked out the living room window. Missy and Busy, the two farm dogs of indiscriminate lineage, ran behind Murphy, her fearless shepherd. Anxiety mingled with anticipation, her constant companion since Henry had gone missing. The emotion rose like a winter tide in her throat, threatening to suffocate her.

At least Dottie was at school, not here. She wouldn't have the scene of being told her father had died a war hero burned into her mind, forcing out all the good memories Sarah had tried to keep alive for her over the past four years.

Tears hovered in her eyes but she blinked them back.

Be strong.

That was her prayer whenever the war had pushed her spirits down.

Her gaze homed in on the interloper. A lone man walked up the dusty drive. They hadn't had rain in weeks and the smell of pine, cedar and dust marked the end of fall. An early winter was around every bend.

The man grew larger as his steady steps brought him closer. Oddly, the dogs followed him as if in unquestioning obedience to this stranger.

She'd heard of other sailors and soldiers returning, how their families didn't recognize them after the years apart.

Her brain knew it *could* be Henry; he could have survived. But this man wasn't him; her heart knew it as surely as she'd recognized Dottie as her own when the nurse had handed the baby girl to her nine years ago. This man was shorter and broader than Henry, his gait different. And his hair—nothing like Henry's blond crew cut.

She should be afraid in that way you were when you feared a thief, or worse, a rapist. But the dogs were her barometer. She saw no weapons in the man's hands. He wore a plain brown leather jacket over basic work pants and a collared shirt. The cold must be blowing right through him but his stride never faltered; he never paused to look around. This was a man on a mission.

She walked out to the porch, her long itchy cardigan wrapped tightly around her. It had been the one luxury she'd knitted herself since Henry left for the war. Her mother had spun the wool for her, from Sarah's two sheep. The kitchen paring knife was in its front pocket, just in case. A woman living alone with her child learned to take precautions.

He looked up once he reached the bottom step. His sharp brown eyes seemed honest, and she knew from somewhere deep inside that she could trust this man.

But he wasn't Henry.

"Mrs. Forsyth?"

"Yes. It's the news about Henry, isn't it? He's… he's…"

She couldn't say the words. The inevitable statement that would end her torment and start her nightmare. He'd been missing for over four years!

"He's alive, Mrs. Forsyth. I came here to tell you that. I didn't wear my Navy uniform, because I didn't want to give you a fright. I didn't want you to think I was bringing a telegram."

Sarah sank to her knees.

"Thank God. Oh, thank God!" She allowed the tears to fall, allowed a complete stranger to witness her like this. What difference did it make anymore?

"Here, ma'am, let me help you." He offered his assistance in the form of two large, capable hands that hoisted her up and then let her sink down onto the steps.

"How do you know Henry?" She didn't look up from her own hands, not yet.

"He was on my ship. Well, not *my* ship. I'm sorry, I forgot to introduce myself."

She peered up at him. His face was handsome and kind, his expression earnest. As far as Sarah was concerned it was the face of an angel. He'd brought her good tidings of Henry, after all.

"I'm Petty Officer Charles Dempsey. Waterman First Class, off LST-19. Our ship pulled into Japan to rescue the G.I.s from the prison camps."

"He was captured in Thailand, in 1942." She whispered the only fact she had, what she'd clung to through almost four years of waiting.

"Yes, he told me that. Henry and I got to be pretty good buddies, crossing the ocean to the Marianas. He was taken to the base hospital there. The Japanese moved him from POW camp to POW camp. He was hopscotched up to Japan, via the Philippines. He's been in Japan the past eighteen months."

"Is he here with you?" She looked past him, willing to see a vehicle with a familiar figure in the passenger seat. She knew the answer before she asked. But the heart hopes.

"No, no, he had to stay at the base hospital until he's strong enough to travel. I think they'll bring him to Hawaii first, then back here. He could even be in Hawaii by now—it's been a few weeks since I got off the ship in Pearl Harbor."

"How is he? How did he look? Why did he send you here?"

Charles Dempsey had a deep, rich laugh. "He looked pretty bad when I first met him. He couldn't talk much, and he needed a lot of care from the nurses and hospital corpsmen. Don't you worry, though, because he was talking every day by the time I left. It was hard to leave him and all the other G.I.s there. They deserved to come home before I did, for sure."

"I'm sure you've done your time, too, Mr. Dempsey. I mean, Petty Officer Dempsey."

"That's okay, ma'am, call me Charles."

"And you must call me Sarah. Can I offer you a meal?"

"That would be very nice, yes. I'll take you up on that. It's been a long drive."

"Where did you drive from?" She suspected Seattle or maybe Portland.

"San Diego."

"California!"

His laughter rang about her. She joined in. Henry was alive!

CHARLES DEMPSEY WAS a generous man who'd traveled thousands of miles out of his way to tell her that Henry still had a chance. More than a chance—he'd made it out of the Japanese POW camps. As Charles told the story that Henry had related to him, tears rolled down her cheeks. Gratitude, sorrow and at times rage at what Henry had endured tightened around her chest. It felt as if the tears were being squeezed out of her. If she could spare Henry any of his pain she would have done it in an instant.

Charles sat with her while she wept, never trying to intrude on her grief.

"Momma, Daddy's alive. We can cry tears of joy now, just like you said we would!" Dottie slipped off her chair and walked around the dinner table to hug Sarah.

"These *are* tears of joy, honey. Your daddy's coming home."

"I know, Momma." Dottie drew back and looked at Charles. "Does my daddy remember me?"

Charles smiled, and tweaked Dottie's nose. "He sure does, honey bunch. He never stopped talking about you."

Sarah's tears multiplied as she watched the relief and happiness flood Dottie's expression. No one had suffered as much as Dottie, not seeing her father for so long. Henry had missed so much.

"I need to stop crying. My husband's coming home."

"Momma, I'm going to go do my chores with the sheep." Dottie was already pulling on her coat and boots. Sarah knew her daughter—Dottie was going to talk to the sheep and dogs about Henry's return. The animals had provided Dottie with moral support throughout the war.

The door slammed shut behind her, thanks to the wind.

Sarah watched Charles as he smiled at Dottie's departure, his expression wistful.

"What are your plans, now that the war's over, Charles?"

"Well, I have a girl in Dubuque, and I hope I'll get my job back as a molder with the same folks, A. Y. MacDonald Company."

"So there's someone special waiting for you, Charles?"

His smile grew subdued and tears formed in his eyes. It reminded Sarah that the war meant long separations for everyone, not just her and Henry.

"Lillian. I hope Lillian's still there for me, yes."

"I do, too."

He cleared his throat and placed his napkin on the table. "This has been a wonderful visit, Sarah, and you make the best egg-salad sandwiches this side of the Mississippi. I won't take any more of your time. I'm hoping to be home by midweek, so I'd best be on my way." He stood, and she walked him to the door.

"Do you have enough gas?"

"Yes, and I've got several cans in the back of my truck, don't you worry. I parked at the end of the drive—I wasn't sure how you'd react to a strange truck rambling up to your house."

He paused at the door. "Henry gave me something for you. Now don't read too much into his shaky writing. He was still pretty feverish when he had me help him write this. It's in his hand, but you'll see where I spelled out the words when he couldn't get his hand to write well enough."

He reached into his jacket inside pocket and pulled out a small envelope.

"He asked me to tell you that no matter what, he loves you with all his heart. Never a day passed while he was in captivity that thoughts of you and your daughter didn't help him through it." Charles sounded unusually formal, as if he'd memorized Henry's message word for word.

He placed the letter in her shaking hands and pressed his own hands around hers.

"You're a dear woman, Sarah, and I have every hope that Henry will be back with you soon."

He kissed her on the cheek and left.

She forgot to get his address in Iowa. Sarah prayed he'd write them. Henry would want to know how he was doing.

CHAPTER TWENTY-ONE

Whidbey Island
One week before Christmas

"MOM, I WANT to put a Transformer at the top of the tree!" Pepé ran around in circles, holding a Transformer toy in each hand, the half-empty ornament boxes and leftover garland no deterrent for his enthusiasm.

"Pepé, slow down, or we're going to have to stop decorating the tree." She didn't have to add that his chances for a mug of hot chocolate were dwindling, as well.

"But, Mom, it's Christmas. Don't be such a grinch." Jonas's voice rumbled low and sexy next to her as he helped reach the higher branches, hanging her icicle collection.

"You're going to be in time-out with him if you don't stop egging him on."

"Look at me when you reprimand me. Bet you can't say it to my face."

Heat washed over her chest, her throat, her cheeks. She didn't dare look at his eyes, not with Pepé in the room. Her willpower around Jonas was being eroded layer by layer, with each ornament he hung, each chore he did.

He'd shown up a couple hours earlier and proclaimed it was time to put their tree up. With the awful "night of the intruder" as she'd started to think of it, decorating for Christmas had taken a backseat for the past several days as she'd focused on getting Pepé to school and preparing to start work in January.

Now with Christmas only a week away, she was lucky Jonas had found the heart to help her. Otherwise, she might have put it off longer, and the extra effort a real tree took made it worth enjoying for a while before Christmas.

"Dare you."

Distracted by her thoughts she forgot her vow and looked at him. His blue eyes sparkled with humor—and a desire that demanded expression.

"Jonas, Pepé's right here," she whispered. Her voice cracked, betraying how deeply he affected her.

His fingers caressed her cheek. "He's in his own Santa dream. And he has a bedtime, doesn't he?"

She didn't misinterpret his question, nor did she play coy. "Yes, he does."

His gaze sent more of that sexy heat right down to her toes, which curled in her fleece-lined slippers.

"Can we use the Transformers as the star, Mom?"

She drew in a quick breath and took a step back from the tree, from Jonas's searing stare.

"No, Pepé. The star goes at the top. But if you want to turn some of your toys into ornaments, that's fine. Go over to my knitting basket and find some yarn. We'll make holders so we can hang the Transformers."

"Great. Got it, Mom!" He darted over to the basket she'd shoved under the coffee table. Since her facial bruises were healing and she'd started to read over some case files that Paul had given her, her knitting had taken a backseat, too.

She had a good feeling that she wouldn't be playing with yarn tonight, either.

JONAS LOVED WATCHING Serena in her role as Pepé's mother. Pepé was a terrific kid, but he had a way of pushing the boundaries of good—and safe— behavior. Jonas had to bite his tongue a lot around the two of them. Pepé came up with the most outrageous ideas, and if not for Serena's reining him in, the boy would've gotten hurt a time or two. Like when he thought tying Ronald's leash to his Razor scooter was an excellent idea. Serena had caught Pepé just after he'd managed to tie the knot in the leather leash.

Jonas grinned at the memory of Serena's eyes going wide, then the wild anger in them that she somehow magically channeled into a calm, firm, no-nonsense voice.

The same tone Dottie had used with him when he'd tried to build a tree house with some of the leftover wood from the back porch his dad had redone. "What's so funny?" Her eyes leveled their challenge at him. When had every look from Serena become a beacon for his libido?

"I'm remembering when Dottie had to all but tan my hide so I wouldn't build a tree house with planks my dad had thrown into a pile after he redid the back porch." He laughed at Serena's stare and Pepé's smile.

"I always wanted a tree house. My brothers said they'd build me one, but then they got interested in girls and football. I was about ten, and my dad had taught me how to use his drill. Dottie found me out back, drilling holes in the planks, with no adult supervision. I could have lost a finger or worse."

Guilt sucker-punched him in the gut when he saw the fascinated admiration in Pepé's eyes.

"Hey, buddy, I was very wrong to do that. You should never, ever play with grown-up tools unless your mom or another adult is around. You know that, right?"

Pepé nodded.

"Did you hear what he said, Pepé?"

Serena shot Jonas an "are you crazy?" look. Crap, he hadn't meant to stir up Pepé's mischievous instincts.

And definitely not Serena's mama-bear self. He was more interested in her hot-mama persona.

"Okay, why don't you go wash your hands and get your pajamas on, *mi hijo?* I'll make your hot chocolate."

"Do you often give him chocolate before bed?"

"Are you questioning my parenting skills, Jonas?" Her hips moved in the way that tightened his jeans across his crotch.

"Um, no."

She shot him a seductive grin. "You're afraid I'll change my mind, aren't you?"

"Frankly, yes."

She chuckled. Low, sexy, throaty. How long would it take Pepé to drink his chocolate and get to bed?

"I give him mostly milk with a touch of cocoa. I make it myself. You're right to ask—if I gave him a full dose of it he'd either be up late or pee in the bed. Neither of which I'm a big fan of."

"Me, neither. I hate when I pee my pajamas."

She giggled at his straight face. "Do you want some coffee or tea, Jonas? Something stronger?"

"I'm good with water. I don't need anything else."

This woman was everything he needed, and she stood at the kitchen counter, mixing cocoa into warmed milk for her son.

"Do you think he's asleep?" Jonas didn't want to overstep his boundaries. He wasn't Pepé's father, nor was he trying out for the part. He did, however, want to take Serena to bed in the worst way. Now that they were most likely only a few minutes away from that, his patience had frayed to its last thread.

"If he isn't he will be. He ran around all day. Before you came over, we played outside with Ronald for a good hour."

The woodstove pumped out its familiar heat, the glow in the small window a hint of the fire that roared inside its cast-iron belly. Serena and Pepé's Christmas tree twinkled to the left of where they sat on her oversize sofa.

"When did you get all this new furniture?" And what had happened to Dottie's?

"I had it shipped from Texas when we were still in the rental closer to town. Once your family had taken the furniture they'd wanted to remember Dottie by, they gave me the option of keeping the rest or selling it."

"Paul told me you didn't have to give my family any of Dottie's possessions. She left the contents of the house to you."

Serena smiled, her gaze on the Christmas tree. The twinkling lights were reflected in her eyes and they made her long hair shimmer.

"I believe in the spirit of the law as well as the letter of the law, Jonas. Dottie's intention was to leave Pepé and me the house, yes, but I don't think she thought out all the repercussions. She probably would have if she'd more time, if her handwritten notes had made it to Paul before she passed away. He would've suggested she allow everyone to take what they wanted. After all, Pepé and I don't have any memories associated with Dottie's things."

"No, your connection is the house. But still, you could have refused. My family wasn't overly friendly to you at the start—I'm sure it would have been easier to say no and to keep us all at arm's length."

The lines between her brows deepened and she tilted her head.

"They weren't unfriendly, Jonas. Once it was clear who Dottie's murderer was, they did nothing but support Pepé and me, as much as could be expected when everyone was hit with the shock and grief of her passing."

Jonas cringed inside. Of course his family had been nice to her. None of them had hoped, or planned, to live here, in this house, for the rest of their lives. Only he did.

And only *he* had been an ass to Serena.

"I owe you an apology. I've been a complete jerk about the house." This came from his gut, deep inside. He wasn't playing her to gain leverage, to manipulate her into selling the house.

The realization stunned him.

"How can I blame you? I'd have done the same thing. Except..." Her lips curved in an impish smile and it was all he could do to keep to his side of the sofa.

"Except what?"

She gave him a slow, seductive smile. "If I were you, I would have contested the will. At the very least, I would've kept you from moving in here. Possession being nine-tenths of the law, and all."

"Possession?"

Her tongue came out to lick her lips.

"I'm not waiting any longer, Serena."

"Don't."

She met him halfway and he threaded his fingers through her long, long hair as he grasped the back of her head. Her lips parted immediately on contact with his and Jonas went after the tongue that had flirted with him moments earlier. "Make love to me, Jonas."

"Pepé's…"

"Asleep. We can stay out here or go to my room. Your choice, sailor."

Her words, whispered next to his ear, gave him all the incentive he'd dreamed of.

"Serena." He leaned back and took her with him, loving the weight of her, the way she pressed her hips into his. She was moving against him in blatant need, until they were both panting like two Olympic runners.

Jonas made quick work of her bra, unsnapping the back and reveling in the feel of her breasts in his palms.

Thump.

Thump, thump.

Serena went still, turning her face toward the front door.

"Did you hear that?"

Yes, damn it, he had.

"Get up, honey," Jonas muttered. "Let me go check it out."

No sooner had Serena raised herself away from him, sitting back against the couch, than several loud knocks sounded on the door, followed by the ringing of the doorbell.

"Impatient guest you have." He tried to sound calm and casual because he saw the immediate panic in her eyes. It was too soon, too close to the night of the intruder.

"Go into the kitchen and wait for me, Serena. I'll answer this."

"But, Jonas, it could be another addict."

"All the more reason for you to go into the other room. Better yet, take your cell and go into Pepé's room. Call the cops if I don't come back immediately after I answer the door."

She didn't hesitate and within thirty seconds had run upstairs.

The doorbell rang again and the sound of feet shuffling on the porch indicated that the visitor wasn't going away.

Jonas looked around. There was a poker lying

next to the woodstove. He grabbed it and held it behind the door as he opened it.

A tall, angry man stood face-to-face with him. "Where the hell's Serena?"

"You should have called, *mi hermano*. You scared the wits out of us, coming here in the dark and pounding on the door like a *loco*." Serena poured more coffee for her brother, Armando, while Jonas sat and watched the family reunion.

Her half brother was lucky Jonas hadn't shoved the poker...

"I wanted to surprise Pepé. When my meeting in Seattle ended early, I hopped in my rental car and drove up. I had no idea getting to this island would take so long. And driving onto a ferry— that's a new one for me."

He had the same dark eyes and hair as Serena, but lacked the taller build she'd obviously inherited from Uncle Todd.

"How many siblings do you have, again?"

Both Serena and Armando turned toward him as if they'd forgotten he was there. He supposed they had; they hadn't seen each other in months, and it was clear that Serena's family was as close as his.

"There are three besides us. Me, the oldest, and then Armando and his twin, Andreo, and two younger sisters, Silvia and Susana." Serena spoke, her expression apologetic.

Jonas knew it wasn't just about not telling him her family details. She'd wanted to make love, too.

He couldn't think about what had almost happened on the sofa or he'd have to stay seated at the table for far too long.

"So you're the guy who wants to take my sister's and nephew's house away from them?"

"Armando!" Serena batted at Armando's forearm, clearly annoyed.

"Hey, I'm only asking for the facts, *mi hermana.* What kind of brother would I be to let someone threaten your well-being?"

"Cut it out, Armando. You mean to tell me you support us living out here?"

"I want you to be happy. You'd never be happy back in our tiny town. Mama and you would be at each other's throats in two seconds flat. Plus the entire town would expect free legal advice."

Serena laughed, throwing her head back in a way that made Jonas long to kiss the hollow of her throat. "True," she said. "But what can you expect—they all more or less raised me since Mama had me as a teen."

"Yes, she was married to Dad by the time we came along. *We've* all stayed." Armando winked at Jonas. "Serena's the black sheep. She left us."

Serena rolled her eyes but Jonas saw the affection she had for her brother.

"How's your love life, brother?"

"Hey, not in front of your *novio,* sister."

"He's not my—"

Jonas didn't speak Spanish but he knew the blush on Serena's face meant her brother had hit pay dirt.

"Novio?"

"It means boyfriend or sweetheart." Serena wouldn't meet his eyes as she interpreted.

"It can mean fiancé, too." Armando grinned slyly. "I'm sorry if I broke up your time together, Serena."

He turned to Jonas. "This is an awkward way to meet but I trust we'll become good friends."

"Sure." Jonas wasn't about to get cozy with Serena's family. He was having a hard enough time keeping her from becoming part of *his* family.

If he was going to get physically involved with her, he had to be more careful…

A feeling of inevitability washed over him as he watched Serena laugh at another of Armando's jokes. It might be too late.

Was he falling for Serena? *More* than physically?

CHAPTER TWENTY-TWO

Whidbey Island
Five days before Christmas

SERENA FOUND JONAS'S house easily enough. His address was written on a sticky note in her kitchen, where he'd left it when he'd gone home after the intruder incident.

Armando had scared the wits out of her last night! She put her car in Park and set the brake. Since it was Saturday, she was betting that Jonas was home, and from the looks of the truck in his driveway, he was.

She could still back out. Start the car, throw it in Reverse and return home.

Armando had offered to take Pepé out for brunch, where Emily was going to meet up with them and then go to the movies. Serena had canceled her plans with Emily, but since Emily had become part of her family, Pepé's family, it was good to have Armando meet her. He'd be able to give her mother a positive report—that Serena and Pepé were happy in Washington State and that it wasn't a temporary arrangement. Maybe

Juanita would find her way out here for a visit at some point.

She flipped down her visor and took a last look at herself. Would her eagerness appear obvious to Jonas? Why didn't she just hang a sign around her neck with Sexually Needy emblazoned on it?

Only after she rang Jonas's doorbell did she wonder if maybe he wouldn't want her at his place, uninvited.

She'd been about to make love to the man last night and had never even seen his home. Maybe she was a little too desperate.

Or maybe she was thinking of Jonas as more than a fling.

Her thoughts slammed to a stop the minute the door opened and tall, sexy, sweaty Jonas looked her over from head to toe.

She'd dressed with care but not so much that her brother would make wisecracks. She'd unbuttoned her blouse to her cleavage in the car, and she'd worn her high-heeled boots. Jonas's hair was damp at the ends, his workout shirt stretched taut over his chest. He was breathing hard, his lips spread wide in a wicked grin. "Are you selling cookies?"

"Something like that. May I come in?"

Jonas glanced over at her SUV. "Where's Pepé?"

"With Armando and Emily." Was he going to make her stand out here, feeling like a desperate fool?

"For how long?"

"The afternoon."

His eyes blazed with comprehension. In one movement Jonas hauled her into his foyer, shut the front door and had her up against it, his lips locked on hers.

Serena could have asked him to shower first, or to get her a glass of water, or to see his house.

Instead, she closed her eyes, wrapped her leg around his hip and kissed him back.

Whether the shivers he sent down her body were from the way he stroked her waist, then moved around to her buttocks, pressing her closer to his erection, or from the thrill of finally letting go of all her reservations, she didn't know.

She didn't care about anything except getting Jonas to keep kissing her, stroking her, arousing her to the heated point she hadn't felt in forever.

Maybe ever.

The realization made her pull back from his kiss and look into his eyes. Jonas breathed in and out for a few heartbeats before he opened his eyes and revealed how much he wanted her.

"It's not always like this, Jonas."

"No, it's not."

"What we have here, it's—"

"Not something that has to be put into words, Serena." He kissed her again and she yielded to the exhilarating sensation of being in his arms. He was the man she found the most attractive since her husband.

The most exciting since she was a teenager and kisses were new.

"Come with me." Jonas stepped back, holding her hand. He waited until she smiled at him before he led her into his home.

She got a glimpse of a gas insert fireplace, a kitchen done in warm cherry wood, an open laptop. A water bottle, almost empty, on the kitchen's black granite counter.

Stairs up to another hallway—into Jonas's bedroom.

Serena paused. "Wow."

"Did you think I slept in a twin bed?"

She gaped at the massive king-size bed with four pillars that would fit as well in a castle as in Jonas's very masculine room.

"Where did you get this?"

He shrugged out of his shirt. The view of his chest, sprinkled with blond hair the same shade as that on his head, made her forget her question about where his furniture came from.

"Antique market, Belgium. Can we talk about it later?" He was next to her, kissing her, undressing her.

"Sure. Oh. My."

His caresses kept her warm as he moved on to her blouse, her jeans.

"I need a shower, and you're coming in with me, Serena."

"Yes."

She stood in front of him in her laciest bra, the one she'd bought online a few weeks ago. When she'd realized her libido had awakened from its long slumber.

When she'd admitted to herself that she wanted to go to bed with Jonas.

"I like this." Jonas had two fingers under the strip of lace that covered her hip, holding her thong in place. He gently tugged on the elastic band until her breasts were crushed against his chest.

"You're beautiful, Serena."

"Thank you." Shyness tried to come up and strangle her arousal, but she fought it. Jonas made her feel beautiful, whole, sexy.

Jonas made her *feel*.

He shucked off his workout shorts and stood in his briefs in front of her.

Serena giggled at the Christmas cartoon characters printed on the cotton fabric.

"Hey, they're my workout underwear! If I'd known you were stopping by I wouldn't have worn anything but a towel to the door."

"Merry Christmas, indeed." She nipped at his lower lip, her hands reaching for his erection.

Jonas's hands covered hers and held her still. She groaned in protest. Feeling Jonas react to her was the biggest thrill she'd had in a long time.

"Let's take it slow, or this will be over before it starts. I've dreamed of this for so long."

He unhooked her bra and pushed her straps off,

sucking in his breath when her breasts spilled out of the red lace cups.

"I've always been, um, endowed."

"Oh, baby, you're perfect." He cupped both breasts reverently and bent to kiss one nipple, then the other. When he sucked on one of them Serena's knees buckled and she leaned against him.

"What was that about taking it slow?"

Jonas laughed and she felt the reverberations as they shook his upper body.

Before she knew what he'd planned, Jonas bent down and hoisted her over his shoulder, holding her steady with a strategically placed hand on her bottom.

"Jonas!" She clung to his waist, his smooth back her view. And his ass…

He set her down on a soft rug in a bathroom with a sleek, modern shower, then turned on the faucets.

"Did the house come like this?"

"No, I did it. I like to work with my hands."

He demonstrated his talent as he led her into the dark brown shower stall. There were at least eight or twelve—who could count when Jonas was about to make love to her—faucet heads, streaming perfectly warmed water all over her body.

It was the most sensual shower Serena had ever experienced.

"Come here."

Body against body, Jonas leaned down and

kissed her, hard. Serena held the back of his neck and kissed him with all the sexual frustration he'd created in her these past few weeks. Since the day she'd walked in on his conversation with Doc Franklin at the clinic.

His erection was against her and she had a moment of clarity.

"Jonas, condoms, we need condoms."

He reached up to a shelf above her head.

"I brought them in with us." His smile was positively wicked, the water running down his head and over his muscled shoulders as though he was the model for a military recruiting poster.

"Well, you *are* a health professional."

"I am."

His hands were on her breasts and, with the protection issue addressed, Serena gave in to the passion Jonas lit inside her. She didn't know if she needed his tongue or his hands on her more—both evoked a simmering sexuality whenever he was near.

"I don't want to wait for the bed, Serena, but I want you to be comfortable."

He'd stopped, caring about her comfort.

"Take me now."

"Put this on me." He handed her the condom packet and she willed her hands to stop shaking.

"My hands are too wet."

Jonas laughed. "Here."

He gave her a washcloth and she dried her fingers quickly before tearing open the package. When she slid the condom over his erection, Serena felt a surge of possessiveness. As if she was staking her claim on him.

He lifted her chin with his finger and looked down at her. "I've wanted this for a long time, Serena."

"Me, too. Please, Jonas. Now."

He moved her against the shower wall and, bending his knees, entered her in one slow, savory motion.

Serena panted with her wanting, her desire. The initial sensations of a climax began and she couldn't hang on. "Look at me, Serena." He stroked in and out, the sensation obliterating her ability to think clearly.

She stared into his sea-blue eyes and let him watch her as she started to come. Only when she reached her full climax did she close her eyes and cry out, her head against the shower wall, water running down her body. The impact of his lovemaking on her sent wave after wave of sensation through her.

Jonas finally surrendered to his own climax, his hoarse shout echoing in the tiled stall.

Serena luxuriated in the weight of him against her, their naked bodies connected as intimately as possible, leaning against the hard wall of the shower. This was how life was meant to be lived.

THEY MADE LOVE two more times before Serena had to return home to Pepé. Armando would be bringing him back from the movies and they were going to have a family dinner before Armando left for Seattle and his flight home to Texas.

"When can I see you again?"

She paused in the middle of pulling on her sock, bent over his bed as she dressed. "I don't know. Can we take it as it comes?"

"I'd prefer to take you as often as I can." Her pupils dilated at his response and male satisfaction coursed through him. He didn't know when, but at some point it had become very important that she was as turned on by him as he was by her.

"That can be arranged, to a point."

"What are you doing for Christmas?"

"On Christmas Day we're having Emily over for brunch, after Pepé opens his gifts from Santa."

"What about Christmas Eve?"

She didn't answer right away, concentrating as she buttoned her blouse. He wanted to pull her back beside him in the bed and rip the blouse open again, make love to her all night long.

"Jonas, I have Pepé. I can't allow anything to distract me from that, and it's not fair to let you think otherwise. He's my priority."

"I'm not questioning that, Serena. I like Pepé a lot, and I don't want him to get hurt, either."

"So you agree it's best to keep this part of our

friendship under wraps?" She scrutinized him with her lawyer stare. Those eyes missed nothing.

"From Pepé, yes. But he's a smart kid, Serena. He'll know."

She zipped up her boots. "No, he won't. Not if we don't act like teenagers in front of him."

"I asked about Christmas Eve because my family has a dinner every year. It's early enough that the little kids can be home in time to get ready for Santa."

"I'll think about it."

"Please do. Serena, we're your family now. Pepé's, too."

She looked at him and he realized, too late, that he'd overstepped, despite his intention to the contrary.

"You're my lover. Your family is our extended family because of Dottie. That won't go away, and I don't want to ruin it with our relationship, Jonas."

"You weren't worried about that for the past couple of hours."

She blushed in the fading daylight that filtered through the plantation shutters that covered his windows.

Her profile was angelic, but her expression fierce with the fire of a woman who knew her strength. And wasn't afraid to use it.

"Let me think about it," she said again.

"HOW WAS YOUR AFTERNOON?" Armando kept an innocent expression on his handsome face, but Serena knew her brother. He was perfectly aware of what she'd been up to.

"Lovely."

"What did you do, Mom?" Pepé spoke through a mouthful of pasta, his eyes starting to droop. Armando and Emily had spoiled him with the movie and bowling afterward. He'd fall asleep the minute he hit his cartoon pillowcase.

"I relaxed, honey. Sometimes Mommy needs time to herself."

"That sounds boring."

"It won't sound boring in about nine years, when you're sixteen, *niño*." Armando laughed at Pepé's confused expression. "I'm teasing your mom, Pepé, ignore me."

"Yes, ignore Tío Armando. He's a funny guy."

"I love you, Tío Armando!" Pepé defended Armando with sincerity. Serena and Armando laughed and Pepé joined in.

"I love him, too, *mi hijo*. It's how we show we love each other—we tease."

"Oh."

"It's nice to see you laughing again, Serena. You were too sad for too long."

"I know. It's good to feel alive. But..." She wasn't sure how much to tell Armando. Everything she told him would end up getting back to Juanita, and she wasn't ready for that. Not yet.

"Yes?"

She looked at her brother and sent a meaningful glance toward Pepé, as in "let's talk about this later." Pepé was asleep, his face practically in his plate.

Serena smiled. "You tuckered him out."

"We did. Your friend Emily is very energetic."

"Maybe I should be asking you how *your* afternoon was?"

"Oh, no. You know me. I'm a bachelor for life. Women, they complicate things."

Serena ignored him. She saw how his eyes lit up when she said Emily's name.

"Do you want to put Pepé to bed, since you'll be leaving?"

"Of course."

She walked behind him as he carried the sleeping boy into his room and laid him on his twin bed.

"I'll miss him. He's a great boy, Serena."

"He misses you, too. You're his favorite uncle."

They walked back into the kitchen and she made Armando a cup of coffee for the road. He was flying back to Texas the next day.

"Tell Mama I'm fine, and Pepé and I will visit this summer once school's out. I promise."

"I will. She's over it, you know."

"Over what?"

"You leaving, taking her grandson away from her. She understands."

Serena didn't reply. Her relationship with her mother had never been easy. They loved each other, but because they were so much alike they needed time apart, too.

Armando drained his cup.

"Okay, sister. Take good care of yourself and don't be a stranger. And remember, life's short. If you find a chance at happiness again, don't hold back."

"Why do you say that?"

"Because I know you, Serena. You think you have to work your ass off for a chance at the good life. Sometimes it gets handed to you and I'd hate to see you turn down a great offer because of your screwed-up early years." He smiled, and she laughed.

It was an ongoing joke in their family that Serena's four years with her mother, before the other kids came along, were Juanita's "messed-up years." The time after their mother got married and gave Serena brothers and sisters were the "normal" years.

"Got it. Don't you suppose I've already done that, moving out here, finding my roots?"

"Sure, but you know I'm not talking about your

biological father. I'm talking about Jonas. He's not a man to take lightly."

"You met him for one night, very briefly, Armando."

"Men know men. Trust me."

He gave her a warm hug and kissed her cheek.

"Tell Pepé I'm going to teach him how to fly a kite the next time I'm out here."

CHAPTER TWENTY-THREE

Whidbey Island
Early November 1945

SARAH ASTONISHED HERSELF with her patience. Or was it stupidity?

The envelope lay unopened on the kitchen table, right where she'd placed it after Charles left.

She coughed as the dust she was beating out of her rag rug blew into her face. Dottie played on the tire swing that hung from the lone oak tree in the front yard, from which Sarah had stretched a clothesline to the back porch post on the corner of the house. Her father had promised to put up poles for her, but steel was scarce.

"Five more minutes, Dottie!" she yelled over to her precious little girl.

Henry was going to make it back. She refused to let the fear creep in again—the voice that reminded her of all the diseases he might not survive while he was in a hospital. They had a daughter to raise, and Dottie needed a sibling. She was going to end up spoiled if she remained her parents' only grandchild.

"Nooooo, Momma!" Point proven. Dottie would settle for nothing less than twenty-four hours a day on that swing.

The package whispered to her, as did the letter she felt in its folds. Like a child on Christmas morning, she'd let her fingers touch, then grope the letter, desperate to know what was inside.

Afraid of it, too.

She never thought of herself as superstitious. Yet she couldn't bring herself to open it. If it was the last thing she ever got from Henry, she wanted to wait as long as possible, as if to prolong his life.

"Stop it." She scolded herself for her worries about him dying. Charles Dempsey had said Henry was really sick, but he had every hope for a full recovery. She should, too.

The sun was starting to peek from behind the clouds and she was glad she'd made the effort to get the rug out here. It was one of the many things she'd made through the long nights that were her life since the war began.

Now it was ending, but it hadn't for her, or for Henry. It wouldn't be over until he was home with them again.

"Time to come in, Dottie!"

Dottie didn't stop immediately her swinging, but waited for the tire to slow into little whirls, first counterclockwise and then clockwise.

Sometimes Sarah would go down to the swing and push her a little longer, or sit on the ground and talk to her. Dottie was almost nine years old and full of life and imagination. Sarah didn't want to miss a minute of it, or at least that was how she felt when she first woke up in the morning. After a day at work and then a few hours of housework that included making dinner, she was ready to crawl under her covers as soon as Dottie was in bed for the night. As if going to sleep early would somehow make the days go faster, bring Henry home sooner.

She lugged the heavy rug up the short distance of lawn to the front porch, then dragged it into the house.

"Momma, is the rug all sunny now?"

Sarah laughed. It was a joke from when Dottie was younger. When she'd believed what her grandmother said—"the sun goes in and the dust goes out."

"Yes, well, it's sunny all right. It's as clean as I'm going to get it for now."

"We're almost ready for Daddy to come home, Momma!"

Dottie made Sarah drop the rug and return the exuberant embrace that she gave her mother.

Sarah's smile froze. Had she been wrong to encourage Dottie's belief that Henry was indeed returning home from the war?

All the other men on island had come back—she'd heard from friends or read it in the paper. All except for Henry. The War Department had sent a notification that had arrived a week after Charles's visit, informing her that Henry was under reha-bilitation in the Marianas and would be moved home as soon as he was physically able. The same things Charles had reported.

The letter had listed his maladies—dysentery, malnutrition, fatigue.

From what Charles had described, Henry was in a lot of pain that wouldn't ease until his bones and muscles got healthy again.

"What's for dinner, Momma?"

"Potato soup, sweetheart."

As she dished up the vegetable chowder, she wished she was filling a bowl for Henry, too.

"Can we open the package, Momma?"

Yes, they could. But should they?

"I suppose so. Maybe after dinner?"

"I'm going to finish my whole bowl!" Dottie slurped up a large spoonful of her soup, her eyes closed as if she were eating her favorite dessert.

Sarah knew better. Dottie had it in her head that the package was a Christmas gift from her father. Sarah wanted to save her daughter the disappoint-ment when they found only a letter or maybe a photo. There couldn't be a toy in the package for Dottie.

Or could there?

Before her irritatingly logical self could grab hold, Sarah put down her spoon and reached for the square packet that had occupied their kitchen table for the better part of a week.

The brown paper was smooth under her fingers, as if it had a coating of wax on it, not unlike the butcher paper her father used to wrap up chicken or deer after he cut it up for freezing.

Tears filled her eyes as her imagination went wild. This had been touched by Henry, and now she and Sarah were touching it, touching Henry.

It was a poor substitute for the husband she so dearly loved, but it was all they had.

"Here, help me."

Dottie needed no further incentive to slide out of her chair and hurry over to Sarah's side, her hands reaching out to finger the package.

"Can I untie the string?"

"Sure, sweetie. If the knot's too tight we'll use the scissors."

The scissors were another joke between mother and daughter. When Dottie was six she'd snuck them out of Sarah's sewing-table drawer and given her doll and herself a new hairdo. Dottie's bangs had taken months to grow back and her school photo from that year showed her bald forehead in stark contrast to her long, curly, shoulder-length hair.

Dottie's face puckered in concentration and Sarah bit back a laugh at her daughter's intensity. It came straight from Sarah's mother, this ability to focus her energy in such a fierce beam of determination.

"This is a tough one."

"Yes, it is, honey. Do you want to get the scissors?"

"No, not yet."

Sarah was impressed by the level of self-control Dottie was demonstrating. Not just for a nine-year-old, but for a girl who would become a young woman in less time than Henry had been gone.

So much time had passed.

"Look, Momma, I got it!"

As Sarah eyed the frayed string, a jolt of understanding made her start. They might very well be looking at the last communication from Henry. She put her hand on her chest, against her pounding heart.

Don't think like that.

She couldn't help it. Weak as Charles had described Henry as being, Sarah knew it wouldn't take a lot to make him ill again, too ill to move. And the longer he stayed on some Pacific island, away from the States...

"Why did you click your teeth, Momma?"

She'd clenched her teeth at the shudder that had raced through her, but she wasn't about to reveal that to Dottie.

"I'm just excited, is all."

The string fell away and Sarah turned the package over so that Dottie could open the folded flaps.

A layer of thin tissue paper covered what was inside. Once it was opened, Sarah held a couple of photographs, a letter and an intricately woven angel. She recognized that palm fronds, similar to the ones used at Palm Sunday service, had been used to make this small ornament.

"Let's put this all on the table." Her hands shook so badly she didn't trust them not to drop the precious cargo.

"Is it a toy, Momma?"

"I don't think so. I think it's a Christmas ornament."

"Look, it has a place to hang it from." Dottie smiled.

"Yes, we can hang it on the tree next month." She was hardly aware of murmuring the words as she opened the letter that had her name scrawled across it. Henry's handwriting was distinct and she had no doubt he'd written the words, but as Charles had warned her, his writing was shaky, as though his hands barely had the strength to form the words.

September 6, 1945
LST-19

My Dearest Sarah,

I'm onboard a Navy vessel on my way to the Marianas. I don't want you or Dottie to worry about me. The Navy nurses are wonderful and the doctors will fix me up real soon.

Forgive my writing. We didn't do a lot of writing in the prison camp. There is a fine Navy sailor helping me write this to you. His name is Charles Dempsey and he has promised to get this posted to you and Dottie as soon as he's back Stateside. I daresay he'll beat me there, as my legs need a little time to get their strength back.

We've made it, Sarah! The war is over and we won. I'll be able to join you and Dottie back on our farm soon. Remember how I used to complain about how I missed Texas and my hometown? I still think of it fondly, but all I've missed these past four years has been you, Dottie and our home on Whidbey Island. It's like heaven in my mind, with the water and mountains all around. I can't wait to see how Dottie likes to pick the raspberries and marionberries at the edges of our property.

I know you've done an amazing job with everything and I'm so proud of you. I'm not the man I was when I left for the war, but I hope you'll love me just the same.

Until we meet again, know I love you with all my heart. I'm giving you a photo of the sailor who has been so kind to me, in case he shows up at your door. His name is Petty Officer Charles Dempsey. He's from Dubuque, Iowa. I don't want you to be afraid. Also, he will give you a photo of me. Don't worry about my bruises. They will be healed by the time you read this.

I carved a little tiger plane for Dottie when I was shot down, but it didn't make it this far. I'll carve her another one once I'm home. I'm enclosing a little angel one of the nurses helped me make for her. It comes with all my love for you both. I can't wait to be home with my two angels.

I'm counting the hours until I hold you in my arms again, my darling Sarah.
All my love and affection,
Henry

Sarah reread the letter at least five times before she put it down on the table next to the photograph of Charles Dempsey in his Navy uniform. He'd looked much the same in his civilian clothes when he'd visited the farmhouse. The war had been kind to him, physically at least.

The photo of Henry took her breath away. Confirmation that he was alive ran through her, thrilling her, making the hair on her forearms prickle with anticipation at his return.

Familiar dread that he might not make it back alive quickly replaced her excitement. The photo was Henry, no question, as he sat up against what she assumed to be the wall of a hospital, or maybe a tent wall, the low back headboard of the bed he was on supporting his torso. His hair was gone, as if he'd been shaved with a razor right through an entire layer of his skin. She made out marks on his scalp, lines on his face and neck that could be cuts. The photo was too grainy to reveal enough information.

The laugh lines around his eyes were deep, as if he were smiling, but his lips were stretched in what looked more like a grimace. As if he'd forgotten how to smile.

Oh, Henry, what hell have you been through?

Whidbey Island
Mid-November 1945

"I THINK YOU'LL enjoy this novel, Mrs. Vanderhosen." Sarah wrote down her patron's name on the book's card, stamped the date and handed it back to her with a smile.

"Thank you so much, Sarah. You always know what I like to read."

"Sure thing."

Sarah watched Cynthia Vanderhosen as she left the small library. Cynthia's husband had returned six months ago, and her figure was starting to show the results of their lovemaking.

Cynthia was pregnant.

Envy stabbed Sarah and she smoothed her work smock. Henry was coming home. He was.

A tall familiar figure walked into the library and up to the desk. Sarah's hands shook and she sat on the stool, since her knees were shaking, too.

"Papa."

"This came for you." He handed out the envelope too many of them had seen. A telegram.

"No."

"It can be good news, too, Sarah. Open it."

She tore open the envelope and scanned the message. Read it again, to make sure it wasn't a dream.

"What does it say, child?"

"He's coming home, Papa!"

Sarah leaped over the library desk and gave her father the biggest bear hug she'd given either of her parents since she was a child and it was Christmas morning.

Her father's arms went around her and he hugged her back, staggering back a step or two from the force of her excitement.

"That's wonderful, honey."

As if her worry and all her questions had conjured him up from the dead, Henry Forsyth walked back into the farmhouse two weeks after Sarah opened his letter.

"Momma, there's a strange car coming up the drive!"

It was Saturday and Dottie was home from school. Sarah had considered leaving her at her parents' for these first few hours—she'd heard how needy, how eager, the men coming home could be. Would Henry understand that they couldn't make love until Dottie was asleep? Or until she sent her over to her grandparents' cottage?

"Momma, come on!"

Sarah ran to the door where Dottie stood, her hair curled and tied with a pretty red ribbon for her father. Sarah had dressed carefully in a new dress her two best girlfriends had insisted on buying for her. She'd secretly purchased some pretty underwear via mail order, to surprise Henry.

The stodgy car pulled to a stop in front of the house and a uniformed man got out of the driver's seat and walked around to the passenger's side.

The shy, diminutive man in the passenger seat *couldn't* be her Henry. He was pale, thin, nothing like the man she'd made love to that night at Moffett Field. Could the Army have made a mistake? Like when newborns got switched at hospitals?

The driver opened the side door, and when Henry stood up Sarah knew it was him. No one had shoulders that broad, no matter how skinny they were. And his eyes—haunted, pained but no doubt Henry's.

"Daddy!" Dottie was ahead of her down the few porch steps and flung herself at Henry, causing him to lean against the car for support.

"Henry." Sarah made the last few steps to her husband. The last few steps of the long, long war years.

He met her gaze and she wondered if it was possible for her heart to swell with love and gratitude while breaking at the same time.

"Oh, Henry, what did they do to you?"

"I've made it back, Sarah. I'm home."

CHAPTER TWENTY-FOUR

Whidbey Island
Four days before Christmas

"I HEARD YOU and Armando had a good time with Pepé."

Emily took the handle of their large cart from Serena. They were off island for a quick trip to the big-box stores in Bellingham, a town about an hour from Oak Harbor.

"That's an understatement. Your brother is a hoot—he had Pepé giggling all afternoon. We almost got kicked out of the movie!"

"I'm sorry he's not your type." Serena looked over a boxed set of Pepé's favorite superhero books. He'd love to find it under the tree Christmas morning.

"Not my type?" Emily stared at Serena. Before she could respond, Emily said, "Oh, you mean he's too young for me." She selected a large tin of Belgian chocolates from the shelf. The toys and the holiday gifts were all displayed together, row after row of brightly wrapped packages vying for their attention.

"I'm sorry, Em. I didn't mean to sound like a bitch."

"But you did." Emily smiled. "I understand—he's your brother. He happens to be eight years younger than me, but you obviously picture him with a woman more his age."

"I can't say I picture him with anyone. Armando is his own person, and he's still young for a guy. He's become a successful software engineer, something no one in our family ever did before."

"You mean before you—you're a lawyer, for heaven's sake."

Serena shrugged. "It's...different."

Emily sighed before putting the chocolates back on the shelf. "Why? Just because you're the one sibling with a different father? So what? Why does it matter?"

"To my mother it does. A lot."

"Your mother sounds like something else. Between what you've mentioned, and what Armando said, you don't deserve the crap she's piled on you. It wasn't your fault who your father was."

"No, and she doesn't blame me for that. It's the fact that I took Pepé and headed west after Phil died. She'd always hoped Phil would get out of the Marine Corps and we'd move back to my hometown and stay there forever. My mother doesn't understand the need to strike out on one's own."

"You know, that's why you and I have bonded. We're the type of personality attracted to the military lifestyle to begin with. We look for what's over the horizon. Some people are quite content to stay in the same place their entire lives."

"Nothing wrong with that." Serena took the cart handle and steered them toward the racks of clothes. She needed to find some new pajamas for Pepé.

"Besides, I didn't choose the military lifestyle. Phil did."

"No, but you chose it when you picked him. Think about it."

"Maybe you're right."

"So, when are you going to tell me how your date with Jonas went?" Emily picked up a pair of slipper-socks as casually as if she wasn't asking for the most private details of Serena's life.

"It was…nice."

"Oh?"

"We did it. Yes, we did. There, is that better? I finally had sex after almost three years of celibacy!"

Emily's eyes widened and she broke into a grin. A woman near them whispered to her husband, and another customer smiled knowingly.

Serena groaned. "What is my problem?"

"You're happy. You're in love?"

"No, no *L*-word, Emily." Serena let out an exclamation of triumph at the pair of cartoon-character pajamas she found in Pepé's size.

"Pepé is going to love these."

"He'll like them, but a boy needs toys." Emily glanced at their cart. "Do you want to go back to the toy section?"

Serena looked at her phone for the first time. "No, we'd better check out. I don't want to risk being late for the school bus."

"Okay, I'm going to run and get a case of tuna. I'll meet you at the cash registers."

"Fine."

Serena watched Emily bounce off and wondered if her friend was seeing something she'd missed.

Was she falling in love with Jonas?

JONAS LOOKED AT his brother as Paul went over the paperwork for the land parcels he'd purchased six months ago.

Right after Dottie died, before he'd met Serena.

Paul skimmed a few more paragraphs, his body relaxed in the executive chair behind his large oak desk. The large window behind him overlooked Puget Sound, where the whitecaps were visible.

Jonas felt most at home in a hospital or clinic situation, but even he had to admit his brother had a great office.

There'd been a gale last night, still evident in the roiling water far below.

Jonas had tried to not worry about Serena and Pepé. They weren't his responsibility.

He'd been called into the hospital to cover the

night shift. It didn't escape him that if he'd been home all night, he might have ended up back at Serena's. To check on them—make sure the pipes weren't freezing.

"Are you sure you're ready to do this? You've been so determined to get that house back." Paul's gaze was clear, but his expression neutral. Full lawyer-mode.

"It's their home now. I have a house, and Dottie's left me a good sum, as you know. In a few years I'll build a place farther out from town, with a little extra land. It's not important where."

Not anymore.

Paul stared at him. Jonas fought the urge to squirm under his scrutiny. Paul didn't know everything, much as he thought he did.

"What?"

"I got the impression you and Serena had something between you."

"Nothing that's going to last."

"Is it because of Pepé?"

Jonas fought the urge to punch the smug look off Paul's face.

"I'm not ready for a family, Paul."

"Why not? You've got your dream orders back here. You can finish up your entire career on Whidbey. If you had a family, they wouldn't have to move."

"Being a father isn't in my DNA." Visions of the children he'd been unable to save flashed in front of him. His body became hot and then cold, and he started to shiver.

"Want to tell me about it?"

"No."

Paul nodded. "Okay." Back to lawyer business, Paul shoved the papers across the table toward Jonas.

"Sign them where my paralegal's put the flags. Initial the bottom of each page. When you're ready, we'll place an ad in the local paper."

"I don't want an ad in the paper. I want to give the land to Serena." He shrugged. "I used the money I saved on my last two deployments to buy the land, and it wasn't a huge expense, since most of it's unworkable and too uneven to put a house on." He took the sheaf of papers and the manila folder and got up to leave.

"Jonas."

He turned back toward his older brother. The boss of their clan. "What?"

"If you won't talk to me, you should talk to someone. Maybe even Serena. Let her know why you aren't going for the prize here."

"Since when did you become an expert in love?"

Paul's eyes widened at the same moment Jonas realized what he'd said.

Son of a bitch.

"Seems to me you're earning your own expertise in that area, little bro."

Jonas stared at Paul for at least a minute before he turned and left. Sometimes his brothers knew him too well.

Serena had to push the speed limit the entire way back to the island, but somehow she dropped off Emily and was back at the farmhouse with a half hour to spare before she had to get Pepé.

"Go run off some steam, boy," she admonished Ronald, who wanted to sniff and inspect every little purchase she hauled into the house.

Back at the SUV she leaned into the back and tugged on a huge bag of dog food. It was Ronald's favorite—a salmon-and-potato mix that did wonders for his coat, which was prone to skin ailments on lesser-quality food.

"Argh." She sounded like a darned pirate, but the bag was heavy. As she started to carry it, she heard a familiar gait on the gravel behind her.

"I'll get it."

She didn't need to turn around to know it was Jonas.

Still, her heart pounded and her hands shook in a combination of surprise and relief. Surprise that he was here. And relief, too, that he was here, that she'd immediately known it was Jonas. She hadn't lied to him or Emily—she felt safe here. During the day. At night, she got a little nervous, but since the sheriff's department and city police had rounded up the meth ring, the incidents of petty crime on island had dwindled.

"Sorry. I left my truck at the bottom of the drive and walked up."

"Oh." She stared at him. He looked too damn good. She knew they'd never make a go of it, not with his aversion to family life and future children. It didn't stop her from reacting to his sheer sensuality.

You'll always react to him.

"Here, I'll get the dog food." He reached around her and heaved the sack onto his shoulder as though it were a pillow instead of forty pounds.

"Thanks." She followed him to the front porch where he turned to her.

"Where to?"

"You can set it here. I can get it into the pantry myself."

He didn't argue, which should have been her first clue that this wasn't going to be a pleasant visit.

Nor were they going to jump into bed. Even if they could, she had to leave to pick up Pepé in twenty minutes.

What was wrong with her? Why was she thinking of making love to Jonas when they had no future and he didn't care enough to bend his rules for her and Pepé.

The bag landed on the porch with a thud. Jonas

came back down the three steps and stood in front of her.

"I came to let you know why I can't be with you, Serena."

"You've already been pretty clear on that, Jonas."

She felt the heat of embarrassment, then told herself that no, she wasn't going to feel ashamed for the way she'd been with Jonas. How she felt about him.

"I haven't been totally honest," he muttered.

"Do you want to come in? I can make you a quick cup of coffee before I have to get Pepé."

"No, this won't take long."

Oh.

He looked past her, at some point in the canopy of the fir trees that made up most of the woods in front of the house.

"I lost two kids when I was assigned down-range."

"What do you mean?"

"Two children came in with injuries from a bombing. I'd saved dozens with the same wounds. It's never easy, or a sure thing, but they should have lived."

"They didn't?"

"No."

"I'm so sorry, Jonas."

He shrugged. "So am I. PTSD and nightmares is part of the coming-home experience. I know that. Hell, I'm trained to treat it. Now that I've been dealing with it myself, I've had to come to terms with who I really am inside. I'm a loner, Serena, and family life isn't in the cards for me."

She watched him. No way was she going to say something soothing or nice to let him off the hook.

"Hasn't anyone ever done something nice for you, Jonas?"

"Of course they have. What does that have to do with this?"

"Your lack of trust, not to mention your assumption that I have to be in a relationship that's headed somewhere permanent, astounds me."

"You're not the friends-with-benefits type, Serena."

"You're so sure about that?"

They stood toe-to-toe, eyes locked, chests rising and falling as they breathed. Serena felt as if she was gasping for air while Jonas looked angrier than she'd ever seen him—maybe even more than the night she attacked the heroin addict.

The sexual energy between them flared as quickly as a spark on dry kindling.

Do. Not. Make. A. Move.

She ordered herself to hang tight, not to react to the desire that pulsed through her.

Jonas's eyes flashed a warning and he lowered his head. Serena closed her eyes in anticipation of his lips on hers.

"I can't do this, Serena." His hot breath registered on her mouth at the same moment she heard the crunch of gravel under his boots.

She opened her eyes in time to see his retreating back as he walked to his Jeep.

Jonas left her standing at the front door of the farmhouse.

She wanted to scream at him for being such a damned coward. But that wasn't going to change anything.

Serena knew what she had to do.

THREE DAYS BEFORE Christmas the Scott law office was decked out with tasteful Northwest-inspired decorations. From the cedar garland around the front entry to the beautiful noble fir in the reception area, the holiday couldn't be denied.

That merry sentiment wasn't reflected in the atmosphere in Paul's office, however. Serena stood at his desk while she tried to explain her logic to him.

"I had to tell you, because you're my boss, even if I haven't started coming into the office yet." Paul had been eager for Serena to begin work, so he'd sent some case files home for her to look at.

She'd taken advantage of the entrée to get some of her personal legal work taken care of.

"I was hoping that if I draw up the papers, you'll look them over for me, for accuracy. It's to show my goodwill in all of this, and to protect Jonas."

Paul Scott was as inscrutable as Jonas. It had to be a family trait.

"Let me get this straight. You want to gift the house to Jonas, yet continue to rent it from him?"

She nodded. "Yes. But only for twelve months. I don't want to move Pepé too soon. We might stay in the area, at which point I'll find us a place in town. Something more modern that won't require so much creativity to maintain." She smiled, hoping Paul would laugh.

He didn't. "What if Jonas won't take it from you?"

"Of course he will, Paul. He wants the house so badly he can taste it." Just not with her and Pepé in it.

As quickly as the hope that she and Jonas might have a future had flared, it had been doused with their last conversation. And that horrible, awful almost-kiss.

Paul quickly read over her papers. "It's all okay from a legal standpoint, Serena."

"But?"

Paul leaned forward and put his elbows on the desk.

"I trust my gut. My gut says there's something more than friendship between you and Jonas. Dottie wouldn't have willed the house to you simply because of the biological ties."

She nodded again. "I know." It had become so painfully obvious to her these past several weeks.

Dottie had known exactly what she was doing. "It hasn't worked out the way she'd hoped, however."

How could Serena not have seen it more clearly when she'd walked in on Jonas in the clinic before Thanksgiving?

"Dottie was going to move out and leave you the house, you know."

Serena's head jerked back. "What?"

Paul gave a sharp nod. "She came in here and told me that she'd been thinking about moving into town, to a smaller ranch-style town house or condo. When I asked her about the house, she was vague. Of course I assumed she was going to leave it for Jonas. Now I know it was for you—and Pepé. And…ultimately, for Jonas, too."

"Did Dottie always play the matchmaker in your family?"

Paul laughed. "No, not so obviously. But she didn't have a problem speaking up when she saw any of us making a mistake. She made it known loud and clear that I'd better get off my high horse and ask Mary to marry me. Dottie was right—if I'd waited, Mary would have taken a position on the east coast and our chances of pulling off a relationship could have died."

"I'm glad you listened to her." And she was. Mary and Paul were a wonderful couple. "But Dottie had no way of knowing how Jonas and I would get along. It was presumptuous of her to assume we'd be friends." Much less lovers.

Saving the ache in her own gut for some time with Ben & Jerry's later, Serena stood up. "So you'll help me do this, Paul?"

"I won't stop you, Serena."

"And our discussion is private."

"Attorney-client privilege." He stood up, as well, ending the serious discussion.

"What are your holiday plans, Serena?"

"Pepé and I are going to have our usual quiet Christmas Eve. Then Santa will come, and Pepé will open his gifts on Christmas morning. My friend Emily is joining us on Christmas Day. You?"

"Oh, the usual Scott craziness. If you think the cookie-baking party was insane, you should see Christmas Eve and Christmas Day. Total mayhem. You know we'd love to have you and Pepé out on Christmas Eve, Serena."

"I appreciate it, Paul, and maybe that will be more feasible in the future. Not this year."

"I understand."

"Merry Christmas." She turned and left his office.

As she sat at her desk in the office the firm had assigned her, she had to admit that her heart felt heavier than it had since Phil's death. It upset her that she was having a hard time shaking off a man she'd really only known for a month or so.

They'd only made love that one time. Okay, that one day, several times.

The legalese in the document was easy enough and she printed out a copy for Paul, which she left in his in-box on her way out.

Whidbey Island
Two days before Christmas

WHEN SERENA PULLED up to the house with Pepé she tried not to cry. They got out of the car and let Ronald out to romp. As she stepped into the entry-way she tried to imagine not living here anymore.

It would soon be reality. By next summer, for sure.

It broke her heart. This had become their home, their destiny.

"Go get your chores done, *mi hijo,* and I'll get supper started after a bit. We'll go down and feed the alpaca later, too."

"Can I have a cookie first?" Pepé was a bottomless pit.

"Sure thing. I made a batch of Dottie's oatmeal chocolate-chip." Her stomach twisted as she uttered her reply. Dottie's home had become their home, too.

She'd learned that destiny rarely worked out as mere mortals expected. The house belonged to Jonas.

Making a cup of coffee, she looked out the window toward the alpaca barn and the area where Jonas had tenderly held her after she'd fallen from her struggle with the intruder. She'd known security and safety in Jonas's arms.

It hadn't been enough. Not for him.

She and Pepé deserved nothing less than 100 percent of any man's commitment.

She grasped the handle of the small pitcher of half-and-half she kept on the top shelf of the refrigerator and poured it into thecoffee. The ceramic piece was a leftover from Dottie's many knickknacks and pantry items.

She couldn't stay in the house with all the memories of Dottie, and Dottie's romantic dreams for her and Jonas. The house had Jonas's memories stamped all over it. Dottie was her biological aunt, yes, but more importantly, she'd been a mother to Jonas and his brothers for over thirty years. Dottie would understand her decision.

She sat at the kitchen table and sorted through the mail.

A large official envelope from the Scott legal office was folded in half in the mailbox, along with an assortment of Christmas cards, mostly from her family and friends in Texas. Serena frowned. She didn't remember having a copy of the lease and house deed sent here; she'd left her copies in her desk at the office.

Probably just Paul being thorough.

She opened the envelope and pulled out the documents. But they didn't have her address on them. In fact, they weren't the house deed and her rental agreement.

They were deeds to the land lots that surrounded the farm.

Serena stood up, took the documents to the woodstove and opened the cold iron door. She shoved the legal papers in with the poker, trying to stoke up some grim satisfaction at crushing Jonas's guilt offering.

It wasn't working.

JONAS STARED AT the legal documents the postman had pushed through the mail slot in his front door. When he'd bent down to pick them up after work, he'd thought they were copies of the land deeds he'd sent Serena.

He wished he'd never opened the envelope.

He finally had it. The deed to the house. With an attached rental agreement from Serena.

He'd fought for this for the past six months. Where was the elation, the satisfaction? Where was his enthusiasm for all the renovations he'd hoped to accomplish?

He held the deed in his shaking hands.

Realization dawned. Chagrin, regret and anger at his sheer stupidity raged through him.

He didn't want the house. It didn't mean anything to him anymore. Not without the right family in it.

He wanted Serena. Needed her.

Pepé, too.

"Who am I kidding?" He spoke to his empty town house.

He loved her.

CHAPTER TWENTY-FIVE

Whidbey Island
December 1945

"Dottie, take this milk and toast in to your father." She stood at the sink as she washed their breakfast dishes.

"Isn't he ever going to eat with us at the table, Momma?" Sarah agreed with Dottie; she wanted Henry to get out of the bedroom more.

"Shush. He'll join us when he's stronger."

Sarah waited until Dottie was out of the kitchen before she sagged against their small refrigerator.

Since his arrival home two weeks ago, Henry hadn't said so much as one word about what he'd been through, or what he wanted to do now. He was terribly thin, but her cooking and Dottie's cheer seemed to improve his appetite. Sarah was relieved to see the color creep back into his skin, too.

But where was Henry? *Her* Henry? The man she'd fallen in love with? Made a baby with?

All her fantasies about a romantic reunion with her beloved were crushed under the reality of what they faced. They'd barely touched each other since he'd returned. He never rejected her, but he didn't invite her, either.

She wiped at her tears with the smelly old dish-cloth. Her tears fell so easily these days. So far she'd managed to keep them hidden from Dottie, but for how long?

Dottie's confident steps sounded in the hall-way and when she skipped back into the kitchen Sarah smiled.

"Did he like the toast?"

"He told me to leave the tray on the bureau."

"But your daddy can't reach it there, honey."

"He said he's getting up today and he'll eat in the chair you usually sit in."

Dottie spoke matter-of-factly, her eyes intent and her posture certain. Was there anything this child wasn't afraid of? Her daddy had come back from war, years after she'd last seen him. Dottie didn't even remember Henry, not really. But she'd gone right up to him and hugged him tight, giving him her love, the love of a nine-year-old, without any limitations.

What Dottie didn't realize was that this was a big step for Henry. He'd decided to get out of bed.

"That's a good thing, honey. Now let's get you ready for school." Sarah might actually have a man to have a conversation with after she dropped Dottie off at the one-room schoolhouse.

"It's been hard, too hard, on you." Henry's words were deliberate, his actions slow but steady, as he drank the milk from the glass she'd filled earlier. Sarah sat on their bed and he sat in the extra kitchen chair she'd dragged into the bedroom.

"War's not easy for anyone, Henry."

"It was selfish of me to leave you here with no help, no means of support."

"We got every paycheck, just as you'd arranged."

"I mean, I didn't tell my brothers to come out and look after you."

"All the way from Texas, Henry? That's too far away to make a trip here. Besides, all but one of them went to war, too." Henry had five brothers, one of whom hadn't made it back. His parents had feared they'd lost Henry, too.

"I still can't believe Jimmy's gone." His voice was even, not revealing the emotion she knew he must feel.

"You can't hang on to it, honey." She stood up and knelt at his feet. "If you need to talk about whatever happened over there, you know you can tell me, sweetheart."

He shook his head. "No."

It was the strongest word he said since his return. Tears stung her eyes, but Sarah wasn't going to let this man see he'd hurt her. He didn't mean to, and he'd lived through hell to get back to her and Dottie. She'd read the papers and the reports of how terrible the prison camps had been. She suspected Henry might have been in the Bataan Death March but was afraid to ask him. Afraid to trigger memories best forgotten.

"You're here now, Henry. You're home, safe. No one is going to hurt you again." She kissed his hands, which remained limp in his lap.

Come back to me, Henry.

December 1945
One week before Christmas

SARAH IDLED THE engine on her father's truck for a few moments after she'd driven up the drive to the farmhouse. A nice big Christmas tree was in its bed, chopped down by her father from their back stretch.

She made a mental note to plant some trees for future Christmases. Because they would have more here on Whidbey.

"Henry!"

She walked down the hallway toward their bedroom when she didn't find him in the kitchen. Her heart started to pound and she fought against the anxiety that had plagued her since his return.

Had he decided that getting better was too hard? She knew of a friend's husband who'd killed himself after he returned. It wasn't public knowledge, and the cause of death had been listed as "heart troubles." But they all knew—it was because of the war memories.

They'd called it *shell shock* in the last World War. Now they called it *combat exhaustion*. Sarah didn't give a damn what the doctors labeled it; she wanted Henry whole again.

Relief flooded her when she didn't find him in the bedroom or the bathroom. Her fear of finding him dead was like a constant unwanted companion. Like a wet sweater in the rain that she needed for warmth but was going to make her feel chilled in the end.

"Henry!"

Panic set in once she determined that he wasn't in the house. She ran out back, toward the shed. Before the war he'd built it and found escape at the workbench, whether repairing the toaster or sanding the wood on Dottie's cradle.

There were so many tools in the shed. So many ways— No!

"Henry!"

As she approached the shed her awareness slowed and it was as if she saw everything in Technicolor. The green of the grass, grown long with the fall rains, the crisp cold air that promised snow, the weathered gray of the shed she'd never gotten around to giving a fresh coat of paint while Henry was gone.

The shed door was ajar and she couldn't call his name—her throat constricted with fear.

Henry sat at the workbench, hunched over his task. When he heard her enter he turned toward her and Sarah saw the blood on his hands, his fingers.

"Henry." The whisper was all she managed before she collapsed.

"I WAS MAKING Dottie this. The darn blade was duller than wax and I cut myself so many times."

Sarah was sitting on a blanket on the shed floor, her back against the wall of the building. Henry sat next to her, his expression expectant.

She looked at the small object he'd placed in her hands. "This is your airplane, isn't it?"

"Yes. It was. It took me on many missions, until the last one when I got shot down."

"Where did you get shot down?"

"Southern Thailand." A faint smile appeared on his whiskered face and Sarah wanted to sob with relief. Instead, she listened.

"Sarah, I constantly wished you were with me and there wasn't a war. It was a paradise. Beautiful white sand, clear blue waters. I survived on coconuts and other fruits for a few weeks."

"And then?"

A dark shadow crossed his face. "Then they caught me. I was in the Philippines after that, and then they shipped us to Japan."

"How did they send you?"

The dark cloud in his eyes threatened to eclipse the spark of life she'd seen.

"Boat. We got fired on, by the Allies. They

didn't know we were aboard. Almost didn't make it to Japan."

"But you did."

"Yes."

She knew most of the rest of the story. He'd survived internment at one of the notorious Japanese prison camps, where he'd watched friend after friend die. Charles Dempsey had warned her that Henry would need time. He'd been right. She really needed to write Charles a letter and let him know they were okay. That Henry was home, and they'd make it.

Somehow.

"I hope we hear from Charles. I don't have his address."

"We will. He's that kind of a man—with a solid-gold heart."

"I'm sorry I fainted. It's just that when I saw the blood…"

"I know, Sarah. It's been hard on you and Dottie. That's why I made the ornament. We can put it on the tree. I want this first Christmas to be special."

"It can't be anything but, Henry."

She looked up from the ornament and into his eyes. He was exhausted and had aged decades in the few years he'd been gone, but he was coming back. Henry was home.

"You've collected some nice decorations since I left." Henry's voice startled her out of her baking reverie. She smiled up from the pie dough she was rolling out for the marionberry pie she planned for Christmas Eve. She'd canned the berries in August, hoping against hope that she'd be able to use them for this pie. Henry's pie.

"Dottie gets one each year. The ornament is the only gift she can open on Christmas Eve. She hangs it on the tree before she goes to bed."

"Does she still believe in Santa Claus?" Henry's voice was lower and she couldn't ignore the trill of excitement in her belly.

Yes, he was coming back to them. This was the Henry she'd fallen in love with.

"She does. Well, let me rephrase that. She acts as if she does. She's not stupid—she knows the source of her gifts. But let's face it—she's nine, she has to know the truth by now, although she's never admitted it to me." She took a sip of water.

Henry didn't need reminders of how much he'd missed.

"I hope a part of her always believes," she whispered.

Henry didn't dwell on her comment and she wanted to throw her arms around him and kiss him for being such a dear.

Not yet. He had to make the first move there. They were sleeping in the same bed again and while they'd started to snuggle for warmth in the middle of the night, lovemaking hadn't happened. His nightmares still came, but he snapped out of them more quickly.

Henry was healing.

"Do you want me to make you a pot of coffee?" One thing he couldn't get enough of since his return was hot coffee. Black and strong, no sugar, no milk.

She imagined it tasted sweet to him just as it was.

"No, I thought I'd drive out to the cottage and talk to your father about what needs doing around here." Henry looked out through the window over the kitchen sink.

"Oh."

She tried to swallow her disappointment.

He turned his gaze on her, his eyes on fire. "Are you upset for the reason I think you are, Sarah?"

A blush crept up her face and she averted her eyes. "I'm fine. Just trying to get everything done in time for Christmas."

"I miss you in that way, too."

Without thought she found herself seeking his gaze again. Were those flickers of *desire* in her husband's eyes?

"Oh."

Henry laughed. The lines around his eyes deepened and he threw his head back. His old laugh hadn't entirely returned but this was close enough.

"Is that all you can say, sweetheart—'oh'?"

"No. I mean, you've been through so much…"

He approached her, never taking his eyes off her face.

"How long until we have to get Dottie from school?" He took the rolling pin from her shaking hands and placed it on the floured butcher block.

"Not till three."

"It's only ten. What on earth could we do until then?"

"You said you're going to meet Papa."

"I never made plans with him. I can easily go see him later."

He untied her apron and removed it, his fingers on the front buttons of her dress before she had a chance to register that Henry wanted her.

Now.

"Henry, are you ready for this?"

"Oh, I've been ready, Sarah. I wanted to make sure you were happy to have me back. That Dottie wasn't scared by me."

"I've missed you so much." There they were again, those dratted tears.

"It's been a long while. I can't promise to go slow these first few times, my love." He wiped her tears before he leaned his forehead against hers and closed his eyes, breathing her in.

Afraid he'd change his mind, she slipped her arms around his waist. He was still too skinny, but he was starting to fill out. Christmas would help.

"Thank you for waiting for me, Sarah."

"Henry, I'd have waited for you until the day I died."

"I know." He kissed her then, and it was the

most erotic kiss of Sarah's life. His lips were at once familiar and new. Her Henry knew how to please her, how to coax her into full passion. Yet the man he'd become was more demanding, strong, thrilling, than the man who'd left her to fly for their country.

For the world, really.

Like him, she wasn't the person he'd left, either. She'd come into her womanhood and her need was an unabashed sexual longing that had gone unsatisfied too long.

This wasn't a time for sweet sentiments or longing caresses.

They'd survived four years apart—with her sleeping alone in their wedding bed and him sleeping through God only knew what.

His tongue wasted no time in reclaiming its prize as he kissed her with complete absorption. Sarah opened her mouth to him and threw open the protective shutters she'd closed over her heart.

"Sarah." Henry's movements became efficient, demanding, needy. Her dress fell to the floor, the air cool on her skin despite the hot oven.

"Here's okay." She knelt down and brought him with her, lying on the kitchen floor. His weight on her, between her legs, almost made her climax right on the dough crumbs. It'd been too, too long.

"Sarah, honey, I don't want to hurt you." But he was already pushing down her panties, his fingers greedy for her. She was starving, too, and angled her hips so that he could better reach her. "You're so wet, so ready for me, so sweet and sexy. I've dreamed of this."

"Hurry, Henry."

Their joining was quick and intense and life-altering. They'd survived the war; they'd waited for each other for four long tortuous years. Their patience was rewarded.

Whidbey Island
Christmas Eve, 1945

"CAREFUL, DOTTIE. YOU know the ornaments shouldn't get too close to the lights." Dottie had exclaimed "ouch" several times as her fingers hit the brightly colored bulbs that were strung on the tree. She knew they were hot, but Sarah wasn't so sure she understood the need for care with the paper chain.

"I'm careful, Momma. Can I hang the angel Daddy made us?"

"Sure." Henry and Sarah replied in unison, and Sarah reveled in the sound. They were Dottie's parents again—together.

"Do we have tinsel?" Henry stood in the middle of the living room, at a loss as to where he fit into the routine that his wife and daughter had established over the past several Christmases.

"I'm sorry, honey." Sarah walked over and hugged him. He kissed the top of her head and she nestled her cheek against his rough flannel shirt. Since their kitchen adventure, they'd made love at every possible opportunity, and gave each other meaningful glances when they weren't alone. It was the honeymoon they'd never had, the exploration many couples would be bored with by now.

The few remaining couples who hadn't gone through a war...

"What are you sorry about?" He stroked her hair as they watched Dottie bounce between the ornament box and the tree, hanging each decoration with care.

"You need your Christmas job, too. I put the lights on the tree, and Dottie hangs the ornaments. You want to do the tinsel, which I have right here." She pulled away and rustled through the seemingly empty box on the sofa, filled with crumpled newspapers that held their glass, paper and tin ornaments the other eleven months of the year.

She felt the sharp edges of the aluminum strips and she pulled her hand out, laughing. "Found it!"

"I suppose there's a special way to put the tinsel on." Sarah smiled at Henry's observation. She did have her own way of doing things and it was a definite adjustment to allow him back into her carefully ordered life.

It was silly. But if she let Henry all the way in, let him take some of the chores off her shoulders, it made her afraid. Afraid he'd have to leave her again, and that she'd never get back to normal.

"Where did you go, Sarah?" His hands were on her shoulders. Usually it was Henry who drifted off.

"Nowhere important. Are you ready to hang the tinsel?"

"Not yet. Tell me, sweetheart. Tell me everything."

"Oh, dear. It's not very Christmassy of me, but I keep thinking I'm going to lose you again. That the minute I believe you're back—really back, here, and safe—the Army's going to call you up for another mission."

"Come here." He wrapped his arms around her and murmured sweet reassurances in her ear. "I'm staying right here, darling. I'm not going anywhere."

"ARE YOU GOING to have to go back to the war, Daddy?"

He looked down at his daughter—his daughter!—whose eyes matched his own and whose expression was straightforward like Sarah's was when he'd first met her.

"No, pumpkin. I'm here to stay. I'm not going anywhere. The war's over, remember?"

Dottie nodded. "Good. Mrs. Albrecht says that we are lucky children to grow up when the war is over."

"Mrs. Albrecht's partially right." Her fourth-grade teacher couldn't possibly understand the number of children who weren't as lucky as Dottie. Who'd lost their fathers, brothers and uncles to the war. He'd even heard of nurses who'd died in the war, right next to the men they served.

His jaw muscles tightened. A distraction was in order. "I made you something, Dottie."

"What, Daddy?"

"Let's see." He made a big show of pulling the tiny plane out of his front pocket where he'd placed it last night when he'd been in the shed.

"Here you go!"

"It's a little airplane! With Santa Claus flying it!"

"Yes, that's right. It's a P-40, the plane I flew. Do you see the name written on its side?"

"D-O-T-T-I-E. It's my name, isn't it?"

"Yes, it is."

"I thought Santa Claus flew his sleigh with the reindeer." The twinkle in her eyes let him know that she was well aware of who Santa was and exactly how her gifts found their way under her tree.

"He does, Dottie. But sometimes he needs help, especially down south where it gets very warm. He has a squadron of airplanes he can hop into whenever he wants. He loads them up with toys for good little girls and boys and then delivers them."

Dottie smiled, a smug look on her face. "Nice story, Daddy."

"Yes, it's an old one, and well-known." He

chuckled. "Will you do me a favor and hang the ornament?"

"Sure thing, Daddy!" She looked like a little fairy, alighting on the coffee table in front of the sofa and then leaning over toward the tree. She hung the tiny P-40 on the highest branch she could reach, in the very front.

He tried to absorb every second as best he could. Dottie had grown so much in his absence, yet he had an inkling that she'd be grown up and starting her own family in a blink.

If only the war years had gone as quickly as the past weeks had.

"You're going to spoil her, Henry." Sarah spoke from her rocking chair, the rocker he'd made her for a wedding present. He'd never forget how beautiful she'd looked sitting in it while she nursed newborn Dottie, or how lovely she was tonight as she knitted some mysterious last-minute Christmas gift. She refused to tell him or Dottie what the object was, or who it was for. It was mostly hidden in a canvas bag she'd fashioned from flour bags, with only the top of the brown wool visible as she worked row after row.

He walked over to her, knelt down and cupped her face in his hands.

"I plan on spoiling you both for the rest of our lives. Together." He kissed her.

"Ewww."

Dottie was growing up indeed.

Henry didn't allow Dottie's disgust at her parents' affection to stop him. He didn't lift his lips from Sarah's until he was sure she'd be as anxious for bedtime as he was.

"Merry Christmas, darling."

CHAPTER TWENTY-SIX

Whidbey Island
Christmas Eve

"YOU REALLY ARE going to pack up and leave this house, Serena?" Emily looked at her over her mug of eggnog. The Christmas tree twinkled behind her and Serena tried to forget her memories of Jonas helping them hang ornaments.

He'd helped with their entire Christmas. Until he'd become possessed by the Grinch, damn it.

"I don't have a choice, Em. But don't worry, we're staying here. I couldn't leave Whidbey now if I wanted to. It's where Pepé and I have healed." Until her current broken heart, but that was another matter.

Emily shook her head. "I can't believe Jonas didn't have the b—"

Serena shushed her with one hand held up in front of her. "Pepé's right here!"

"Mom, is Jonas coming over for Christmas? He said he would."

First strike to her heart.

Damn you, Jonas Scott.

"No, honey, he'll be busy with his own family, and besides, we have to get ready for Santa and tomorrow morning. Do you still want cinnamon rolls for breakfast?"

"Mmm, yes!"

Ronald barked.

His tail thumped the floor.

The doorbell rang.

Emily looked at her, frowning. "Expecting someone?"

"No." As Serena replied, she got up from the easy chair and tried to see through the door's beveled glass. All she could make out in the dark was a red blob.

They'd missed the firehouse delivery of candy canes; maybe the firefighters had come back.

"Pepé, see if there's a fire truck in the driveway." Meanwhile she made sure she had her fireplace poker in hand. Christmas Eve didn't mean anything to drug addicts or criminals.

Thump, thump.

"Coming. Ronald, stay."

Serena opened the front door a crack at first, careful and wary.

"Ho, ho, ho!"

Santa Claus, in full red velvet apparel, complete with a snowy white beard, stood on her porch. She opened the door wider.

Eyes as blue as Texas bluebonnets gleamed at her.

"I understand there's a little boy here named Pepé."

"There is! It's me!" Pepé squeezed between Serena and Ronald. Ronald, damn that dog, had ~lled on his back, waiting for a belly rub from "Santa."

"Santa, I thought we made it clear that...that there's nothing left—"

"Let Santa in out of the cold, Serena," Emily interrupted her. "Pepé, go get some of those cookies you frosted with your mom. I'll get Santa some eggnog."

"I think Santa likes milk, Auntie Em." Pepé was serious about Santa's needs.

"He can have a little bit of eggnog, I think. It'll probably do him good before his big ride of the night." Emily laughed at her double entendre as she urged Pepé into the kitchen with her.

Serena allowed Santa to enter, wondering if they could hide his real identity from Pepé. Pepé's feelings were paramount.

"Trust me, Serena. You have no reason to, but trust me."

His eyes were on her and she couldn't look anywhere else. "I burned the land deeds."

"You didn't!"

"I don't need your land, Jonas."

"I know, you need…" He looked over his shoulder toward the kitchen and she followed his gaze.

Emily and Pepé were mysteriously gone. Vanished.

"Did Em know you were doing this?"

He took her hands. "You need me, Serena. Pepé needs me. Admit it."

She stared at him, speechless.

"Wait, let me do this over." He took off his hat and beard, and shrugged out of his red coat. Jonas placed all the items in her small coat closet, out of sight.

Jonas, in a thermal shirt and jeans, stood in front of her, his eyes blazing and the smile on his face incredibly irritating.

"This isn't funny, Jonas. Pepé's going to come back out here and wonder where Santa is. And you're leading him on."

He took her hands again and pulled her toward him.

"I'm not leading him on—or you, Serena. I am so sorry to have put us both through my angst. I've never been so deeply in love before, and I didn't know how to deal with it, especially when the woman I love was basically thrown into my life by Dottie."

He knelt down and pulled a box out of his front pocket.

"I love you, Serena. I don't give a damn where we live, whether it's in my town house or a cottage by the beach. I only want to be with you. Will you marry me?"

Oh, no. He wasn't getting off this easily.

"What about the house?"

"Do you mean *your* house?"

"How much moving around will we have to do, with the Navy?"

"Not much. Maybe none. I'm a Navy man, so I can't promise anything on that score until I'm out."

"Will you come to Texas with me to meet my family?"

"Yes."

"Then, yes, Jonas, I'll marry you."

Jonas stood up and placed the largest diamond she'd ever seen on her finger.

"This was Dottie's mother's. Your grandmother's. Your grandfather did well after he came back from the war and he bought this for her when your father was born. Mary had it and Emily helped me figure out your ring size."

Tears blurred her vision and Serena wiped away her tears with her sweater sleeves.

"I'm so happy, Jonas."

"I know. Me, too."

He kissed her, then kissed her again. It was the best Christmas Eve. Ever.

"Hey, where's Santa?"

"Sorry, I tried to keep him upstairs—" Emily's

words reached Serena's ears but she didn't want to stop kissing Jonas.

Jonas lifted his lips from hers but maintained eye contact. Pure love and the promise of Christmas future, shone in his gaze.

"Come here, Pepé. Santa's coming back later, but first, your mom and I have something to tell you."

* * * * *